THE SECRET DIARY OF ELEANOR COBHAM

TONY RICHES

ALSO BY TONY RICHES

COPYRIGHT

Copyright © Tony Riches

Published by Preseli Press

ISBN-13: 978-1502822031
ISBN-10: 1502822032
BISAC: Fiction / Historical

ABOUT THE AUTHOR

Tony Riches is a full-time writer and lives with his wife in Pembrokeshire, West Wales, UK. After several successful non-fiction books, Tony turned to novel-writing and wrote *Queen Sacrifice*, set in tenth-century Wales, followed by *The Shell*, a thriller set in present day Kenya.

A specialist in the history of the early Tudors, Tony is best known for his Tudor Trilogy. His other international best-sellers include *Warwick ~ The Man Behind the Wars of the Roses* and *The Secret Diary of Eleanor Cobham*.

For more information please visit Tony's author website www.tonyriches.com and his blog at www.tonyriches.co.uk. He can also be found at Tony Riches Author on Facebook and Twitter: @tonyriches.

To my wife
Liz

Henry VI. Part ii Act ii. Scene 3:

King Henry:

Stand forth dame Eleanor Cobham,
Glouster's wife.
In sight of God and us, your guilt is great:
Receive the sentence of the law, for sins
Such as by God's book are adjudged to death.
You, madam, for you are more nobly born,
Despoiled of your honour in your life,
Shall, after three days' open penance done,
Live in your country here, in banishment.

William Shakespeare

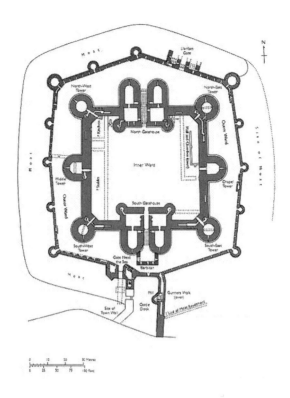

Map of Beaumaris Castle

1

JULY 1450

ARCANUM

W hoever reads this, my secret journal and only true companion, should know I am unjustly condemned to end my days within these castle walls. I am forgotten by the world and my poor beloved husband, once Regent and the Lord Protector of all England, is dead these past three years. My hope is, through these words, people of a time so far away I cannot comprehend will know the truth of how my good and loyal friends were most cruelly tortured and murdered by my enemies.

Loneliness is the worst of my punishment, as though this castle is in a beautiful place it is my prison. I am held as prisoner of Sir William Beauchamp, Constable of Beaumaris, and know Sir William receives my allowance. It is a hundred marks each year, from the dues for fishing on the River Dee and is supposed to cover my expenses. Little of that money finds its way to me. When first at Leeds Castle I had my own allowance and servants to help me. They left one by one and were not replaced. Now I have only the cook who brings my food and the maids who come to clean my room and wash my clothes. They speak to me in the Welsh language and are afraid to look at me. I fear they have been told I am a sorceress and will put some curse on them.

My only company most days are the rough soldiers who have the duty of guarding my prison and the elderly priest who sometimes visits me. Less welcome are the visits from my jailor, William Bulkeley, the Serjeant-at-Arms here at Beaumaris. Bulkeley is an educated man, although ambitious and disliked by the men he commands. He is well married though. Bulkeley's good wife Lady Ellen is the daughter of a powerful Welshman Gwilym ap Gruffydd. She is kind to visit me and the closest I have to a friend in this castle.

It was after one of the visits from the priest that I confided to him I needed to occupy myself more fully, as I have been imprisoned here some three months now, with little else to do apart from dwell on my memories. When the old priest first came to visit he would not look me properly in the eye, a sure sign he believed the stories of my witch-craft. A good man, with white hair and stubble of grey beard, he leans heavily on a stick to walk.

Slowly, over the weeks, he has come to know me a little better. At Easter he kindly brought me an old Latin prayer book, illustrated with brightly coloured pictures of the saints. The priest put the leather bound book solemnly in my hands with the suggestion that I may use it to find answers in God. It has been many years since I studied Latin and I care less for praying for salvation, but as I studied the little book I saw it was a version of the Christian devotional Book of Hours, probably copied by monks in the nearby priory.

I am grateful to the priest as it has uses for me. You may imagine it is better not to note the passing of the months, yet I find time passes more quickly if I do. The little book contains a calendar of the feast-days, helping me to keep track of the year and also serves as a bridge between me and one of my few visitors, the priest. It offers a small way to show I am not entirely as evil as people would have him believe.

I amuse myself by translating excerpts from the gospels and the seven Penitential Psalms. My imprisonment has given me the one thing I never had in excess, the time to study and reflect on such things. I am surprised to find unexpected comfort in the sixth of the psalms of confession. The neatly written Latin of the last line read *'Erubescant et conturbentur vehementer omnes inimici mei; convertantur et erubescant valde velociter.'* This means *'May my enemies be put to shame and come to ruin. May they be turned away and be swiftly put to shame'*. As fitting a spell for any witch to curse her enemies.

On the days I am granted permission to visit the chapel tower, I kneel and devoutly recite psalm six from my Book of Hours. I pray for the eternal damnation of the souls of those who killed my husband by their wicked plots and would have me end my days forgotten here on this island of Anglesey. I was not a witch but they have made me one.

My eyes are also opened to an opportunity by my book of prayers. I contrived my plan to keep this journal. It will be my best company and maybe one day help to correct lies that are written of me. I asked the priest if he would kindly request a small payment from Sir William Bulkeley for some parchment, a quill and ink, so I may translate and copy out the prayers to pass the long summer days. The priest seemed pleased with my new-found religious conviction. He smiled at me for the first time in four long months and promised to help me improve my Latin. I believe there is a softening of his previously cold manner towards me, so perhaps I do still have some powers over men after all.

On his next visit I could see the priest had brought me no parchment. I concealed my disappointment and asked what reply he had from William Bulkeley. The priest explained that my jailor had refused his request, as he is under orders to provide me with nothing that could be used for the purposes of witchcraft or necromancy. He had also informed the priest he is concerned I would write letters that could by some means find their way to supporters outside the castle. I had to hide my disappointment and listened carefully as the priest began to help me with my Latin texts.

It was some weeks before my next walk in the castle grounds with Lady Ellen but I reasoned that Sir William Bulkeley would listen to the opinion of his wife. I carried my Book of Hours and showed it to her, explaining my wish to occupy my time more usefully by translating the Latin. I had to share with her my request sent by the priest and her husband's concerns, yet I am able to say in truth that after nearly nine long years of incarceration any supporters I had were either dead or have long since forgotten me. Ellen was at first reluctant to intervene on my behalf yet could see the virtue of my planned religious study. I know she feels sorry for my dreadful imprisonment. She promised to speak to her husband but warned me he could be a stubborn man.

I know William Bulkeley was already a wealthy landowner in Cheshire before he married Ellen and has ambition to one day become the Constable of Beaumaris Castle. He is in the habit of coming to see me as a jailer not as a friend. He is not an unkindly man but apart from checking I am properly fed and not unwell, he rarely speaks to me. When he does, his manner is one of professional detachment. I suspect he justifies his role in the knowledge that I am a traitor, even though I am certain he knows I was never convicted of treason. William Bulkeley would not be easily persuaded to risk his reputation by agreeing my request.

When I next saw the priest, I pleaded with him to reassure Lady Ellen my intentions were sincere. It seemed he had taken to heart his role as my reformer, for on the following Sunday he greeted me with a parcel of parchment of fine quality. He told me it had been provided by the Augustinian friars of St Seiriol's Priory at Penmon. The quill he provided is also new and holds a sharp point. I shall take good care of it, as I cannot be certain if it will be replaced when it is worn. The ink is good and black iron gall, probably also made by the monks at the priory from oak galls and vinegar, with iron to make it so black. They have given me a good quantity in a pottery flask with an airtight stopper, which I must be most careful not to break.

The priest was unsure if the guards would object but he also let me have a small blade to trim the end of the quill. He showed me how it could be kept sharp on the stone sill of my window and how to score the parchment for trimming into folded pages, which I can sew with my needles to bind together. Although my mother taught me to read and write in French and Latin from an early age, I am out of practice and happy to let the priest act as my tutor, a role he does seem comfortable with. I shall take care to have some verses to show him when he visits so he is also less likely to ask questions about other uses I may have for his materials.

I have found a secret place to hide my writing, where it will be safe. My room is on the second floor of the tower and follows its circular shape, with a high, vaulted ceiling that gives a sense of space. I have little furniture, just my wooden cot with a straw mattress and rough blankets, my table and one wooden chair. I am grateful my room has a large hearth to keep me warm and a window which looks out across the inner ward. The heavy oak door is always bolted on the outside and has an iron grill near the top through which the guards can check on me. I wait until I am certain they have gone, then prise up the loose floor board which can be lifted to reveal a dry space beneath.

My guards are unable to read and have no reason to search but before I started writing I determined to use this cipher, taught to me by a princess. I must prevent my jailors from discovering my work as it is my wish to speak freely of the events of my life, without fear of recrimination while I still live. I believe the only other people who knew this encoded writing are long since dead and I am certain it will be beyond the wit of even William Bulkeley to read. My hope is that whoever understands this journal will also take the time to ensure it is used to ensure the truth of my story is not forgotten.

I am fortunate that when the weather is fine Sir William has permitted me to walk within the castle grounds, although escorted by his soldiers of the guard. I need the sun and fresh air, as it clears my head and makes me feel alive once more, if only for a few hours. The castle of Beaumaris is close to the sea and has a little harbour so that boats can bring supplies right to the wall. Although I cannot see them from my windows, I wonder if ever I were to find a way to escape it would be by boat, then perhaps over the sea to find some sanctuary in Ireland.

Such daydreams are of course no good for me as I have

a dozen men trained to guard me, yet the sea is so close. I wake each morning to the calling of gulls and when the wind is in the right direction I taste the salt in the sea air. My only comfort is to know the king is frail and most unpopular with the people, so the fortunes of my enemies may change. I have been imprisoned for too long now to hope of sympathisers to come to my rescue, but the thought does cross my mind, usually on these good summer days.

Lady Ellen has been on this walk with me and tells me this is the last and largest castle built by King Edward the first on his conquest of Wales. I can sense her mixed feelings about the history of this place. Her father is descended from a long line of Welsh lords and chieftains, but she told me her blue-grey eyes and auburn hair come from her mother, who is English of Norman descent. King Edward's devoted young wife was another Eleanor, of Castile, the daughter of a Spanish king. She would have visited Beaumaris, his finest castle. Eleanor of Castile would have walked these same paths, but as a free woman and Queen of England, as I should now also be.

My walk is usually confined to the vast square courtyard of the inner ward, flanked by the six tall stone towers of which one is my prison. This inner ward has interesting diversions for me as it houses the castle kitchens and stables, as well as the banqueting halls and barracks for those who work in the castle. My guards are under orders from William Bulkeley to ensure I speak to no one, even those who cook and clean in the steaming kitchens or the young grooms from the stables.

Last week I saw the horses being taken out for their exercise through the south gatehouse and wondered if my jailor would one day let me ride. Sir William Beauchamp has a good dozen horses in his care and I overheard one of the guards say he treats them better than he does me. I look the unruly soldier directly in the eye and know he fears I will use my powers over him.

I take my time on my walk and usually end in the chapel tower. It is simply furnished but a quiet, peaceful place. Always cool even in this summer heat, the chapel has a high vaulted stone ceiling and carved wooden panelling. Lady Ellen said it was built by King Edward for his personal use. I am grateful for his piety, as his chapel is where I can find some peace from the soldiers and my jailers. I kneel in contemplation but do not pray. God has long since forsaken me. Instead I remember those who have treated me well, the few who have been kind to me and those who have died in the nine long years since I was last a free woman.

My husband taught me history is written by the victors. If I have been foolish it was to trust those around me who had so much to gain by discrediting his good name and reputation through their false allegations against me. They have called me many things, witch, traitor and harlot, but I am a lady of noble birthright. It saddened me to hear my family scorned and my good father called a 'mere knight' at my trial. He would tell me the stories of his famous grandfather, my great-grandfather, the first Baron of Cobham.

My father Sir Reynold, the third Baron of Sterborough, inherited his title when his brother died. He taught me to take pride in my great-grandfather, one of the most important knights of his day, who was richly rewarded for his support of the new King Edward. He took part in grand royal tournaments and jousting with horses and was a brave man, proving his courage in the savage wars against the

Scots. My great-grandfather distinguished himself at the battle of Crecy and negotiated the surrender of the French at Calais. My father told me the first Sir Reynold's proudest achievement was to be summoned to parliament as a Lord.

My own grandfather, the second Baron, died before I was old enough to remember him. As a young girl I would visit his memorial in our old Saxon parish church at Lingfield in Surrey. I always read the Latin epitaph on his tomb and committed it to memory. I would like to think I have inherited some of his determination, as it read '*Here lies Reginald, Lord Cobham of Starborough. As a soldier he was brave as a leopard, wary in council, yet bold enough when occasion required.*'

My mother was Lady Eleanor Culpeper. Beautiful and well educated, she was the daughter of the wealthy knight Sir Thomas Culpeper. I have happy memories of her and of my childhood at our family estate of Sterborough Castle in Surrey. A fine castle set in extensive grounds; it was built by my great-grandfather and improved by each generation.

A wide moat was crossed by a long wooden drawbridge and my rooms were in one of the two towers with French style conical roofs each side of the gatehouse. I would watch from my window as I waited for my father to return from his journeys to London. He would always bring gifts from the city for me, my little sister Elizabeth and my brothers Reginald and Thomas.

I wear my mother's simple gold ring to this day. She was sadly taken from me by a sudden illness when she was only thirty-seven. My father was heartbroken. He threw himself into his work and began to spend much of his time at court, achieving a knighthood for his services to the infant king. As well as bringing him closer to the centre of power in the land, my father's renewed importance also led him to remarry. His unlikely new wife, Lady Anne, was the daughter of Sir Thomas, fifth Baron Bardolf of Wormegay. She was neither beautiful or rich, as her father's wealth was confiscated after he took part in the ill-judged insurrection against King Henry IV and died of terrible wounds.

I saw little of my father after he remarried. I think it was because I reminded him too much of my mother and what he had lost. One of the sad consequences of the ill luck that befell me was that the last time I ever saw him was before my trial. He was not able to visit me before he died four years ago, so now I am alone in the world.

Apart, that is, from my children. It saddens me to write of it but I fear my son Arthur was murdered by men who knew of his innocence, yet I know my beautiful daughter Antigone lives. My three young grandchildren are part of the reason this journal must be in code, as I still have enemies who would delight in spoiling their young lives.

Lady Ellen came to see me with exciting news from London. I miss being at the centre of things but it seems bad news travels quickly. I know Henry VI is one of the least able kings to ever have ruled this country and England has been ruined by taxes raised to pay for the futile wars with France. The signs of his mismanagement are everywhere, so I was not surprised when Lady Ellen told me the people of Kent have rebelled against the king. Last month an army of commoner workers marched on London but the king had been warned and fled to safety in Warwickshire.

She was unclear of the details but Ellen heard that the Tower of London was overtaken and several of the king's men roughly executed, their heads displayed on spikes for all to see. She heard the Archbishop of York bravely ended the rioting by agreeing to the rebels' demands, although it seems more likely he has been used as a device to end this revolt. The rumour in the city is that the king has ordered the leaders to be hunted down and given a treasoner's execution, a horrific way for any man to die.

I am most grateful to Ellen and look forward to her visits. I have yet to determine where her loyalty lies, so am careful not to criticise the king by calling him a madman, although of course he is. I pity his young French wife Margaret of Anjou, who is little more than twenty years old and has to try to rule the country when King Henry VI suffers from his bouts of insanity. It makes me sad to consider how different the world would be if my husband had been able to take his rightful place as king, with me at his side to guide him.

Ellen is not much travelled, although she is well tutored and well connected, so must surely have heard the dreadful allegations of my witchcraft, yet she shows no regard for it. One day I would like to see if she will hear the truth of it but that can keep. She has done much to benefit her husband William Bulkeley, as her father helped him secure his position in Beaumaris. For now, I am content to listen to her opinion of the world outside this castle and form my own in secret.

AUGUST 1450

FRATRE REGIS

The summer has fortunately been dry and hot in Beaumaris. The sun has warmed the stones of this old castle so I can keep the shutters open, even at night. It is good to feel the salty air fresh from the sea and remember to be grateful I still have my health. Lady Ellen has not been to see me for some weeks but sent a servant with one of her gowns for me. The plain style and dull material is far from the beautiful dresses I once wore, yet it was a simple matter to alter so it fitted my more slender form. I doubt Ellen realises the worn blue dress it replaces was all I had to wear or that my cotton shifts are threadbare from washing as often as I am able.

At least I look like a lady of some value again, although the poor food in this place has made me thin. When first imprisoned I ate so well and exercised so little I put on weight. Now I can feel my ribs and have little appetite for the rough bread and salty stew the Welsh cook brings me almost every day. I have learned they call it 'cawl' and I suspect it is made from kitchen scraps. I use my little Book of Hours to note the saints days in advance and ask for special meals to be prepared, or a jug of wine instead of milk. One day Lady Ellen sent me a bowl of delicious strawberries, which I hadn't tasted since I was at Greenwich.

When her husband, my jailer William Bulkeley, visited me and enquired in his usual way if I was well, I asked if he could kindly tell the cook to make me something else to eat. Bulkeley seemed dismissive but sent a servant carrying half a fine cured ham and a dozen sweet green apples, so he may have some pity for me after all. I must keep on the right side of him, as it is within his power to make my life more bearable or most miserable. I shall wait until I know him better but my dearest wish is for a visit from my precious daughter Antigone.

Now I must explain how I became a lady-in-waiting to Jacqueline, Countess of Hainault, Holland and Zeeland, Dauphine of Viennois, Duchess of Touraine, Duchess of Brabant and then Duchess of Gloucester, wife of one of the most powerful men in England. The countess had sought sanctuary and arrived in England at the personal invitation of the king, as an honoured guest of his court. Jacqueline was glad to escape the threat to her life from civil wars in her home countries of Holland and France. She also needed to prove her marriage to her dislikeable husband John, the Duke of Brabant, illegal on the grounds he was also her first cousin.

In the year 1423, following the death of my mother, my father decided it was time I joined London society. He was concerned to find some way to improve my prospects of marriage and see me become a respectable lady. The fortunes of my family were to be inherited by my brother, so my father thought it unlikely I would find a wealthy suitor. Instead he sought a place for me as a lady-in-waiting. Fortunately, he was at court and heard talk of the imminent arrival of the Countess of Hainault from France. Her husband had replaced her ladies-in-waiting with those of his own choosing and Jacqueline arrived with only a few servants and the most essential items, such was her haste. It was not a simple matter to arrange an introduction, as there were many others wishing to join such a powerful woman who enjoyed the protection of the king.

Before I was invited to meet the countess, I spent long hours preparing with a tutor paid for by my father, to learn as much as I could of her family. I found out she had not had an easy life, as her father died horribly before she was sixteen, making her the sovereign of Holland and Hainaut before she was prepared for the responsibility. Her father's death, quite likely from poisoning, was soon followed by that of her husband, whom she had been engaged to since she was four years old. My tutor explained that they had been betrothed as children and her husband was the son of the French King Charles, so the boy had the title 'dauphin' as the heir apparent to the crown. The marriage had been arranged by the Duke of Burgundy, at the suggestion of his sister Margaret, Countess of Holland, who was of course Jacqueline's mother.

When I met her I was surprised at how young and attractive the countess was, full of life and lively humour, with no trace of her troubled past. Her blonde hair was always braided in the latest fashion and diamond necklaces sparkled at her neck. The countess had an infectious laugh and a talent for seeing the amusing side of everything, so I was delighted to be asked if I would care to take my place at her side as her new companion.

I must admit my life had not been easy after my mother died. I followed my father to London and had fallen into difficult times, living in a rented house. The allowance he provided was barely enough to live on, and I met men who took advantage of my circumstances. They didn't treat me well and damaged my reputation, so my father's intervention was most timely.

I found the countess good company once I was used to her condescending manner towards me. She told me her ladies at her Castle Le Quesnoy were of course of high degree and noble blood, ladies of good life and reputation, wise, honest and in all respects worthy. They were also for the most part educated with her from childhood, so had a proper understanding of their place. Although by implication I was not 'in all respects worthy', I knew better than to point out none of them seemed to have been loyal enough to accompany her to England. I later learned that the king had only granted safe passage through the English lines for herself and her mother, so only a few servants came with her from France.

The countess was a woman of more names and titles than any I have known. Baptised 'Jacoba' in Hainaut, her mother the Dowager Countess of Margaret of Burgundy called her 'Jac' and the French 'Jacqueline', the name she chose to use here in England. She told me once her enemies called her 'Dame Jake' and worse. As well as being the sovereign Countess of Hainaut, Holland and Zeeland, she was also a Dauphine of the house of Viennois and held the title of Duchess of Brabant through her ill-chosen husband.

I soon learned to call her different names, depending on her mood and circumstances. She told me her people called her Domina Jacoha but nothing seemed to please her more than to be referred to as 'la princesse' in company, although she was more properly known as 'the countess' at court.

Jacqueline quickly came to regard me as her most trusted friend and confidante, which made the future turn of events more painful for us both. We were the same age and had both been born and grown up in country castle estates. She was a skilled horsewoman and we enjoyed riding fast in the royal parks, often leaving our armed escort far behind us. The countess was grateful for my help with her English and understanding of our manners, our English customs and fashions. In return she helped me to improve my French and Latin and started teaching me the Hainault dialect of her homeland.

There was little similarity in our upbringing or circum-stances. My family were wealthy enough for comfort but of declining status since the glory of my great-grandfather's time. Jacqueline came from a different world. She told me that in truth the modern ways had yet to reach the wooded hills of Hainault. The countess loved to talk about how her household numbered more than two hundred servants and was defended by an army of six thousand fighting men. She said her family home at Quesnoy was richly furnished, with priceless tapestries, exotic peacocks and maidens playing on golden harps. I realised listening to her stories that her family had ruled as feudal lords, demanding absolute obedi-ence and enjoying the highest privileges.

Jacqueline was also a wealthy woman. In addition to her income from inherited lands in France and Holland, King Henry V ordered a provision of one hundred pounds a month for her expenses so long as she sojourned in England. Once she told me the king had sent an envoy, Sir William Esturmy to proceed to Holland to offer the hand of his brother John, Duke of Bedford, to Jacqueline. It seems Sir

William took his time and arrived too late, as by then she was married to the Duke of Brabant. I wonder if I would be in this prison now if he had reached Hainault in time.

When her marriage to the Duke of Brabant proved a disaster, Jacqueline's mother encouraged her to seek refuge at the English court. She confided in me they had been afraid the king would be angry, but he was not. The king at once sent a personal letter of authority to permit her and her mother to pass safely through the English lines in France and entry into Calais. Jacqueline said that when she crossed the English Channel she was full of hope the tide might turn for her at last.

As the weather was fine I was permitted to walk the outer ward of the castle and climb the stone steps to the high battlement, watched by my ever vigilant guards. As I reached the top I could see two pairs of pure white swans on the dark moat which surrounds the castle on all sides. One of the soldiers told me the castle moat is deep and some eighteen feet wide at the narrowest point. I also learned that all the latrines empty into the moat, a thought I do not wish to dwell upon.

From my high vantage-point I can also see the blue-green mountains of Wales and the shimmering expanse of the Irish Sea. Anglesey is of course an island, divided from the Welsh mainland by the narrow but fast flowing Afon Menai. A large sailing boat was unloading in Beaumaris harbour and the sounds of men's voices carried well in the still air. It took a moment for me to realise they talk in Welsh and I wonder if Lady Ellen will teach their language to me.

If I were not a prisoner here I would think it a good

place to be on a sunny day. Lady Ellen told me this spot was originally the thriving Welsh coastal village of Llanfaes. King Edward decided it was the ideal site for his castle and forcibly moved the entire village some twelve miles away to a place he called 'Newborough'.

English kings have indeed shown scant regard for the local people, as even the Franciscan monastery here was plundered and destroyed by the men of King Henry IV, with many of the friars put to the sword for supporting the Welsh cause in their last uprising. It may be Ellen's influence but I feel sympathy for the people of Wales, who have been punished so severely for trying to defend their homeland.

It was through Jacqueline that I first met Humphrey Plantagenet, Duke of Gloucester, Earl of Pembroke and brother to Henry V, King of England. Of course I knew him by reputation, as he was a champion of the victory at Agincourt and second in line to the throne. I don't know what I was expecting when I first met him but I was taken completely by surprise. Countess Jacqueline had been invited to stay at the duke's London mansion, a fine building called Baynard's Castle near Paul's Wharf on the banks of the River Thames. The duke was not in residence when I arrived to take up my position as her lady-in-waiting, as he had been called away to deal with his business in Dover but Jacqueline was happy to tell me all about him.

She told me when she arrived at the white cliffs of Dover, she found Humphrey waiting to welcome her and escort her to his brother's court. He had brought Jacqueline a fine thoroughbred palfrey for the ride to London, which they reached at an early hour on the following day. She told me the king had received her most graciously, as a grand princess, former dauphiness of Vienne and one who might have been the queen of France.

I was able to explore the duke's London residence in his absence and knew from the library he was much more than a soldier. The walls were lined with the finest collection of books I had ever seen. Many of the duke's books were beautifully written on fine vellum with many illuminated letters and bound in gold tooled leather. I marvelled at the French translations of classical Greek volumes next to early illustrated manuscripts and collections of the work of most of the modern poets. There were piles of books on his table and it was clear he was making a study of them. My mother, who was also my tutor, would have loved to see the duke's books if she had still been alive.

The duke was also a lover of music, as he retained a talented group of minstrels in his household and they would play for us in the evenings. I was surprised when I spoke to the musicians and found they were well educated scholars, fluent in several languages. Some had travelled to London from Italy and Spain and spoke highly of the duke, apparently more like companions of his household than simply the minstrels I had taken them for. As with all his servants, they seemed to hold the duke in great esteem and were proud to be in his service.

Most of all, I could see he had enormous wealth, as the furnishings were all of the finest quality, with ornaments of silver and gold. The walls of his mansion were covered with richly carved wooden panels. Rich tapestries were displayed in every room, with the whole wall of the banqueting hall covered by a dazzling depiction of the Battle of Agincourt. The mansion had wonderful views of the busy river, with its own jetty where the duke had a fine golden barge, and there were extensive parks and gardens on all sides. I later found that the duke had many homes, including castles at Pembroke and Devizes and manor houses in Kent and St Albans.

We had been staying in his mansion for barely a week when the servants told us the duke had sent a messenger to say he was returning home. The countess was greatly concerned to look her best and I could tell she saw him as more than simply her host in London. Jacqueline confided to me she considered Humphrey would make an eminently suitable husband and she intended to marry him. I asked if it was true she was already married but she waved her hand in the air and said she would have it annulled by the pope.

People have accused me of using witchcraft to secure Duke Humphrey's affection, that I seduced him through political ambition and even that I was paid by his enemies to come between him and the countess. As with most things, there is a simple explanation. I fell for him as soon as I saw him. I would not say he was particularly handsome. He was ten years older than me and tired from the long ride from Dover. He had the thin, clean shaven face of the House of Lancaster and was wearing ordinary riding clothes. Yet as he stepped into the room I sensed his power and intelligence. His keen eyes took in every detail of what I was wearing. He listened attentively to every word I said. I knew we would become lovers.

Looking back I can see how Jacqueline's deeply superstitious beliefs influenced me and might have brought about my downfall. She once told me how she had visited the capital city of Mons in splendour after inheriting her father's title.

The people turned out in great numbers, cheering and celebrating, but at the height of the festivities the most severe hailstorm had deluged the city. The countess looked serious as she described how the sky grew black and the wind howled through the city, with hail so heavy it killed many cattle and ruined the harvest. The people of Mons had claimed it was of ill omen to Jacqueline, who had met misfortune beyond her years.

Jacqueline told me the sudden death of her father had been seen as a bad portent but when her husband also fell ill with a strange fever and died, the superstitious people of Hainault had said it was a sure sign there was a curse on the family. Jacqueline told me her mother suspected a servant, bribed by the Armagnacs, had found some way to poison him but I could tell from the haunted look on Jacqueline's face she still believed she was cursed.

Her next arranged marriage to the Duke of Brabant had led to three years of abject misery and she told me how she had many times wished him dead. This darker side to Jacqueline's stories emerged as I began to become her confidante. I could soon see why she had sought sanctuary in England and learned the truth of this through the letters which she sent to her mother. As there was a real risk of letters to France falling into the wrong hands, she taught me to write them for her in this special code, based on the old dialect known only to her family.

My father's plan to bring me to court as the lady of Countess Jacqueline proved better judgement than even he had hoped. Soon after I first met him, the Duke of Gloucester was sent back to Dover by the king to prepare his next campaign, procuring a fleet of ships to carry a thousand men to war in France. The king sailed with him to Calais as soon as the men were ready, so the countess was invited to join the queen at her confinement in Windsor Castle. Queen Catherine had only been crowned in February but was already expecting the next heir to the throne. We were all the same age and, as the daughter of King Charles of France, the queen was Jacqueline's sister-in-law through her first ill-fated marriage. They had many interests in common and quickly became close friends.

Thanks to Jacqueline's good word for me I also soon became part of the queen's inner circle at Windsor. It was difficult for me at first, as although my mother had taught me French she had barely prepared me for the rich sophistication of Queen Catherine's court. I learned to listen though, and observe. The complex intrigues of the queen's court fascinated me and it proved to be an excellent preparation for what was to come later. Most exciting of all was to be so close to the centre of power and wealth in the land. I longed to see the duke once more and felt a strange frisson of anticipation and excitement at the thought of his return.

There was a moment in November at Windsor I remember clearly. I was alone with the countess in her apartment, helping her to write another of her coded letters to the Dowager Margaret in France. She surprised me with her frank description of our situation, clearly placing much trust in my discretion and her certainty the letter would never be read by anyone other than her mother. She was telling her mother Humphrey was as good as betrothed to her and if the queen and the baby were not to survive the impending birth, he would become King of England, France and Holland, with her as his queen.

I must confess I was happy she was wrong, as I had

grown to like Queen Catherine. The new heir to the throne, a strong and healthy boy, was born safely in the first week of December. By then the king and Duke Humphrey were embattled with their campaign in France and unable to return. An exhausted messenger eventually returned with the news that the king was engaged in the siege of Meaux, north of Paris.

Despite the freezing winter rains, the king was determined to defeat Jean de Gast, the Bastard de Vaurus, who had been capturing travellers on their way to Paris and hanging them in the market-place if a ransom wasn't paid. The king's reputation in France depended on his success, so he had resolved to take Meaux whatever the cost. The king commanded the queen to bring the new prince to France once she was well enough. We had a joyous Christmas at Windsor and the countess was invited to be godmother to the new prince, holding him at the font as he was christened Henry, after his father and grandfather, next in the line of kings of England.

In the spring of 1422 the queen felt ready to make the long journey to France with her infant son and was to be escorted by John, Duke of Bedford, who had been acting as regent. This meant Duke Humphrey was commanded to replace his elder brother as the new Regent and Lord Protector in King Henry V's continued absence. I returned to Humphrey's London mansion by the Thames with the countess and was waiting there to welcome him on his arrival.

I was now truly close to the heart of power, as Humphrey was king in all but name, the most important person in the land. The countess now openly sought his attention and made no secret of her intention to marry him. She asked me to arrange a banquet fit for a king to celebrate his new appointment and safe return from the war in France. My time at the queen's court at Windsor Castle had been well spent, as I had attended many royal banquets and had no difficulty in fulfilling the wishes of the countess. I also had the advantage of having gained some insight into Duke Humphrey's tastes in music and the arts.

The king's own trumpeters played a rousing royal fanfare to herald the entry of the duke with the countess on his arm. The food was the finest ever seen in London, with every type of wild bird and venison from the king's royal parks. At the beginning of each course minstrels and jugglers entertained the diners and for the highlight of the banquet I had arranged players to put on a pageant. They performed the tale of Sir Gawain and the Green Knight, with expensive costumes and a golden crown for Duke Humphrey, who played the part of King Arthur of Camelot.

Countess Jacqueline chose for herself the role of the young Queen Guinevere but had little to do other than sit at King Arthur's side and remain silent. I chose to play Lady Bertilak, the flirtatious and intelligent young wife who tempts the chivalrous knight Sir Gawain. As required by the play, in each of my three seduction scenes I changed my costumes, from the elegant dress of a modest lady in the first, to voluptuous and revealing at the end. The effect was not wasted on the duke, and I watched his eyes as I recited my lines of courtly love.

As a finale, I arranged for the duke's talented minstrels to play his favourite songs, with dancing and music to end the evening. Much fine wine was drunk and the duke clearly enjoyed himself, joining in the rousing chorus and congratulating Countess Jacqueline on her success. She had never looked happier and had shown good judgement by her plan, as from that moment on it was clear they would marry.

Many years later I confessed to him she had almost no part in the arrangements, and that I had secretly managed to include amongst the specially invited guests my father and his new wife, as well as my sister and two brothers, who really had no place at court. I also took the opportunity to have the queen's own seamstress make me a gown of rare Persian silk edged with gold. Humphrey had admitted Jacqueline had taken credit for every detail of the banquet, but he had hardly been able to take his eyes off me the entire evening. That was, he said, the moment he fell in love with me.

3

SEPTEMBER 1450

INIMICI AUTEM MEI VIVUNT

The coming of autumn to the castle has also brought a visitor of such importance I begin to hope I may be rescued after all. Late one afternoon a noisy commotion came from the direction of the south gatehouse. There was much loud shouting and I could hear the heavy boots of soldiers running in the corridor. They had placed guards at my door. It had never happened before, so I knew something important was happening. I listened for over an hour but the castle walls are thick. I could hear nothing of what was happening outside and could see nothing from the narrow windows of my tower.

My first thought was that the king had been overthrown for his incompetence. The rioting that started in Kent reached London last month, so it could be it has finally reached Anglesey. I asked the servant who brought my supper if she could tell me what was going on. She was younger than the others and one of the few English speaking women working at Beaumaris who did not seem afraid of me. She told me a ship from Ireland had tried to land at the castle quay and was turned away by the

26

sergeant-at-arms and soldiers of the guard. The gatehouses had been sealed off and no one allowed in or out since. Even those who lived outside the castle had been told they must remain, by order of William Bulkeley. The rumour in the kitchens was that the ship carried no less than Richard, the Duke of York.

Richard is a Plantagenet, one of the wealthiest land owners and most powerful men in the country. He is a cousin of my husband and once supported his open opposition to the policies of our enemy, Cardinal Henry Beaufort. I find it hard not to believe his attempted landing at the castle means he intended to see me. His father Richard, Earl of Cambridge, was beheaded by my husband's brother King Henry V for his part in the Southampton Plot, so although Richard claims loyalty to the king, he may see his chance. There is still no heir to the throne and it is possible he intends to take advantage of the public dissent. Now my husband is dead, the way is clear to put himself forward as heir apparent to the crown.

It was nearly a whole week later that I was visited by Lady Ellen, who was in some distress. She told me it was indeed Richard, Duke of York, who had sailed that day into Beaumaris from his castle in Ireland. It had fallen to her husband and the castle guard to arrest him, on orders from the king. The duke was determined to land at the castle dock, the safest landing place for his ship on this side of the island.

Lady Ellen confided that her husband was in a quandary, as he had no wish to arrest and imprison such a powerful and important man. He had shown true courage, as he ordered the barbican on the south gatehouse to be closed off, remaining with a small force of armed men outside to prevent the duke's ship from landing or entering the castle dock, at great risk to himself.

Richard had threatened he would report this interference by her husband and his men to the king, but William Bulkeley did not give in. The duke eventually moored in the small harbour at Beaumaris, a shallow place used by the ferry and fishing boats. Ellen told me Thomas Norris, captain of the town of Beaumaris, met the duke there with five soldiers and denied him landing for supplies. Duke Richard then crossed to the mainland where Ellen's own father barred his way with Lord Sudeley, the king's captain in Conway town, surrounded by his garrison of soldiers.

The duke and his small group of armed men forced their way through, as no one cared much for the inept king or his incompetent parliament, so made no move to fight or detain him. He is now thought to be heading to his castle in Ludlow to rally his supporters. Ellen fears that if Richard of York claims the throne he will remember his threat to deal harshly with those who had dared to bar his way. She has heard rumours that rebels in Kent and Sussex claim to be acting in the names of Mortimer and York. The riots in London have given him the cause he needed, so I am sure Richard is capable of raising an army of fighting men and marching against the king.

Lady Ellen's husband, my jailer, told her Duke Richard did not ask to see me or even mention my name. Although he clearly wished to moor his ship in the castle dock, he and his crew were seeking a safe haven and supplies for a journey. The duke himself made no move to enter the castle. He has been here before, so knows how easily it can be defended against his small force. I could tell from the look in her eyes that Ellen doubted the duke had cared about me.

He was simply passing through Wales on his way to confront King Henry VI.

Duke Humphrey's house in London became one of the most important places in the country, with many high-ranking people coming and going. Some wanted favours, calling to renew their relations with the new regent. Others needed decisions made, disputes settled and guidance on matters of state. At the centre of it all, enjoying all the attention and false compliments, was the Countess Jacqueline, supported by her ladies-in-waiting. She had taken effortlessly to the role of the duke's hostess, entertaining the most distinguished visitors while Humphrey was in meetings.

The duke was also enjoying his new importance. He later told me of his frustration having to share the role of regent with his brother John. Although Humphrey was a prince in the line of royal succession, he was the youngest of four sons of the king and had never been expected to take the role. Instead, he had been given the best possible education, in preparation for a life as a scholar knight or even in the church. He had also not been expected to prove such an able military commander and all he had achieved had prepared him well for the challenging task of the temporary regency.

As well as overseeing the meetings of Parliament, Humphrey was empowered to do all things necessary for the welfare of the country and to exercise the royal prerogative in ecclesiastical matters, giving him effective control of church and state. Looking back I can see he presided over one of the most peaceful times I can remember in England.

The king's war in France was beginning to outlive its

popularity and had none of the glamour of a victory such as Agincourt. There were signs the soldiers were tiring of the endless sieges and Humphrey realised most people in England had no idea of the patient diplomacy needed to secure peace in France.

Countess Jacqueline longed to see more of the towns and cities of England, so she persuaded Humphrey it would be a good idea for us to embark on a grand 'progress', taking a vast retinue of supporters to visit the most important towns and cities of the land. The king had last toured the country when he married Catherine, but that had been a different matter. He was preoccupied with the war and only interested in gathering support for his next campaign in France. Humphrey was visiting the towns and cities to show the people he understood the changes that were sweeping through the country, and aimed to win new friends and supporters. Wealthy merchants and traders competed with each other to secure titles and favour.

It was an exciting time for me, as I had never travelled far before and we were welcomed as royalty everywhere we went. Countess Jacqueline paid for the finest seamstresses in London to make silk dresses for her ladies-in-waiting. She even loaned me her gold and silver jewellery, diamond rings, pearl necklaces, worth more than I could ever dream of owning.

I needed to take care, for more than once I was mistaken for the countess herself. The duke also flattered me with his attention and began to take an interest in improving my education. He let me have my pick of his books, one of the finest collections in the country, and promised to introduce me to his favourite poets.

I now have to wear my thick woollen cloak on my walks, as protection from the biting autumn winds. The early morning skies are grey with mist and the noisy gulls circle my tower and roost on the battlements, like huddled grey harbingers of the cold winter to come. The castle has grown quieter now. No more important visitors are expected now the nights draw in and I am alone and forgotten. Writing about the events that changed my life makes me melancholy but the fresh air reminds me how fortunate I am to be one of the few survivors of those times.

Cardinal Beaufort, for all his clever scheming and trickery, is now dead, managing to outlive my poor husband by barely one month. I was right to fear Henry Beaufort and know he was the man behind my downfall. My imprisonment makes it hard for me to be certain of rumours, but Lady Ellen heard he was terrified of meeting his maker and died screaming, offering the whole treasury of England in return for living a while longer.

I wonder if his many sins gave him a heavy conscience. As well as plotting the ruin of my family, he was guilty of cruelly burning young Joan, Maid of Orleans. It was my husband's long dead brother John, Duke of Bedford, who paid the Burgundians ten thousand francs for Joan but the cardinal presided over the deceit of her long trial.

As with me, they charged her with heresy, using magic and witchcraft. Cardinal Beaufort refused her appeal for mercy to the pope, knowing she would be saved. Henry Beaufort condoned the torture of the devoutly Christian girl and planned the trickery of her confession. John signed the order, in the king's name, sentencing her to be burned at the stake as a witch, and it was by Cardinal Beaufort's order that her ashes were put into a sack and thrown into the River Seine.

I stop at the castle chapel and light a candle in memory of poor Joan. Not because I believe in God, but because like me she was cruelly wronged and should not be forgotten. A second candle flickers in the cold chapel for my beloved Duke Humphrey. I do not know how he met his end; only that he was arrested and died in custody. A third candle is lit for my son Arthur, hanged by the Duke of Suffolk for treason against the king. I grieve for his innocent soul.

It was on our tour of England that the first signs of the duke's enemies began to emerge. He was careful to be sure his duties did not exceed the official business of the kingdom and representation of the king at ceremonial functions, but he was also ambitious. It was only natural, having had a taste of power, to wonder if he might be able to change the country for the good. The gossiping nobles accused him of 'pandering to the populace' and as his popularity increased, so did the opposition shown to him by his peers, the ruling class and of course the highest ranking members of the church, led by Cardinal Henry Beaufort.

I also watched as the duke and countess became closer and Jacqueline began planning for a new life as his future bride. There was of course an obstacle to their marriage. Jacqueline was still officially married to the Duke of Brabant. She told me Duke John had agreed to the arranged marriage for her money and lands, and had treated her badly. She conveniently decided the marriage was cursed because they committed a mortal sin, so it should be annulled as soon as possible so she could be free to marry Humphrey.

Advisors helped her to prepare a statement of reasons

why the union was invalid. They argued that as the children of a brother and sister, the duke and countess were first cousins. Jacqueline's first husband, John of Touraine, was a blood relation of John of Brabant and Jacqueline's mother was godmother to John of Brabant. So, he argued, John and Jacqueline were therefore spiritual brother and sister. Finally and most importantly, the first papal dispensation allowing their marriage had been annulled by the pope.

Humphrey first came to my room when we were in the city of York. I pretended surprise but had been eagerly antici- pating his visit, as I had seen how he looked at me across the room as he spoke to some civic dignitary or made a speech. I was happy to encourage his attentions. We had been spending every waking moment together and he was opening my mind to a whole new world, riding together from one town to the next, with only Countess Jacqueline between us.

In most of the places we stayed, my room adjoined that of the countess, but on our visit to the city of York the duke arranged that I stayed the night in the house of a wealthy merchant. It was several streets away from Jacqueline and I thought there had been some mistake. My room was far too grand for a lady-in-waiting, even accounting for my sudden rise in status. It was only when I opened the door to the duke that I knew of his plan.

My mother told me the secret of a woman's power over men was to always be hard to get. I know she meant well with her advice but I forgot it in an instant. It didn't matter. I wanted him perhaps even more than he desired me. My life changed from the moment he stepped into the room and

I closed the door behind him. The memory of that night is still fresh despite the troubles I have known since. He brought a fine bottle of French brandy and two crystal glasses, which he filled generously, leaving me in no doubt of his intentions.

The servants lit a blazing fire in the hearth and we lay together in the warm bed. His body bore the savage scars of battle, but he was gentle and I was completely and hopelessly in love with him. I felt a powerful attraction the first time our eyes met and a strange feeling I can recall even now, twenty-eight years later. When he touched me, I knew I would spend the rest of my life at his side. I had watched Duke Humphrey closely and saw how he could win over a room with his knowledge and charm. He was more intelligent than anyone I had met before and his new-found power made him seem even more attractive. The most amazing thing of all was that as well as everything else, he was the most sensitive and caring lover.

We talked long into that special and memorable night, sharing our hopes and dreams, admitting to past loves and insecurities. He told me how he had been out of his mind with longing for me. I told him how I had loved him from the first moment I saw him at his mansion in London. Humphrey said we could never marry but he would keep me as his only mistress. He confessed he had already promised the countess before she even left Valenciennes that he would marry her once her annulment was confirmed. He asked that we could meet as often as possible, but in absolute secrecy. No one must ever suspect I was his lover.

I had little choice but knew to be grateful for this new life I had chosen, the path my destiny had driven me inexorably towards. For the next few months we lived a happy double life, both of us indulging the countess but secretly relishing the risky excitement of the precious moments we could spend together. There was always the danger of discovery but the more I could have, the more I wanted, and Humphrey's support in the country seemed to grow in proportion to his happiness. The people had tired of a king preoccupied with war and welcomed him with open arms. I was of course jealous of the countess but was no match for her, except in Duke Humphrey's true affection.

After barely six months of this strangely idyllic life, news arrived from France that changed everything in an instant. The king was dead, after nine short years on the throne. He had not died a heroic death in battle, but in his bed at the Château de Vincennes near Paris. The rumour was that, like so many of his men, his reign had been ended by that most un-kingly of deaths, the bloody flux.

It was the scourge of his long campaigns and had caused the death of many good men in France. King Henry V suffered the illness during the long winter siege of Meaux. He was only thirty-five years old and never saw his son. The messenger told us the king had named his brother John, Duke of Bedford, regent of France and Duke Humphrey the guardian of the young prince and protector of all England.

Humphrey told me it was all a matter of chance, for if he had been at his dying brother's bedside he could have been asked to take command of the war in France and John made regent in England. At first I saw this as a good outcome for Humphrey. The war was proving costly and unpopular and he was learning how to make the best of his temporary role of regent. The heir to the throne was barely nine months old, so the regency would last at least ten years, with him as king in all but name.

We soon learned how wrong I had been. The real power in England was now with his enemies and Humphrey's uncle, Cardinal Henry Beaufort, Bishop of Winchester. The title of cardinal had been granted as a favour by the pope, as Beaufort was one of the richest men in England. His deeply lined face betrayed how rarely he smiled and how often he frowned, yet it was his dark eyes that scared me, with their burning hatred of Duke Humphrey and all he stood for.

The king had allowed the cardinal to take control of the royal council of advisors, in return for large sums of money to pay for the war in France, secured against the royal crown jewels. Henry Beaufort was a skilled and cunning man who had built his experience and support over twenty years, serving for two successive kings and knew this was the opportunity he had been waiting for. He persuaded the Council they should immediately limit the duke's power in any way they could, for the good of England.

They started by insisting that any royal functions would be carried out only with the assent of the Council, which made it almost impossible for the duke to do anything. When Humphrey tested the resolve of parliament to back his opposition to Beaufort, his peers voted against him. He knew this was the price for his success in recognising the merchant class despite the warnings from his enemies. He told me later that he considered persuading his brother to establish the regency while he took control of France, but the moment had passed. The sudden and unexpected death of the king had not allowed any time to prepare.

The final straw that made the duke angry was when Parliament decided his brother John would be made Lord Protector of the kingdom and Humphrey should only be allowed to hold the office when he was not in England. He saw the hand of Henry Beaufort behind the plan to rob him of any power and put his own family forward. Parliament even denied Humphrey the right to be consulted by the Council, except on matters where they would have consulted the king. He had been completely outmanoeuvred by the cardinal and swore to honour the dying wishes of his brother the king, whatever the cost.

From my tower I can see the wooded hills of Wales turning gold and brown in the setting sun. A skylark hovers high over me, delighting all who can hear its song. Perhaps it is because I am in the autumn of my life, this is my favourite season, the harvest time, the autumn equinox. As a young girl, the harvest festival in our parish church at Lingfield marked Michaelmas, but as I grew older I learned the deeper meaning. Autumn is the time of balance and of sacrifice, a time when the light is defeated by darkness, a time when night takes over and brings the coming winter. The ancient wisdom says that those who long for light must face their inner darkness and overcome it.

To keep the pretence of my new-found faith I must take time from writing my journal, to copy prayers and psalms from my Book of Hours. The priest has failing eyesight and asked if I would kindly read to him on Sunday. I chose psalm thirty-seven from my little book and was struck by the truth within it. The priest has no doubt heard it many times, so the words are but a litany to him, yet when he heard the vengeance in my voice he almost shrank back in horror. I must learn to be gentle with him, as apart from Lady Ellen, he is my only true supporter in this place.

I committed the psalm to memory as I copied it out on my parchment:

But mine enemies live, and are confirmed over me: and they are multiplied that hate me unjustly. They that repay evil things for good, did backbite me: because I followed goodness. Forsake me not O Lord my God: depart not from me.

Has my God departed from me, I wonder? He has taken my freedom but let me live, taken my beloved husband but allowed my daughter to prosper and bear my grandchildren. My Antigone, married to Sir Henry Grey, Earl of Tankerville and Lord of Powys, is a countess and the lady of a knight, with three children, my grandchildren, Richard, Humphrey and little Elizabeth. I did my best to teach my Antigone as my mother taught me. I live in hope that one day she will visit me. I shall live on through them and pray their descendants remember me, not as a sorceress but as a lady who was wrongly accused.

4

OCTOBER 1450

MATRIMONIUM

I take my early morning walk round the inner ward of the castle, trying to shelter from the breeze that whips up from the Irish Sea and chills my bones. Seagulls shriek in alarm and flap into the air as I disturb their vigil by the castle kitchens, where they have learned to wait for scraps. My head is full of the news from Lady Ellen about Richard of York, who has now arrived in London and is recruiting supporters from all over the country. He continues the work of my husband and claims to be a reformer, demanding the king should act firmly with men such as Edmund Beaufort, Duke of Somerset, presently in disgrace for the loss of Normandy. The talk is that Richard has offered to deal with any traitors himself, if the king lacks the will to do so.

Ellen's father told her that both he and her husband William have been reported to the king by Duke Richard for their obstruction when he landed here at Beaumaris. These are dangerous times and they are right to fear for their safety. It is possible Duke Richard may choose to make an example of them. I hope the king will know they would have acted on his own orders. I must admit I have no love for the dour William Bulkeley, but I do rely so much on his wife Ellen's visits and they have a young family, so I wish no harm to come to them for their actions.

I stop to watch the gathering storms over the dark, brooding shape of the mainland of Wales. The wooded hills are shrouded in low clouds, heavy with rain. This name of this place was once the port of savage Vikings and the island is known as Anglesey, an old Viking name. The people here call it by the older Welsh name of Ynys Mon, which Ellen told me comes from long before the Roman times. They call the fast flowing water that makes this place an island Afon Menai. It is no river but the sea that has channelled deep, cutting me off from the mainland. Another impassable moat to keep me imprisoned here.

Ynys Mon seems to have more than its share of rain and the biting frost lies heavy on the ground even in October. I fear we are set for a hard winter, a worry because I start to feel the cold more each year now. Although there is a good sized hearth to heat my room, I am at the mercy of my captors for my supply of roughly hewn logs and the black Welsh coal, which I am trying to save for when the winter is at its worst. I hope they would not see me die of a chill to save them the trouble of looking after me.

As I walk on toward the towering southern gate of the castle, I ponder on the consequences for Duke Richard, now he seems to have made an enemy of the young French queen, Margaret of Anjou. I don't know Queen Margaret. I was imprisoned at Kenilworth Castle when she arrived from Anjou, so never met her, but feel saddened she has taken my beautiful home in Greenwich for herself. She was an unpopular choice for the king because, instead of a dowry, the French were given the lands of Maine and

Anjou. This was kept secret until it was too late and the people rioted once word got out. I suspect she now sides with Edmund Beaufort, nephew of our old enemy, Cardinal Henry Beaufort, who no doubt ensured his nephew Edmund's disastrous appointment as Lieutenant of France.

My mother was a wonderfully tolerant woman and taught me to learn to forgive, but I can never find it in my heart to forgive the cardinal. He did not act alone, but I am certain it was he who directed those who sought to ruin my husband through tormenting me. At my trial I learned the cardinal had spies and informants in my household from the moment I married Duke Humphrey, possibly even before. They had always been enemies but we did underestimate the lengths the cardinal was prepared to go to.

I have to deduce what I can from Ellen's second-hand accounts of events at court, but it seems this devious queen is manipulating the simple-minded king to her advantage. Once again there is also an evil Beaufort hand at work, as Richard was sent to Ireland as the King's Lieutenant as soon as Duke Edmund Beaufort came to power. It was easy to see they had wanted to get him out of the way. The king's orders to arrest him if he tried to return might have been inspired by the scheming queen, who really wanted to make sure he stayed in Ireland. That means she knows him to be a threat as the heir apparent.

I imagine Richard has ambition and sees a way to claim the throne for himself but fears the dangers of open rebellion. Queen Margaret is still childless, after six years of marriage, so Richard needs to act before someone else does. I still have no idea what this means for me, or if Richard of York even knows or cares that I am here. After nine years in so many dismal prisons you may think I should give up all hope of rescue, but hope is all I really have to keep me going.

I always knew of course Duke Humphrey must marry the countess, but when he did it felt like a knife had been plunged into my heart. He was my lover and could have married me. He didn't need her money or influence. He was in direct line of succession to the throne of England and wealthy beyond the dreams of most men. He didn't have to own her lands in France and Holland. He had more than enough land in England and knew Hainault was a trouble-some place. I realise now he was attracted by the sheer adventure of it all. He loved the challenge of claiming his rights by force and longed for the chance to re-kindle some-thing of his victory at Agincourt.

It was not an arranged marriage, except that it was arranged by the countess herself. She told me it would be the first time she had married for love, to a man of her own choosing. I wonder, though, if it really was chance that sent the duke to meet her at Dover. His now dead brother King Henry V had forbidden the marriage until her previous marriage had been annulled, but he had also seen the chance to bring her lands within his family and knew Humphrey would be a worthy match for her. I think Humphrey probably loved her in his way but showed me little sign of that, so I knew he married her because he had promised to.

One morning as I helped the countess to dress she was in a bright and carefree mood and told me she was expecting a child. I cannot say I was surprised, as I knew the duke had been going to her rooms late at night and was seeing less of me. The duke hadn't shared the news with me though, and I realised how innocent I was to think there were no secrets between us. Jacqueline's condition explained the reason for their haste. There would be no time for a state wedding that could take many months to plan, and there was too much at stake for the child to be born out of wedlock.

It was a freezing January when we travelled from London to the old Norman church of St James the Less in Hadleigh, where the duke owned a fine castle. The horses slid and stumbled on the icy ground and the men had to dig a path through the snow to reach the church. The white painted church was filled by men and women of the duke's household. The young priest conducting the ceremony looked like he feared he was committing a mortal sin. He stumbled on his words and nervously watched the door, as if expecting soldiers to burst in at any moment.

There was no heating in the church and the Duke kept his heavy black cloak on the whole time, but Jacqueline took off her woollen shawl to reveal her beautiful wedding dress. It had been specially made for her in London, from expensive Ottoman white silk, but was poorly suited to the freezing conditions and I saw her shiver as she waited at the altar. Humphrey cast a look back at me as if expecting a nod of approval but I kept my eyes straight ahead, unable to bless their marriage.

I watched and listened as Humphrey and Jacqueline exchanged their solemn vows, their voices echoing in the cold, half-empty church. They married without waiting for the confirmation of the annulment from the pope. Jacqueline had tired of waiting and simply declared herself free to marry Duke Humphrey. The only guests were a few of Humphrey's close and trusted friends from good families in

Essex. I knew there could be trouble for them both once the word got out.

Countess Jacqueline had been through two weddings where no expense was spared and confided that she preferred the simplicity of the English ceremony. I was puzzled at first, then realised she thought her wedding in the modest church was simply how we did things in England. I nearly explained that it would have played straight into the hands of Humphrey's enemies if they had risked a more public ceremony, yet decided to keep my silence. Jacqueline was so clever and worldly wise, with so much experience of life for her age, it was easy to forget she really knew little of our English ways.

Their first night as man and wife was accompanied by drinking and music in the private apartments of the castle which Humphrey had inherited from the Dukes of York. The countess seemed happy and relieved she had finally married someone of her own choosing, and made good her promise of all her lands to Humphrey on that day. He added Count of Holland, Zealand and Hainault to his many titles but seemed unconcerned of my feelings, merrily singing with his musicians and attentive to his happy new wife.

I pull my dark woollen cloak more closely around me, thinking of my husband. I miss him most of all when I see the trees turning to the golden brown of autumn and know I have to face another long winter alone. He was my lover, my chivalrous knight, my tutor, my husband. I was so certain he would find a way to free me but the days grew long and I knew he must be gone. Soon it will be winter, and I will miss his strong arms to keep me warm.

I tried so hard to send my husband messages, carefully written in the code only he would understand, but still at great risk. I pleaded with him to find some way to come and visit me. Once, when I still had my own allowance, I sent one of my most loyal and trusted servants to find out where he was, and what was being done to free me. I waited in hope for my servant's return but never saw or heard from her again. I suppose I will never know if any of my messages reached my husband or how he was stopped from seeing me.

Writing my journal gives my life new purpose but also dredges powerful memories of times past I would rather forget. Like the recollection of that fateful day the man I loved married the countess. She was my mistress and I was his, a secret tryst that our many enemies would surely one day discover. I would not do it now, but we were young and he was an adventurer. I remember how the duke and I lay in the marital bed, knowing Jacqueline was close, taking the most audacious risks, with everything at stake.

I have heard it said their marriage was wondered at by the common people, detested by the nobility and abhorred by the clergy. If that is true they hid it well from me. Countess Jacqueline, with Duchess of Gloucester to add to her many titles, had long let it be known they were to marry, so when they did it surprised no one. The common people already knew her as a royal, the nobility may have hoped she would curb the duke's excesses and the clergy seemed to disapprove of everything he did.

Countess Jacqueline wasted no time in writing to her match-making mother, the Dowager Margaret, to convene a meeting of the important nobles of her estates at Mons for her marriage to be announced. She also declared that she was with child and wished to return to Quesnoy for her confinement. Jacqueline became excited and full of antici-pation at the prospect of returning home and invited me to accompany her. She told me she would order an army of six thousand archers to protect us on the journey and we would be welcomed as royalty.

Although the duke was civil to me, he was doing his best to make his new bride happy and had resolved to remain faithful to her. Although his powers had been limited, he was not without influence at Parliament and ensured his new wife was recognised as Duchess of Gloucester. He made her a citizen of England by a special Act of Parliament, with the full rights of an English subject. She was well known by that time and had already been accepted by the duke's wide circle of friends. Even his critics, including Cardinal Beau-fort, who had confronted Humphrey at every turn, seemed to grudgingly accept the new duchess.

There were plenty of dissenters to the marriage in France, of course, the most significant being the duke's brother John, Regent of France. John had just married Anne of Burgundy at Troyes to strengthen the vitally important alliance with her brother, the powerful and manipulative Duke Philip of Burgundy. Humphrey was no ambassador and wrote a deliberately provocative letter to the Duke of Burgundy, telling him that he had married the countess and all her territories now belonged to him. Poor Anne died horribly of the plague and all John's plans died with her, but we were not to know that at the time.

The excitement turned to deep sadness when Jacqueline gave birth to a stillborn child. It was the only child of her three marriages and brought back dark superstitions she had almost been able to forget. She was distraught and told me her family had been cursed. I was starting to believe her. I regret to say Humphrey never seemed to treat Jacqueline the same after he was told the sad news. It was a boy, his son and heir who could have even one day been King of England. He once confided to me that his son would have been christened Humphrey, the name handed down through four generations from his mother's Norman de Bohun family.

The tragedy meant I had my lover back. I had missed being the centre of his world, missed his loving embrace. We returned to taking risks, back to our secret double lives. The duke needed time to grieve but he wanted me to help him through it. The countess wasn't well enough to ride, but I went with him to exercise the horses and we would gallop recklessly through the woods to leave our escort far behind, just as I had done with Jacqueline in the London parks.

This time it was different though, as the duke started talking about how we could one day be married. Physicians had told him the countess might not be able to have more children, but he had proved he was capable of fathering them. He began talking of how their marriage may not be legal and how easily Jacqueline would find a new husband in France. I listened, not daring to hope, but knowing my future happiness depended on his wishful thinking.

The duke was a good friend of the powerful Abbot of St Albans, John of Wheathampstead, as they had studied together at Balliol College in Oxford and St Albans was one of Humphrey's favourite places. On that frosty Christmas Eve I travelled with Humphrey and Jacqueline and our growing retinue in grand procession to the priory of St Albans. The prior made us welcome and formally acknowledged the countess as Humphrey's true and legitimate wife. I watched as the prior blessed their union and admitted the countess into the fraternity of the abbey, confirming her official acceptance by the church.

We stayed on at St Albans for the twelve days of Christmas, but it was not the peaceful celebration we would have wished. Our household had now grown to over three hundred servants and soldiers, many of them Dutch and Flemish mercenaries who had seen an opportunity and travelled across the English Channel to serve their rich new count. The duke was also building his personal guard of soldiers into a small private army, recruiting good loyal Englishmen who had fought with him on his campaigns in France.

The Christmas festivities were hardly underway when a servant rushed in to tell the Duke that the men of our household had become drunk and rowdy, the English fighting with the Dutch over an argument. Humphrey immediately sent some men of his personal guard to sort it out. They returned some time later, having thrown the ringleaders in irons. They also had more serious news. Others had apparently been caught red-handed, blatantly poaching deer and rabbits in the abbey woods, an offence punishable by death.

I had never seen Humphrey in such an incandescent rage. He said he had to make an example and ordered one of the men put into the stocks. I watched with Jacqueline from a high window overlooking the courtyard as he proceeded to hit the defenceless man over the head and ordered that his dog, a fine hunting greyhound, should be hung as a punishment. It was a side of him I had never witnessed before. He was normally so charming it was easy to forget the sights he must have seen as a soldier fighting in France. I know the countess was shocked at his brutality, although she knew better than to intervene. It was hardly the happy and peaceful Christmas we had expected.

Another surprising side of the duke was his sudden determination to take control of his new territories abroad. His friends warned him to take care and his enemies watched with interest to see what he would do. John, Duke of Bedford, wanted to settle the dispute between the Dukes of Brabant and his brother Humphrey, with himself and the Duke of Burgundy as arbitrators. John had already given French territories to the Duke of Burgundy and Humphrey hesitated to put his case in the hands of judges.

He saw his case as beyond dispute and knew he could be bound by whatever decision they made. Philip of Burgundy was hardly neutral, as he was the heir to Jacqueline's former husband, John of Brabant. Humphrey insisted that he and Jacqueline had been recognised as man and wife by the laws of the Church in England. His brother John wrote a letter to the pope, urging him to confirm the divorce of Jacqueline and Brabant and pointing out the loss of life that could result if he failed to do so. He was right, as Humphrey was already busily raising an army, strengthening his retinue with good men who had fought at his side in France, as well as mercenary fighters who would be loyal to him at a price.

The man who could most easily finance Humphrey's claiming his newly acquired lands was Cardinal Henry Beaufort, who was then the Bishop of Winchester and also the man who took delight in stopping any funding from the state. Humphrey had anticipated this but he was still disappointed, as it meant he would have to pay for the campaign from his own income. I am not sure even he knew the full extent of his wealth, as he had been granted huge areas of the country when his brother was king, including the Isle of Wight and estates in Wales. As well as his mansion in London and the castle in Essex he had a castle at Pembroke. The income from these was complex, as he was also responsible for their upkeep.

There was one last visit to make before we set sail for France, to see Humphrey's stepmother, Queen Joanna at King's Langley Palace. It was the first time I met Queen Joanna, who had been imprisoned for three years for witchcraft and necromancy, although she had of course never been tried by any court. I travelled with Countess Jacqueline and an escort of twenty-four horsemen, as the Duke was delayed by his work. Word of our approach seemed to travel before us, as we caused quite a stir as we passed through towns and villages.

The countess was surprisingly well informed about Queen Joanna and explained to me that although she had never met her, they were distantly related to both her own mother and her father's line. Humphrey's brother King Henry V had seen a way to deprive her of her over generous allowance of ten thousand marks, which he needed to finance his campaigning in France. Jacqueline had heard that Henry soon changed his mind and ordered the restoration of her freedom and her property, so I was not surprised to see the obvious wealth and comfort provided to her.

Queen Joanna kept us waiting in her well-appointed outer chamber room for some time before making a grand entrance, wearing a fine rosary and girdle of gold over a dress of black satin, sparkling with small jewels. She welcomed us both warmly and spoke quickly to the countess in a dialect I found hard to understand, despite my greatly improved French speaking. I think she was questioning Jacqueline about the details of her annulment of her previous marriage. There was clearly a tension between the two women. I suspected it had to do with Queen Joanna's concern for her stepson, but her manner towards me was engaging and I was intrigued by this enigmatic woman.

Later, as we dined in her palatial banqueting hall, Queen Joanna spoke openly about her interest in astrology and how she had come to be accused of necromancy by her own stepson. She was knowledgeable and persuasive; pointing out there was no more evidence to support the Christian faith than there was to deny the ability of anyone to foretell the future. Looking back I can see it was over that first dinner with Humphrey's stepmother, with the expensive Rhenish wine flowing freely, that set me on the path which led to this cold prison so many years later.

5

NOVEMBER 1450

INCURSIO

My days grow shorter now and I am careful to conserve the tallow candles provided to light my room. I have taken to lying awake on my bed in the darkness, planning what next to include in my secret journal. My writing has become so much more than just a way to pass the time. It has become my confessor, my own account of the happiest days of my life – and the saddest. I know I must record these memories while I can, even though I find myself wondering if anyone will ever take the trouble to decipher my code and read this diary.

On one of my walks I found an iridescent feather from one of the noisy magpies that swoop into the castle grounds. I hope it will make a good quill, once I have boiled it in a little of my precious store of salt and left it on the sill of the window to harden in the sunlight. I remember when I only used the finest goose feather quills, discarding them after a single use. Now I take the greatest care to make them last as long as possible. My favourite quill now is this black feather from one of the castle's sinister crows. This quill is smaller than I am used to but comfortable in my hand and particularly good at making the fine lines of my secret code.

I have become skilled at keeping my writing small to make best use of this fine parchment, as I don't know if the priest will be able to bring me more. I sharpen the iron blade the priest gave me against the stone of my window-sill with gentle strokes as he showed me to do. Then I trim the smallest of shavings from the worn nib of the quill, being careful to preserve its shape and length. My sight is not as good as it was and I struggle to make out the details of the mainland across the water. I am fortunate though, as I can see close up as clearly as when I was young and the coded words come naturally to me now with little effort.

On his last visit the old priest brought me another small clay pot of the special black ink, sealed with red wax to stop the contents spilling or drying out. He handed it to me almost hesitantly, as if he suspected the real purpose it was to be put to. Taking his old hand in gratitude for his kindness towards me, I was surprised to find it cold to the touch. I looked into his slate-blue eyes and saw acknowledgement, so invited him to take a seat by my good fire and warm his hands for a while. After sitting in silence, looking into the glowing embers, he began telling me something of his circumstances.

'I am not originally from this island, you know. I was born in the Welsh heartlands beyond the mountains.' He spoke slowly, with a note of regret in his voice.

I nodded in understanding. 'I often look out over the mountains and wonder what lies beyond them.'

He looked into the flames. 'My father was a tenant farmer, raising sheep. We lived comfortably enough,' he continued, 'until my mother and my younger brother both fell... victim to the plague.' He made the sign of the cross on his chest at the memory.

'I am sorry.' I could see he was still deeply troubled by his loss.

The priest looked at me. 'My father was a good man.' He seemed to struggle to find the words. 'He fell into dark moods after that. He eventually sailed off to sea. I never heard from him again.'

I looked into his sad eyes. 'That is why you chose to become a priest?'

He nodded. 'It was always my ambition. My mother used to say I should have a *proper* education.' He smiled, for the first time. 'My happiest memories are of my time at the seminary, where I learned to read and write, as well as learning the ways and rules of the priesthood.'

I understood. His choice meant sacrificing the things men hold most dear, yet it had been a way out of the hardships of the life his father had led. All the same, I suspected he had lived a lonely life since taking up his parish in Beaumaris all those years ago.

The priest continued looking into the fire, as if deep in thought, before speaking again. 'Now I dedicate my time to serving the people of Ynys Mon, supporting the poor and the sick as best I can.'

'It is good work you do, and I am most grateful for your visits.' It was true. I looked forward to seeing him now.

'My needs are modest, but,' he shook his head and frowned, 'the greater share of the tithes paid by the villagers are... appropriated by the bishop, who lives in a grand palace.'

I found myself recalling the wealth of my enemy Cardinal Beaufort, who used his position in the church to build such wealth and power that he could even bring down the brother of the king. I also remembered the bishops at my trial, in their gold-trimmed robes.

The priest looked at me again. 'I should tell you, my lady, I am paid a small allowance by Sir William Beauchamp, Constable of Beaumaris, because of your presence here.' He smiled at me again. 'It means I am able to eat well in the castle kitchens.'

I had never thought of it before. I realised that I must also provide an easy living for the soldiers who guard me and the servants who wash my clothes and prepare my food. It was comforting to know that even now, locked up in my tower and cut off from the world, I am of some small use.

As I listened to the priest's story, I wondered if this was my time to risk taking him into my confidence. My only wish is that my daughter Antigone would be allowed to come and see me, or at least send a note to let me know she is safe and well. The priest could perhaps find some way to help. The danger was that he may stop visiting me with supplies, or worse, he could feel obliged to report me to the sergeant-at-arms. I decided to wait a while, for time is something I have plenty of.

I stood at the window and watched the priest as he shuffled back to his lodgings in the gathering gloom, his hunched posture making him look even older than his years. Just as I was about to look away he turned and raised a hand. I raised my own hand back to him, surprised to feel comfort from such a small gesture of companionship after my lonely imprisonment. I hadn't even asked his name.

Duke Humphrey became preoccupied, perhaps even obsessed with securing his wife's lands in Hainault. He worked late into the night, sending long letters bearing his royal seal to potential allies in far off Hainault. He spent every spare moment in careful study of the maps he had obtained of the country and questioned the countess about any detail that could be of advantage. I always suspected his motivation was largely because his older brother had forbidden him to even try. There had been no love between the brothers since the premature death of King Henry V in France.

Humphrey watched impotently from England as his elder brother John continued to rule over their French territories, which he seemed to have done remarkably well. For his own part, Humphrey was struggling to act as Regent with most of parliament opposed to him and his uncle Cardinal Beaufort openly challenging his authority.

Raising an army needed all the favours the duke could call on, as Cardinal Beaufort persuaded the government that the state should not finance what they saw as his self-serving adventure. At first it looked impossible to find enough good men, but he had influential friends and was able to persuade Sir John de Mobray, Duke of Norfolk and the Earl Marshall of England, to support his claims, in return for Sir John's appointment as commander once the army arrived in France.

I disliked Sir John, a humourless man, who looked at me with an appraising eye, but I was glad of this turn of events, as many years had passed since Humphrey was last in a battle of any kind. I worried for his safety and also for his judgement, as he had little patience for the manipulative politics of the Hollanders. Sir John de Mobray was a valuable supporter, as he had recent and successful experience both as a soldier and ambassador in France. Although he had not fought with Humphrey at Agincourt, he knew how to command men on the battlefield.

Humphrey took us on the long ride from London to his apartments in Dover Castle. As well as the countess and myself, he ordered our full retinue of servants to accompany us to France, including his personal guard and over a thousand fighting men. More joined us on the journey, so by the time we arrived at the coast the line of marching soldiers, horses and wagons following us stretched back far into the distance, further than I could see. Like never before, this was a reminder of Humphrey's true wealth and influence.

As warden of the port he had been able to commandeer a fleet of forty-two warships, but mustering good men prepared to sail to France with him had not been so easy. He spent a fortune recruiting men, arming them and securing provisions for what we all knew could be a long and dangerous campaign. I watched from the high window of Dover Castle with Jacqueline as Sir John de Mobray prepared this sizeable but ill-disciplined army. I knew they consisted mostly of mercenaries and opportunists, yet he appeared to regard them as if they were loyal soldiers of the crown.

It was the middle of October and even the elements were against us. Stormy winds and heavy rain made it impossible to sail for many days. Humphrey was frustrated yet well used to the changeable weather of the English Channel, but Jacqueline's superstition got the better of her. She saw the gathering black clouds as another ill omen and confided to me that she doubted we would receive a warm reception in her homeland. Her people had a deep distrust of the English and she worried they would accuse her of abandoning them, even though it had been far too dangerous for her to stay in Hainault.

Soon after we had arrived in Dover, Jacqueline showed me another of the secret messages which had arrived from her mother, the Dowager Margaret. It did little to reassure her anxiety about the trip. It transpired that the merchants had become used to prosperity under the peaceful rule of John of Bavaria and had no wish to see Humphrey reclaim their lands. The message said they offered to raise the considerable sum of thirty thousand pounds a year for Humphrey to remain in England. If the message had arrived when we were still in London it might have been possible to try to persuade Humphrey, but it was too late now we were almost ready to sail.

Despite the thick walls of Dover Castle I could clearly hear his furious reaction when she told him the news. He shouted that he was insulted by the suggestion he could be so easily 'bought off' reclaiming her rightful inheritance. As I expected, the message strengthened his resolve. It also marked the moment when I first heard him raise his voice at the countess. He accused her mother of being a scheming trouble maker. When I saw Jacqueline soon afterwards her eyes were red, as if she had been crying. It was a long time ago, but looking back I think that day in Dover was when she began to change her attitude towards me.

It was twenty-six years ago and my memory of some things is failing, yet I recall our departure from Dover that day so clearly. It proved, of course, to be the turning-point in my life and on that chilly autumn morning in the busy harbour I sensed nothing would ever be quite the same again. It was the first time I had set out on a sea voyage and I had always longed to see France, having heard so much about it at the court of Queen Catherine.

When the storm finally calmed we made our way to the bustling harbour. I knew Humphrey would not rest until he had secured Jacqueline's lands, so we were going to be in France for a long time and our servants laden down with as much as they could carry. A soldier shouted something to us as we made our way to our ship. I couldn't hear over the noise but Humphrey grinned and I suspected he was glad to be back with his comrades. Agincourt had been the making of him but that was some time ago now and I know he missed the life of a soldier.

Ours was one of the grandest ships and proudly flew Humphrey's royal standard, a splash of colour against the dark clouds. I followed the countess up the narrow gang-plank and wondered when I would next set foot on English soil. Every ship in the harbour was crammed with young soldiers, their equipment piled high. More waited on the quayside, huddled in noisy groups. Men-at-arms stood apart from archers, who in turn distanced themselves from the duke's mercenary foot soldiers. I was amazed at how quickly the sailors climbed the towering masts to set the sails. The men in command were shouting orders. Sailors were heaving on ropes with a clever arrangement of blocks and tackles to raise the sails and all around the harbour I could see other ships being readied for the journey.

Horses protested loudly as they were hauled up gang-planks and tethered on the decks. Some of the families of the men had gathered on the quayside to say farewell and I remembered my father's warning. He had worried when I told him of our plans but knew it was my duty to accompany the countess. That was the first time I met Anne, my father's third wife. She seemed wary of me, as if I would somehow turn him against her. I remember thinking my father looked older, his grey hair thinning and his face deeply lined. He privately handed me a velvet purse, heavy with gold coins. He told me it was the last of my once great inheritance, so I must guard it well and use it only in an emergency.

Despite our ship being the largest of the fleet in the harbour, our cabin space below decks was cramped and soon filled with our supplies and belongings. As it was my first time at sea I wanted to be on deck when we sailed, so I put on my cape with a hood that would give me some protection if it rained. I left Jacqueline in her cabin and went to find Duke Humphrey. He was in good spirits, clearly glad to be sailing to France at last, standing high on the stern of the ship talking with the captain, who pointed to the approaching black clouds.

The experienced sea captain was right, as we had barely cleared the safe shelter of the harbour walls when a violent storm hit us, making the sails flap loudly and causing waves to break alarmingly over the bows. The soldiers on the deck had no shelter and were quickly soaked through to the skin, some hanging over the side to be sick. I was scared the ship would be swamped but the sailors continued on their course and the sea water simply washed off the deck. I gripped the wooden railing with both hands but was nearly thrown off my feet as the ship pitched to one side. I clearly remember how Humphrey put his arm around my waist to steady me. It had been some time since we had been together, so I felt safe in his embrace, although I knew he was no sailor.

One of the ships to our side turned suddenly in the strong breeze and came straight for us, its sails full and barely under control. I braced myself for the impact but both ships had good men on the helm and passed with a few feet to spare. I could hear the captain shouting for the sails to be reefed and the ship slowly settled back on course. Such near-misses must be commonplace with ships sailing so closely but it made me realise how vulnerable we were, even on this short journey.

It began raining heavily and Humphrey led me back to the cabin, where we found Jacqueline on her knees in prayer. I saw that Humphrey made no effort to comfort her and he seemed more concerned about my need to change into dry clothes than he was for his wife. I carefully chose an expensive deep blue velvet gown which I had been saving for a special occasion. Humphrey looked at me approvingly once I had changed and took my hand, leading me to the captain's cabin. I suspected that some of the crew who saw us together could have mistaken me for the countess.

The captain had a nautical chart spread out on his table and was carefully checking the position of the other ships. The storm had scattered the fleet but the strong breeze was in our favour and their captains showed great skill in bringing them into line again. As one came closer to our side I could see the deck was crowded with soldiers, wet through but in good humour, as we heard them give a rousing cheer as they recognised the flagship.

It was mid-afternoon before we heard a shout from the lookout and could make out the distant shape of Calais on the horizon. Duke Humphrey led me back up to the deck so we could have a better view. A small patch of blue brightened up the sky and the rain had passed. We watched as the green fields of France slowly became visible. Soon we could see the harbour. Small fishing boats set out to greet us and I could sense the heightened anticipation amongst the crew. I began to wonder what fate awaited us in Hainault.

6

DECEMBER 1450

NON FECIT MISERICORDIAM

Winter has come to Beaumaris Castle, chilling the air so I see my frozen breath as I take my walk in the inner ward. My guards are under orders to tend my fire and I hear them curse as they carry heavy logs up the winding stone steps of my tower. They are simple men and their superstition reminds me of my mistress Jacqueline so long ago. A single glance from me is enough to silence them. I watch the guards closely to see a way to get to know them better, as I know it may be useful some day.

One of the guards reminds me a little of Arthur, my long lost only son. He has the same beguiling innocence and I see a question in his eye as he looks at me. It gives me hope. The other guards regard me as little more than an inconvenience, despite the fact I am the reason for their occupation. Also unlike the others, who speak only in Welsh, I have heard him speak in English. He seems popular and to be respected by them, even though some are clearly older than him. When the time is right I will ask his name and see what more I can learn.

Now I look forward to the winter solstice, when the sun begins its northward journey in the sky and the days will finally begin to grow longer again. From my translation of the little Book of Hours, which also must serve as my calendar to mark the passing days, I see it is the holy day of the martyr Saint Barbara on the fourth of December. Like me, she is unjustly locked up in a tower, hidden from the world and closely guarded. She was able to bring down thunderbolts and is made a saint for her faith. I wish I could do the same but know it would instead be taken as certain proof of my necromancy.

I continue to carefully translate the Latin script to keep my mind sharp and pass the long hours. The priest takes comfort from my apparent return to the church, but my faith is long since gone. When I was young I remember being entranced by the sermons, delivered with such conviction in our family parish church at Lingfield. December was when we would listen in wonder at the story of the nativity, yet now I wonder how anyone could hear that tale of immaculate conception without questions forming in their mind.

As I write I recall instead the wonderful Christmas and New Year celebrations of my childhood. We would have a golden goose, the magical yellow colour created by covering it in butter and precious saffron. My mother told me the saffron had been brought back from the Holy Lands by brave Crusaders and it was even more precious than real gold. Years later Humphrey laughed at my innocence and told me saffron is expensive but grown in a place named Saffron Walden in Suffolk.

I also loved the special treat of Christmas puddings. The steaming kitchens at Starborough Castle were a hot and busy place, yet in my mother's time they were also happy and exciting to a young girl. I was not supposed to visit the kitchens when I was young, yet I knew the cooks would let me help them make the puddings at Christmas and New Year. I remember they boiled a thick porridge of wheat, which they sweetened with sugar, currants and dried fruit, then spiced with cinnamon and nutmeg.

Years later I would plan special Christmas feasts for Humphrey. We would have banquets in our great hall, with all our friends and family. There would be venison and hot mulled wine. Travelling mummers would perform plays and dances, their faces painted and wearing colourful costumes, so one could only guess at their true identity. A favourite of the duke in those happy times were what we called the mystery plays. The story of Christ was turned to simple entertainment, with Humphrey easily persuaded to take the part of King Herod as an evil villain and I would sometimes play the innocent virgin Mary, much to his amusement.

Another of Humphrey's favourite pastimes was to regale us all with reminiscences of the victory at Agincourt. It had been the making of him, and of course his brother King Henry V. He repeated the story when he had been drinking, so I was well used to his account of how the French were so completely defeated on that victorious battlefield in Normandy. He would tell how the English were outnumbered twenty to one by the French army, yet won the day through courage and bravery. Duke Humphrey was modest about his own role in the battle, but would admit to taking part in hand-to-hand fighting with his men at the front.

Many years later he gave me quite a different account of

the events of that fateful day. I had known of the deep scars on his body but when I asked about them he was usually dismissive, calling them his 'war wounds'. One evening, long after we were finally married, he had drunk a few glasses of his favourite wine and was in a reflective mood. I asked him to tell me what it really had been like for him in that muddy French field at Agincourt. He was finally ready to talk.

He told me how proud he was to be chosen to sail with his brother, King Henry V, on his splendid flagship the Trinity Royal in support of his claim for the French crown. It was the autumn of 1415 and Henry had raised one of the biggest English fleets ever assembled, numbering over one thousand four hundred vessels. They needed every seaworthy ship because they were carrying two thousand men-at-arms and some eight thousand of the finest long-bowmen from England and Wales.

Humphrey said their army was accompanied by Welsh miners and master masons, experts at besieging castles, as well as heavy horses to haul a dozen of the new great cannons and siege equipment, which were loaded with much difficulty onto the decks of the biggest ships. The king brought his entire retinue of servants, including his trumpeters and minstrels, a sure sign to Humphrey it was to be a long campaign. Also on board the king's flagship were the most respected surgeons and apothecaries in England, a more worrying sign that his brother the king expected his mission to claim the crown and kingdoms of France to also be a bloody one.

Their destination was the city port of Harfleur, one of the most important harbours on the coast of Normandy, which they planned to use as a base for a march up the banks of the Seine, all the way to Paris. It was a great adventure to Humphrey, who until then had always lived in the shadow of his brothers, King Henry and John, Duke of Bedford, who was to take charge of the country in the king's absence. It was also his chance to show his military skill to those who dismissed him as a scholar, and prove he was a fit and able heir to the throne, if the succession was ever to pass to him.

The voyage started with a bad omen, as one of the ships caught fire and was quickly ablaze when it was barely underway. A good breeze caused the flames to set light to the sails of the ships closest to each side before they could manoeuvre away. All three ships were lost, with most of those on board, as few could swim to safety. Despite himself, Humphrey saw this as a portent that all would not be easy in the months to come, but the same winds that had fanned the flames also sped the fleet quickly across the English Channel. They anchored in the bay of the Seine a few miles from Harfleur, without further incident.

The port town of Harfleur was found to be small but well defended, taking advantage of the land and protected by a high stone wall with tall towers overlooking each of the gates. Humphrey's men established a chain across the mouth of the harbour and stockades at the gates to prevent anyone from entering or leaving. The giant siege canons they had brought were unloaded and hauled into position using teams of horses. He described how these fearsome cannons kept up their noisy barrage day and night, deafening the men who worked them, blasting huge stone balls at the walls and towers. The siege should have been over quickly, but the garrison was commanded by two experienced knights, who defended it bravely.

Humphrey confessed to me that all was not well for the English army. As the weeks of siege fighting drew on, their supplies of food and water ran worryingly low. His men started to desert in the night and many fell ill from drinking bad water. All were tormented by a host of black flies and weak from their poor diet. They began pillaging the farms and villages around Harfleur, against the strict orders of the king, who commanded that looters were to be hanged on the spot. King Henry V also ordered that any harlots and camp followers who came to corrupt his men were to have their left arms broken as a punishment. This did little for morale and several men were severely punished for fighting their own side.

Despite their greatly inferior numbers, the Harfleur garrison continued to make successful night-time raids against the English, using their local knowledge to ambush the English guards and picking off those who came within range of their deadly crossbows. It began to look as if this small force of barely three hundred men were going to see off the might of the English army, if they could hold out until reinforcements arrived.

A breakthrough came when the Duke of Clarence captured a French convoy carrying supplies and ammunition for the beleaguered port. The small garrison of Harfleur tried a desperate last attack but many were killed, badly wounded or taken prisoner. There was no sign of the French army and after a month of fighting the garrison surrendered, raising a white flag of surrender and throwing open the gates. It was a costly victory, as Henry had lost a third of his army, but like Calais, Harfleur became an English port.

King Henry V sent more than half his army back to England by way of Calais, with many French prisoners and carrying cases of gold and other booty taken from the people of Harfleur. Humphrey assisted with overseeing the repairs to the walls and ditches of the town, so it could be defended by the new garrison. He stayed in Harfleur for two weeks then left with his brother King Henry V, with nearly two thousand men-at-arms and thirteen thousand archers. Sir Thomas Beaufort, Earl of Dorset and Humphrey's uncle was left in command of some three hundred English men-at-arms and a thousand archers who had been chosen to remain in Harfleur.

They were in no condition to march on Paris and instead followed the rest of the English force north to the safety of Calais, to wait out the winter and recover their strength. As they marched, more men died from what they called the bloody flux and lack of proper food. Even worse, a good many men deserted in the night, rather than face the risk of catching the flux or the prospect of facing the French army that was rumoured to be waiting for them.

As Humphrey feared, the French were camped in great numbers on the opposite bank when they reached the wide River Somme. This meant a long detour to cross the river at Bethencourt. It was mid-October and the sick and wounded soldiers had marched two hundred miles in twelve days, with barely enough provisions for one week. It rained heavily and supplies were running low, so it was an exhausted army that found their way completely blocked by the French at Agincourt.

Humphrey remembered that the French encampment stretched far into the distance. From their many banners he could see a great army of men had marched from all over the country. Knights on horseback paraded around the camp and men-at-arms practiced advancing in tight formation. The sheer number of soldiers facing them was too much for Henry. He released some of the remaining prisoners they had been intending to ransom, with a message for the French commander, offering to return Harfleur and make good the damage caused in the siege. In return they asked for safe passage to Calais, where they would embark for England.

His answer was the sound of the French celebrating, the sounds of revelry continuing long into a cold and sleepless night. There were no celebrations in the English camp. Henry's future had never looked so bleak and Humphrey told me he wondered how any of them could expect to live through the next day. He recalled that the last meeting with King Henry before the battle was a sombre affair, made bleaker by news that reinforcements sent from Calais to aid them had been captured on route, with many men killed. King Henry commanded they would die fighting, to the last man, rather than face the shame of capture by their enemies.

Early the next morning the two armies lined up to fight at a place called Agincourt. Humphrey said the French were close enough to shout insults while the English waited in heavy rain, every archer tasked with setting sharpened wooden stakes to slow the expected cavalry charge. He remembered how hard it was to dispel the sense of impending doom. Henry had ordered his siege cannons back to Calais, so they watched in despair as the French prepared to use new cannons against hungry and tired men armed with bows and arrows.

Worst of all, Humphrey recalled the feeling of dread at the sight of the French 'Oriflamme', a huge red banner that meant they could expect no quarter was to be given, no mercy would be shown and no prisoners to be taken. The best he could hope for was to be taken for ransom or a quick death, although he knew that neither was likely when the two sides met in battle.

The French forces were well fed and well-armed, but not well led, as their choice of Agincourt as the place to block the English march to the coast proved a poor one. The recently ploughed fields turned to deep mud after so much heavy rain. After hours of waiting the French foot soldiers advanced in waves. They were accompanied by the sounds of an ominous drum beat, with mounted cavalry galloping on each side.

Humphrey described how it seemed his men would be overwhelmed by sheer force of numbers. Then the tide turned in his favour. The air was filled with more arrows than he had ever seen as the English made their desperate last stand. The front ranks of the French broke formation as men fell, mortally wounded. Inhuman shrieks rang out as the sharpened stakes proved horribly effective, impaling the charging war horses. He watched as his archers deliberately aimed at the flanks of the horses, causing them to rear into the air and throw their riders into the mud. Some of the French had heavy armour and sank into the freshly ploughed field, starting a crush where they trampled over each other, driven on by the pressing force from behind. Now within range of the longbows, this made for an easy target for the skilled English bowmen.

Humphrey could have stayed in the relative safety of the rearguard, but he was young and adventurous. He dismounted from his horse to fight at the front, with his best men on either side, using his sword on any of the approaching enemy who made it through to the English lines. He shook his head as he described the carnage, with his archers using mallets and billhooks to finish off wounded Frenchmen. In the heat of the battle he somehow advanced too far into the enemy ranks and suddenly found himself surrounded by French soldiers.

He was well trained but had little experience of this close combat and told me he was soon battling for his life. He remembered killing several men in the fierce fighting before he met his match. He later found it was no less than the commander of the French second wave, the Duke of Alencon, who struck him down with a savage blow. Humphrey said he fell backwards in the deep mud, severely wounded in the groin. He was losing a lot of blood and couldn't stand. Word reached King Henry, who rushed forward to save him, surrounded by his personal guard.

His brother told him the rescue nearly cost him his own life, as he received a heavy strike on his bascinet from a French axe that could have been fatal. The Duke of Alencon was eventually disarmed and knelt before Henry in surrender, expecting to be ransomed, but was swiftly executed by one of his guards before Henry could respond. Humphrey later heard this was not the last of the executions. The cousin of the King of France, Antoine of Burgundy, Duke of Brabant had his throat cut as he lay wounded on the field.

Many French had been taken prisoner and while Humphrey was being carried off to have his wounds tended, six hundred French cavalry charged to free them. At the same moment a band of armed peasants from Agincourt attacked from the rear, ransacking the king's supplies and taking his crown jewels and all the gold and silver carried from England. Henry was outraged but there was nothing he could do, as he didn't even have enough men to guard the prisoners, and reluctantly ordered that they all be killed.

Humphrey told me he passed out with the pain, resigned to his fate. If he had not been the king's youngest brother he would surely have died from loss of blood, as his wounds were deep and the risk of infection from the mud of the battlefield was high. The king's own physicians cleaned his wounds and tended him until he was well enough to return home. He had been twenty-five at the time of the battle and quickly recovered, with the deep scar to show for his adventure, but he never fought in a battle again.

Our arrival in Calais nearly ten years after that victory in Agincourt was welcomed by most of the population, some who turned out to show their loyalty but most I suspect out of curiosity. We had brought nearly half of Humphrey's army with us, over five hundred archers and twice as many foot soldiers. Some cheered and shouted to us but others looked anxious, perhaps conscious of the precarious hold the English had over the walled town.

The fleet had returned to Dover with the tide to collect the rest of Humphrey's men, leaving us to wait in the French port. Humphrey had secured us a fine mansion in the middle of Calais and established his men in the barracks. He sent riders to the city of Mons to announce our presence and set out our demands for the reinstatement of Countess Jacqueline's rightful inheritance.

Humphrey knew Calais well, having been there many times. He explained how it had first been taken by his great-grandfather, King Edward III after a short but brutal siege. The town's leaders had refused to surrender and faced execution, but the English had taken anyone of rank hostage and evicted all other inhabitants, sending messages to England for people to come and take such property as they wished.

At Christmas time I had a visit from Lady Ellen, whom I have not seen for nearly two months. She gave no reason for not visiting me for so long and I didn't ask, but she brought her little son to see me, carrying a present. Named William after his father, Ellen's son is a confident boy with his father's dark hair and at six years old, grown enough to be curious about my presence in this castle. He handed me his present, a small basket of fruit and spiced gingerbread. I thanked them both, as it was a long time since I had seen a ripe peach or eaten sweet ginger. I was grateful for their kindness.

Ellen told me how she was teaching young William to read and that he could already write his own name, after a fashion. He took great interest in my writing desk and my small collection of feathers that will be soon made into quills, so I made him a present of my small iridescent feather. It had cost me nothing but a little time, of which I have plenty, and it clearly gave him great pleasure, as he admired it as if it were the most precious of gifts.

His mother also appreciated my gesture and I think it helped build a little trust between us. She told me there was little news from London since we had last met but Ellen had learned more of the fall of Queen Margaret's main supporter, William de la Pole, Duke of Suffolk. It was William who had negotiated the king's marriage to the four-teen-year-old Margaret of Anjou and was rewarded by being made Duke of Suffolk two years ago.

The lives of Humphrey and William de la Pole had been intertwined since they fought together at the siege of Harfleur. Humphrey told me once he never trusted William's father, the Earl of Suffolk, who was one of the many who died an unheroic death at Harfleur from the bloody flux. William himself was so badly wounded during a counter-attack by the French garrison that he was amongst those shipped home. He therefore missed the carnage of Agincourt but his older brother Michael de la Pole, heir to the family title, who became the new Earl of Suffolk, was one of those killed in the battle.

I cursed the man who was suspected of the murder of my beloved Humphrey and now it is unlikely we will ever hear the truth. Suffolk is dead, executed by an unknown hand for his scheming. He had been on the ascendant, a powerful advisor to Queen Margaret, appointed Lord Chamberlain, Lord High Admiral and of course made Duke of Suffolk. His sudden fall was probably due to public anger at the loss of the hard won English territories in northern France.

Ellen was uncertain of the details but told me how he had been arrested and imprisoned in the Tower of London for alleged plotting with the French against the king. Suffolk must have had some influence to avoid being executed for treason. It was rumoured that the queen had intervened, as he was instead sentenced to five years' banishment from court.

The story she told me was he protested his innocence but fled by sea to Calais and was apprehended by a faster ship, possibly sent by the Constable of the Tower, acting on secret orders from the king, or even Richard, Duke of York. She looked to see her young son wasn't listening. He was happily playing in front of my fire with his brightly painted wooden toy soldiers, a Christmas gift from his father. Ellen whispered to me that the headless body of William de la Pole, once one of the most powerful men in England, had been found on the beach at Dover.

After my visitor had gone my mind returned to another Christmas, so long ago in Windsor, and I wondered what the country would have been like if events had taken a different turn. If Queen Catherine had given birth to a daughter, instead of Henry VI with his ambitious French wife, the throne would have rightfully been inherited by my Humphrey, with me at his side.

7

JANUARY 1451

AD PORTAS CIVITATIS

The new year is marked by snowflakes drifting in the air. They melt as soon as they settle but I sense we are in for a hard winter. My first visitor of the year was my jailer, William Bulkeley. He arrived early one morning, knocking noisily on my wooden door and dressed in a fine new uniform. There was a new confidence about him I had not noticed before and I saw he was quite handsome in a rugged, Welsh way. He looked around my cold room, noting the soot blackened hearth and the thin ice which had formed on the earthenware jug of water left for me the previous night.

What he had to tell me made my heart beat faster. He announced his decision that I was to be moved the next day and told me I should make ready my few possessions. Since my so-called trial and sentence over ten years ago I have been moved many times, but I have become used to this peaceful place and feared the move may not be for the better. At the same time, I could not resist a sudden unexpected feeling of hope that I may be released at last, having served penance enough for my mistakes. This will be my tenth long year of imprisonment, my husband and even my enemies are now dead and I am forgotten by the world. Even when Richard, Duke of York came to this place he seemed unaware of my presence here, or worse, indifferent to it.

The king's advisors surely see me as no threat. I could be allowed to end my days in the company of my daughter Antigone and to see my little grandchildren. William Bulkeley must have noticed the look of hope in my eyes, as he quickly explained I was simply to be moved to a room in the south-east tower. He gave me no reason and I knew better than to ask.

My immediate concern was for the safety of this journal, so I took it from the secret hiding place under the loose floorboard and hid it in the folds of my dress, making a bundle of the rest of my poor possessions. My guards did not bother to search me when I left my room for the last time, and although a small victory, it gave me some comfort.

The designer of Beaumaris Castle loved symmetry, so much that my new room is almost identical, with one important difference. My windows which looked out across the inner ward with nothing particular to engage me, now provide a view through a slit in the outer wall of the castle, across the Menai Strait to the mountains of mainland Wales. It catches the early winter sun which brightens my mornings. For a long time now I have woken with the cry of the gulls at dawn and gone to sleep at sunset. I much prefer writing at my window in sunlight and am carefully conserving my tallow candles, as I don't know when I will have more. I have learned to be grateful for the little I have. Who knows what the future holds for any of us?

∾

My recollection of that first time I visited France is a happy one. There was a great sense of anticipation in our new house in Calais. Duke Humphrey even spoke of the possibility of building a mansion in his new lands in Hainault and making it our main residence. Even Jacqueline was in a brighter mood once we were on our way to her homeland. She was full of stories of the wonderful palaces she had lived in as a child. The duke and I had heard them all before but listened with new interest, needing to know as much as we could about our potentially dangerous destination.

While we waited for our fleet of ships to return with the rest of Humphrey's army, I accompanied the countess on an exploration of the bustling town of Calais. It had always been a trading port and the centre was busy with noisy merchants selling everything from fresh fish and fruit to fine silks from the Orient. Although the local people were probably used to strangers, Humphrey had insisted we were followed by a well-armed band of soldiers from his personal guard, so we drew unwanted attention wherever we went.

In the evenings Jacqueline would be visited by the ladies of the town and we entertained ourselves sharing news and gossip of events in England and France. They welcomed me to join in, which helped me to further practice my French, as they spoke little English where we were going. It was from the ladies of Calais that I learned more of how Philip, the powerful Duke of Burgundy, had formed an alliance with Humphrey's brother John, Duke of Bedford. John had married the duke's sister Anne the previous year and I realised how Humphrey now threatened to undo all John's careful peace-making with our arrival in France to pursue his claims.

Duke Humphrey kept busy writing letters to the influential men of Mons, setting out his claims to Countess Jacqueline's territories. He was impatient to be heading for Hainault, as every day in Calais was costing him, in precious time, as well as wages for his mercenary army. He grew restless; complaining that every day we delayed would allow his enemies more time to plot against him. We knew his brother John was working on a diplomatic agreement but Humphrey was in no mood for compromise.

Even when we received a deputation of finely dressed nobles from Flanders, refusing passage through their country, Duke Humphrey would not be deterred. It was of course a setback but not unexpected. We treated them to a splendid banquet, with music and dancing and flagons of good French wine. I think they understood the Duke's position, even if they didn't support him, and we parted on good terms with agreement that we would respect their wishes. I think it was the closest I ever saw Humphrey come to diplomacy.

When the remainder of his men arrived, we travelled to their camp outside Calais. Although I had seen the preparations in Dover I was surprised at how many of them there were. The encampment was a huge sprawling place, like a temporary town, the surest reminder he was ready to fight if necessary. The air was thick with the smell of wood smoke from the many camp fires, which made my eyes sting and lingered on my clothes. At least it masked the rank odour of men and animals.

I could feel many eyes upon me as I stood with Jacqueline at a discreet distance from Duke Humphrey as he addressed his men. They gathered round him, eager for news of when they would see some action. I remember how he revealed little of his plans but instead warned them not to pillage the local area when foraging for food and fodder for the horses. He showed his skill in winning over the men with promises of glory and reward and raised their spirits when he announced extra rations of ale and ordered a whole ox to be roasted.

Baron John Mowbray, the Earl Marshal, finally arrived in the early morning on the second day of November. We watched from the harbour wall and I counted forty-two heavily laden ships, four of them having been delayed or blown off course. I had enjoyed our stay in Calais but knew Humphrey had been counting the days until the arrival of the rest of our mercenary army. I might not have liked Mowbray but he was Humphrey's appointed commander, with experience of the war in France, and had fought at the side of King Henry V at the siege of Harfleur but was glad to see him, as it marked the start of our new adventure.

Baron Mowbray wasted no time organising the unloading of the ships. It was good to see the men respected him and there were no complaints as our supplies and equipment were carried to our camp. As well as many good warhorses, I noticed that the ships had brought carts laden with siege equipment and some small cannons. Duke Humphrey had told us he was prepared for whatever awaited us in Hainault but this was the first time I had appreciated the scale of what he had in mind or the possible dangers for us all.

It was the middle of November when Mowbray led us out of Calais on the long march to the city of Mons and on to Hainault. I rode with the duke and countess and remember looking back to an impressive sight, as we had brought nearly two thousand horses, followed by over four thousand men-at-arms, archers and foot soldiers. At the rear we had a motley assortment of camp followers and the supply wagons stretching all the way back to Calais.

I would have expected the duke to ride alongside Baron Mowbray at the head of the army he had worked so hard to raise, yet he rode with us in silence behind the main cavalry, a grim expression on his face, a sign his recurring illness had returned. He had brought with him his own physician, but the potions seemed to be having little effect as we made our way to the county of Artois and the lands of the Dukes of Burgundy.

We were unsure of the welcome we would receive in Burgundian territory. Countess Jacqueline was in good spirits after so long away from her homeland but Duke Humphrey had told us the men were at full readiness to fight if they had to. The sheer size of our army meant there was no chance of our arrival passing unnoticed, or that our intentions could possibly be seen as peaceful.

Those days in Calais seem so long ago now as I watch from my high window. The tops of the Welsh hills are white with a fresh fall of snow and the people retreat into their homes to escape the chill of winter. There are no visitors to the castle today, so my only distraction is to watch the herring gulls as they swoop so effortlessly over the battlements, as if mocking my imprisonment in this unfinished castle.

The builders of Beaumaris castle have included corridors within the thick walls which connect my new room to the chapel tower. Lit only by the tall window openings to the inner ward, these passages are mainly used by the guards to avoid the winter rains. In places the corridors are so narrow

I can easily touch the cold stones on both sides as I feel my way to the chapel at dusk.

The last time I passed through the corridor I noticed a movement in the poor light and saw it was a small bird sheltering in the passageway. I bent down to take a closer look and realised it was a bedraggled pigeon. It had made a little nest at the side of the corridor from twigs and straw. The pigeon's bright eyes looked back at me without concern and I left it in peace, taking some comfort from the way it seemed to sense I would do it no harm.

Like that small bird, I feel safe in the sanctuary of the chapel. I can imagine in King Edward's time it would have been a magnificent sight, but the once colourful wall paintings have now faded and where there may have been a golden crucifix now stands a poor replacement made from wood. My guards wait at a respectful distance while I kneel at the altar, not in prayer but in quiet contemplation. I found my mind returning to our reception in Hainault. It was such a long journey for so little reward, but one which changed the course of my life forever.

When our tired army finally arrived in Hainault we were refused entry into the old Burgundian city of Valenciennes. Our arrival had obviously been expected by the people of Valenciennes, as the huge city gates were barred and the city looked ready to withstand a siege. An unseen voice shouted from the ramparts, imploring us to depart, first in French then in English. Our reply, that we came in peace to claim the birthright of Countess Jacqueline, seemed to strengthen the resolve of the men defending the city walls.

Duke Humphrey was in a black mood but unsurprised

and had expected trouble, which is why he brought a mercenary army to Hainault. He was already discussing plans with Baron Mowbray to lay siege to the city. Countess Jacqueline persuaded him to leave Valenciennes and argued it was no longer the capital of Hainault. Duke Humphrey realised he should save his energies for the bigger prize of a triumphal entry into the true capital, the city of Mons. Jacqueline reminded us how she had left Mons in such unhappy circumstances, in fear of her life, so it was agreed.

We reached Mons on a misty autumnal morning, having camped for the night at a small border town called Crespin, where we were joined by Jacqueline's mother, the Dowager Margaret. To our surprise she met us with her escort of several hundred fully armed Hainault troopers, as well as her full entourage of servants. Most importantly, she also had many supporters amongst the old noble families of Hainault who remained loyal to the memory of her father, Philip the Bold, the Burgundian branch of the House of Valois.

The gates to the city were opened to us after long negotiation, on condition that our army remained outside the city. Baron Mowbray had anticipated this and had personally selected three hundred of his best cavalrymen as a bodyguard to ensure our safety. He offered to garrison the men in the nearby towns and we rode through the gates where we were met by a deputation of the most important nobles in Mons.

After such a long ride it was pleasant to be provided with fine apartments in the heart of the city of Mons, where I was able to take a hot bath for the first time since we had left Calais. We were made welcome with gifts of rich Burgundian wine and Countess Jacqueline and her mother were kept busy receiving many visitors and restoring old alliances.

Duke Humphrey was treated with deference but it was easy to see the tension and distrust behind the insincere smiles of the Hainault nobles.

There was time to explore the city while we waited for the diplomacy to take its course. Countess Jacqueline was proud to show her husband her capital and insisted we visited the castle and the gardens of the archery guild. Humphrey was recovering from the illness that troubled him on our journey from Calais and was keen to learn as much about Mons as he could. He asked many questions and impressed our hosts with a generous donation towards the completion of the guild's new chapel. We climbed the hill in the park to have the best view of Mons and for the first time I realised the scale of what Humphrey wanted to achieve, for the lands he was claiming as his by right extended to the distant horizon.

I remember it was on the first day of December that the nobles of Hainaut finally convened to discuss Humphrey's claim. Some still questioned the legitimacy of his marriage to the countess and were reminded that she had a dispensation from Rome. The duke was now her true and legitimate husband, so he should be recognised as Regent and Protector of Hainault. The dissenters argued long into the night on detailed points of precedence and legal procedure. Jacqueline explained this was typical of her people and was unsurprised when we were told that they were unable to reach agreement.

We learned that the objectors had absented themselves, meaning that those who remained had no authority to make such an important decision. It was just a matter of time. Three days later the nobles, aware of the fact our restless army was camped outside the city gates, agreed to send letters to the Duke of Brabant renouncing allegiance to him.

Humphrey was greatly relieved that he had achieved this without the need to use force, although it was far from over, as we knew Holland and Zealand would not give in so easily. Jacqueline's mother also pointed out that many important Hainault nobles still refused to acknowledge Humphrey as Regent, including the powerful Count of Conversan and the Lord of Jeumont, whose father Duke William had been amongst the many nobles murdered by the English after surrendering at the battle of Agincourt.

There was little that could be done about those who had always opposed Countess Jacqueline and remained loyal to the Duke of Brabant. Humphrey decided we would visit those towns which had accepted him as the declared governor of the county and Lord of Hainault. We also returned to Valenciennes, which he had so nearly attacked when we had previously been barred from entry. This time the gates to the old city were thrown open and the nobles and merchants greeted us with a cautious welcome. Humphrey promised to guard the citizens and respect their laws.

It was in Valenciennes that Humphrey found his way to my rooms one night, something which he had not done since we left England. I of course understood how he had needed to show his loyalty to Jacqueline but now he shared his true feelings with me. He was scathing about the nobles who acknowledged him merely as regent for his wife. I remember him telling me the only way he was going to truly inherit her lands would be on her death. There was menace in his voice as he said this and I wondered if this marked the end of our adventure in Hainault.

I will never regret what I did then, as it was clear he was never going to be accepted. I reminded him of a promise he had once made to me. The details are hard to recall, as we had drunk more than a little wine and it was late, but he took my hand and asked me to marry him. I pointed out he was already married and he laughed, as for having spent so much time and energy proving his marriage to Countess Jacqueline to be legal, he would now have to find some way to justify a divorce. I worried what his enemies would make of it but Humphrey was resolute. There was no shame in marrying me, even though I had been his mistress. It was what his grandfather had done before him, and his enemy in England, Cardinal Beaufort, could not possibly object, as his own claims to legitimacy were based on such a union. Humphrey was used to having his own way and I was beginning to realise this was no hollow promise.

The raising of the army and the journey to Hainault had cost him dearly. As well as the cost to his reputation, he had invested heavily in the expectation he would be inheriting vast new estates. Unknown to me, while we had been seeing the sights of Mons, the Earl Marshal had taken Humphrey's army deep into the territory of Brabant as far as Brussels, dealing ruthlessly with the limited resistance they met and pillaging anything of value.

Humphrey had been impassive when the news of this reached us. I knew he must have ordered it, for he would have been furious if he hadn't known how his men were breaking his promises to the nobles of Hainault. He had told me once how his own brother King Henry V had ordered men hanged from the nearest tree for less, as an example to others.

It was now no longer possible to pretend he was anything other than an invader and he warned me it was simply a matter of time before the nobles organised their resistance and our lives could be at risk. Countess Jacqueline had often told us how her people were renowned for their skill with administering deadly poisons and how she suspected that both her father and husband had been served poisoned food. It was time to return to the safety of England, so we had to find a way to do so with some dignity.

The next morning we rode back to Mons and Humphrey began negotiations for the terms of his withdrawal. The duke demanded restitution of forty thousand gold crowns, a huge sum of money but his mercenary army needed payment and there was still the return journey home. It was Christmas and the nobles of Hainault had other things to think about, finding endless reasons to delay making a proper response to Humphrey's demands.

As the year drew to a close without any progress, a deputation arrived in Mons from the citizens of Valenciennes who were complaining about the drunken and rowdy behaviour of our soldiers, who now occupied the city. The looting had now resulted in several deaths. People were being arrested on questionable charges and held as prisoners for ransom. By then I knew Humphrey had encouraged the men, as we also received urgent pleas from Soignies and its surrounding villages to restrain our English troops.

His ploy worked, as the nobles reluctantly agreed terms, but only on condition the oaths he had sworn to keep law and order in the county were respected. Humphrey lacked the diplomatic skills of his brother John, the Duke of Bedford, but he seemed to enjoy taking his revenge on the nobles of Hainault. Mindful of Jacqueline's warnings, we quickly packed the few belongings we had brought with us to Mons and prepared to depart the city for home.

Looking back on those events after so many years I realise he was putting a brave face on what must have been a hard decision. Humphrey had publicly declared his intention to claim what was his by right, so to return to England empty handed was potentially ruinous for his social and political reputation. Our ships were laden with treasures looted from the lands that could have been his but there was one notable person who had not returned with us—Countess Jacqueline.

I had watched, with increasing hope for my own position, as the distance between them grew greater each day. Once Humphrey realised his wife was not going to win him his estates in Hainault, his manner to her changed to one of patient tolerance. He was always respectful toward her but chose her company only when he really had to, preferring instead to ride the hunt with his men, writing long letters and spending his nights secretly visiting my own apartments. Then her people fought back and everything changed.

We had grown used to the regular complaints about the increasingly harsh treatment of the local townspeople. The resistance had always been vocal but suddenly it turned into an organised army. News arrived from one of the frontier towns that the Count of St Pol had easily over-run our small garrison with a force of over forty thousand men. As well as Burgundian soldiers, this new army was reportedly attracting Hainault men who were tired of Humphrey's presence, as well as French mercenaries.

This is how we found ourselves camped on an easily defended hilltop not far from the besieged town of Soignies, facing an uncertain future. Countess Jacqueline and her mother had remained in Mons but I felt safer taking my chances with Baron Mowbray and Duke Humphrey. He issued a challenge to the Burgundian army to come and fight him, confident of our superiority. The Count of St Pol had more men but, thanks largely to the Earl-Marshall, our army was better disciplined and organised. The Burgundian army assembled on a nearby hill and we waited for their attack, our entire future in the balance.

8

FEBRUARY 1451

OMNIA VINCIT AMOR

Blizzards pack drifts of snow hard against the castle walls and trap me in my room for several days at a time. I am grateful the fire in my hearth is kept well-stocked with seasoned logs as it keeps the chill of winter from these cold stone walls. Unable to take my walks in the inner ward, I am also grateful for my secret journal that makes me feel I am using my time well. As I write the story of my life I feel great sadness and suffer the pain of many regrets, yet I know there is also so much to be grateful for.

It was a freezing March day, which chilled us all to the bone as we anxiously waited on that hill in distant Hainault, wondering when we would have to be ready to fight. I remember how the heavy canvas of our tent flapped in the bitter breeze and my future husband put his warm, fur-lined cloak around my shoulders. He made a pretence of cheerfulness but his dark eyes showed his true feelings. To me he was an open book, no secrets to hide. I knew how deeply he worried about our safety and the likely cost of our failed enterprise to his reputation and his purse. I also sensed he was troubled by the dry cough that ensured neither of us had much sleep, as it presaged the return of his illness when he most needed to be strong and well.

Humphrey recalled how this was not the first time his path to Calais and the welcome safety of a ship home to England had been blocked. Ten years had passed since Agincourt but I could see the events of that day had left mental as well as physical scars. His voice was hushed as he told me again how men trampled over their dying comrades in that muddy battlefield. A life could end in the flash of a single arrow or be spared, as his was, by the bravery of others. He had watched as wave after wave of Frenchmen were beaten back by the king's body guard or surrendered, little realising the English would show no mercy to any prisoners they could not hold for ransom. Humphrey remembered little of how he was dragged from the battlefield, but told me he heard them call for the priest to pray for his soul, so certain was his fate.

I will never know if it was recounting the story of Agincourt or his returning illness that weakened his resolve to fight the Burgundians. I wonder if he knew to do so could put my life at risk. I did not expect good treatment from the Burgundians if they had succeeded in an attack. We had grown close since he had made the decision to leave for Calais and his talk now was full of the things we would do when we finally returned home. Despite the unhappy outcome of our time in Hainault he was still regent of England and hoped to start a new life in English politics, away from the mud of battlefields.

The duke spent long hours discussing tactics with Baron Mowbray, the Earl Marshal, listening carefully to the reports from the scouts who had made the journey across the valley to spy on the activities of the Burgundian army. I had grown to like the Baron and once, when alone with him, I asked about his family. His father was Sir Ralph Neville, also Earl Marshall and one of the most powerful knights in the north of England, yet it was the story of his mother, Lady Katherine Neville, Duchess of Norfolk, which really interested me. Joan Beaufort, Countess of Westmorland, was the illegitimate daughter of John of Gaunt, Duke of Lancaster, and his mistress, later wife, Katherine Swynford. I wondered if this was why the Earl Marshall was one of the few men of rank who seemed unconcerned I was Humphrey's mistress and treated me as a lady.

Baron Mowbray had recalled all the men garrisoned in the villages. They seemed in good spirits, having travelled to Hainault expecting to fight, and were ready for a battle. John Mowbray's experience of fighting in France really counted now we were in such a perilous position. He had already sent several successful forays across the open ground between the two hills to test the enemy strength. Men had been killed on both sides in these skirmishes, yet each time the Count of St Pol's disorganised soldiers had been no match for our mercenaries. These small victories were an important boost to morale.

After long hours of patient waiting, word finally reached us that the enemy was retreating. A rousing cheer went up. The duke thanked the men for upholding the honour of the English and ordered that those who wished to see off the Burgundians could do so. He did not follow them, preferring instead to write a response to the nobles of Hainault in negotiation of our safe passage to England. A messenger arrived before nightfall bearing the news that a truce had been declared. We were free at last to begin the return journey to Calais, where our ships were waiting.

It was just as well I had kept up my work of translating my old Latin prayer book, as the priest made a welcome yet unexpected return after a long absence. Melting snowflakes adorned his cloak, like tiny diamonds set in the rough wool. Grey stubble on his chin made him look much older and he leaned heavily on his wooden staff as if he would fall without its support. The priest apologised that the harsh weather and parish work had kept him away from the castle. He inspected my writing approvingly, complimenting me on my progress. I realised from the way he held the work close to his face that his eyesight was failing and he was finding it difficult to read.

He told me he had finally been able to visit the Augustinian monks of nearby Penmon Priory to obtain more writing materials, during a break in the weather. He reached in his bag and handed me a bundle of good thin parchment, as well as spare quills and a small bottle of black ink. I thanked him for his kindness, as my supplies were running low and I had feared I would soon run out. It was some time since I'd had any company, so I asked the priest to stay and tell me more about my neighbours at the priory. I sat on my wooden cot and pulled the chair closer to the fire to keep him warm. He looked into the flames in contemplative silence for a moment, then began speaking in his soft Welsh accent.

He told me Penmon has barely a dozen monks yet is wealthy, thanks to a good income from the priory lands and from their quarry, the best source of millstones on the island. It seemed the priory was going through difficult times. The tolerant but ageing prior, Thomas Godfrey, had fallen ill and was unable to properly carry out his duties. His deputy, an ambitious Canon, William Whalley, was therefore acting as prior but without the proper authority. He had promptly moved into the prior's house and was making all decisions in his name, increasing the rents, much to the distress of the poor tenants and consternation of the monks.

The old priest disapproved of Canon Whalley. He must have seen my look and explained that canons were ordained priests who took vows of poverty, chastity and obedience. They lived as monks but had closer contact with the lay community, helping pilgrims and looking after the upkeep of churches in the area. Canon Whalley justified his unpopular rent raising by claiming it was his sworn duty to secure the future of the priory, even if this was at the expense of the hard-working people of Beaumaris.

As I watched the priest struggle to find his path back through the deep snow of the inner ward I remembered how Cardinal Henry Beaufort used to plot and scheme against Humphrey, always claiming his actions were for the good of the church. I am certain he was the man behind the false accusations that led to my downfall and possibly the murder of my good husband. I will not forget it. I curse his memory and hope his reward was eternal damnation. Not for the first time, I wish I really had the powers of witchcraft I was accused of.

I watched the coast of France fade into the distance as we sailed for Dover in a freshening breeze. I remember the feeling of anticipation and excitement at the prospect of the new life ahead of me in England. No longer the lady-in-waiting to a countess, I had the personal protection of the King's Regent, who promised to marry me as soon as his divorce from Jacqueline had been granted by papal decree. Even now I smile to myself at the irony that, after going to so much trouble to prove the marriage legal, he was so quickly obliged to claim it invalid.

I knew this would be impossible to do in any hurry without drawing the criticism of his enemies in parliament, so I would have to live as Humphrey's mistress. Cardinal Henry Beaufort would be waiting for any excuse to limit Duke Humphrey's powers as regent and promote his own considerable influence in court and parliament. This meant continuing our assignations in strictest secrecy for as long as possible to prevent further damage to the duke's reputation. This was no great hardship, as I had become well used to the necessary subterfuge and knew how to avoid the watchful servants in the duke's household.

At the same time I longed to live with him openly as his wife yet had to learn patience. Countess Jacqueline still petitioned the pope to recognise her marriage, as her status in Hainaut would depend on the outcome. My last memory of her was a tearful farewell as our ramshackle army rode out of Mons. She had of course expected to accompany us but her mother, the Dowager Margaret, persuaded the nobles of Hainault that she should not leave the country and Humphrey had agreed, on condition they would ensure her safety at all times. We had once been close friends and she confided many secrets to me, including the special code she used to write in secret to her mother. Now, like Duke Humphrey, I had tired of her often repeated stories of her extravagant upbringing.

Our arrival at the busy harbour of Dover drew more attention than expected and was followed by a hasty departure to Humphrey's riverside London mansion. Accompanied only by the loyal armed escort of the duke's bodyguards that had been our company since leaving Mons, we rode hard, late into the night, without waiting for our ships to be unloaded. Duke Humphrey had been increasingly concerned about developments in parliament during his absence and our future together depended on reclaiming his role as regent and protector of his young nephew Henry.

I should have been happier than ever now my life had changed so much for the better, yet I sensed the disapproval of the servants. The duke's London housekeeper, a large, red-faced woman, clearly used to having her own way, seemed to particularly resent my presence. She showed her hand when she tried to allocate me to one of the smaller guest rooms on the coldest side of the house, furthest from the duke's own room. I was young and strong-willed, so I threatened her with dismissal and instructed her to make the countess's room ready for me. Looking back I see how this mistake cost me dearly. The duke trusted and relied on her and she could have become a good friend. Later she appeared as a witness against me, damming me with her fanciful recollections of my sorcery.

Duke Humphrey was also not of good spirit, having lost many supporters with our exploits in Hainault. His costly mercenary army was spending the pay they had barely earned in the taverns, regaling shocked Londoners with tales of looting, rape and pillage and painting Duke Humphrey in the poorest possible light. Rumours spread quickly through the city, damaging half-truths and lies, of how he had 'abandoned' his wife to her enemies and cowardly ran for home when he should have stood and fought.

The duke returned from a meeting in Westminster in a dark mood and drank several glasses of brandy before I could console him. As well as incurring the disapproval of his brother John, Duke of Bedford, it seemed he had gained many new enemies at court. There was frustration and sadness in his voice as he confided that he feared the balance of power had shifted too far in favour of the Beaufort faction. He wished to somehow restore his good name, yet I knew it was highly likely they would make some hostile move against him. I was determined to support him through this difficult time so we contrived a plan to remind the people of London of his importance.

The young King Henry VI was to be brought to London from Windsor, to be officially welcomed by the duke, as his spiritual guardian and protector of his kingdom, at the gates of St Paul's Cathedral. Although Henry was now five years old and perfectly capable of walking, Humphrey made a great show of carrying him through the cheering crowds while the cathedral choir sang popular hymns. The Bishop of St Paul's led a service of thanksgiving to a packed congregation and there at the centre was Humphrey, with the King of England.

The timing was perfect, as at the grand opening of Parliament the following week it seemed the duke was ready to begin a new life, our sojourn to Hainault almost forgotten. As a sign of his restored influence, the Parliament and Council voted to grant him a generous loan of forty thousand marks. He was also granted the wardship of the considerable estates of the young Duke of York, following the death without issue of Sir Edmund Mortimer, the Earl of March, from plague in Ireland, much to the annoyance of the Chancellor, Cardinal Beaufort.

Even his brother John agreed to a reconciliation, yet although we had escaped the worst consequences, it seemed the ghost of Countess Jacqueline would continue to haunt our lives. The stories of her courage in adversity had gained her unexpectedly sympathetic support and fuelled the fires lit by Humphrey's enemies. I regret to say my own part in all of this did his fragile reputation more harm than good, as I refused to become an invisible paramour, demanding to live openly as his mistress.

There was also the matter of our mysterious house guest, John Randolph. A Franciscan friar, he had served for many years as the personal confessor to Humphrey's step-mother, Queen Joanna of Navarre. I visited her with Countess Jacqueline before we set sail for France and knew it was by Randolph's testimony that she had been found guilty of practising witchcraft. In a twist of circumstance Randolph had been imprisoned in the Tower of London as a heretic, accused of his own treasonous use of 'the Black Art'. I was therefore astounded to learn Humphrey had ordered Randolph's release.

When Cardinal Beaufort heard his prisoner was to be freed, he had his men cause a riot on London Bridge. Beaufort accused the duke of planning to seize the king and threatening his own life. To 'defend himself' he fortified the alleyways leading to the bridge with barricades and assembled an armed force to guard them. The people of London set watches night and day to protect their property from the fighting they expected.

Duke Humphrey ignored the cardinal's antics and secretly removed Friar Randolph from prison, inviting him to stay as our guest. Of course, news of this arrangement soon reached the cardinal, who saw it as an opportunity to blight our reputation. He publicly demanded that Friar Randolph must be returned to detention in the Tower immediately and accused the duke of exceeding his authority, a call which Humphrey of course ignored.

Randolph was a thin, quietly spoken man with bright, intelligent eyes, who looked at me as if he could read my private thoughts. He was fluent in several languages and extremely well read, so it soon became evident why

Humphrey wished to spend time with him. On the evening of his arrival at our home we sat by the fireside in the grand study, listening to his account of how Humphrey's brother, then King Henry V, compromised his own stepmother for personal gain. The friar seemed hesitant at first, possibly unsure of how Duke Humphrey would react. He pointed out that if there had been any evidence of his treason by using sorcery against the king he would have been executed by now, not imprisoned. Randolph also noted he had been unable to make any comment on Queen Joanna's words in the confessional. Far from giving evidence against her, he had been forced to remain silent.

This had not, of course, troubled the king's judiciary, who had been tasked to find the queen guilty, thus forfeiting her fortune to the crown. It was enough for them that he would not deny using astrology to predict the future. There was no bitterness in Randolph's voice when he described how he had been tortured and half-starved, although he clearly disapproved of King Henry's treatment of Queen Joanna and the use of his ill-gotten funds to wage further war in France.

Humphrey was intrigued and full of questions. He owned several rare books on the art of astrology, one in handwritten Latin and others in old French, illustrated with esoteric charts which were impossible to understand. He showed them to Friar Randolph, who studied them with keen interest but said little. It was then I realised why the duke had risked so much in releasing the friar and bringing him to our London house for his personal protection. There was a price for his freedom; he would have to share his secrets.

At first, the friar was cautious and evasive, and then it seemed he had made a decision. He asked for writing materials and for the duke to ensure we could not be overheard. We had no other visitors in the house at the time, so Humphrey dismissed the servants for the night and locked us in his study, bolting the room from the inside. He cleared a space for Friar Randolph at the oak table by the window, lighting several candles so he could see to do his work.

For every question he had a ready answer. Was he really an astrologer? He confirmed that he was well versed in the science. Was he able to foretell the future? Under some circumstances, he believed it might indeed be possible, he told us. Friar Randolph became a changed man, talking compellingly about the need to be open to new ideas and how cosmology could show destiny is pre-ordained. I remember being captivated with the notion that there could be some way to foretell the future and had many questions of my own. Would Humphrey and I ever marry? Would we have children? Randolph fanned the flames of our curiosity with his knowledge of the wisdom of the Greeks and ancient Egypt.

Spreading a sheet of parchment on the table, the friar took a sharpened quill and began drawing a detailed astrological chart from memory. It looked to me as if he was casting a magical spell. Marking positions with Greek letters and special symbols, he explained this ancient learning was used by Babylonian priests to decipher the will of their gods. This knowledge was adopted by the Greeks, who understood that the arrangement of the stars could predict the seasons. I remember how Friar Randolph lowered his voice when he said it was but a short step to create oracles to foretell the future.

So that was the moment when the seed of my downfall was sown. Was it so wrong of us to be curious, to wish to learn, to have an open mind? The sad postscript to this tale is that Cardinal Beaufort had his way, as he always did. Shouting soldiers came to arrest our friend John Randolph and he was soon returned to his prison. We later heard he had been allegedly murdered there by his cell-mate, another friar said to have gone mad. I remember Humphrey had procured a rare and precious book, written by Randolph, which he treasured above all others. They have killed the man, yet his words live on.

9

MARCH 1451

FILIOLI MEI

At last the snow has melted, washed away by spring showers. Now a thick mist hangs over the dark Welsh mountains like an ethereal shroud, turning the view from my window to a swirling greyness. Fat, wild-looking pigs have been released inside the inner castle ward and squeal and hungrily root for scraps thrown from the kitchens. My guards chase the pigs off for sport and, together with the rain and heavy-booted feet of sentries, they churn my courtyard walk to a slippery mud which spoils the hem of my dress.

I am cheered by the sight of bright yellow daffodils, standing bravely against the downpour near the entrance to the chapel, a heart-warming sign of hope that winter is nearly over and spring is on the way. The daffodils are ignored by the feral pigs and I wonder how they know they are poisonous. I also wonder who had the care to plant daffodils in this otherwise gloomy and barren place. I hope, perhaps, it was done in the memory of someone long forgotten, like myself.

Each time on my return from my walk I busy myself

cleaning the thick mud from my boots and trying to dry my damp cloak by the fire. Even in mid-afternoon my room is dark in the poor light. I have to conserve my candles, as I have no idea when they will be replaced, so now my log fire sends strange shadows dancing on the cold stone walls. Staring into orange flames I recall again the fervent passion of Friar John Randolph and the glint in his eyes as he found in us a receptive audience.

I knew it was another turning-point in my life, the exciting realisation that, far from wandering as victims of chance events, we could be following a pre-ordained destiny. I wanted to believe what I heard from the persuasive and knowledgeable friar. Humphrey wanted to know how the friar reconciled astrology with his faith. Randolph had eyed us with guarded caution as he made a judgement.

He told us he spent many years studying scriptures and the writings of Friar Thomas Aquinas, searching for answers. He looked directly at me and told us how, in the Book of Deuteronomy it warns, 'There shall not be found among you anyone who practices divination or tells fortunes or interprets omens, or a sorcerer or a charmer or necro-mancer.' Humphrey knew the quotation, for he continued: 'Whoever does these things is an abomination to the Lord.'

The three of us remained silent as his words echoed round the room. I cannot pretend not to have understood the dangers of what we were discussing. I have witnessed heretics being burned at the stake, an unforgettable, haunting sight. The victims seemed incredibly brave, accepting of their fate. Until the flames reach them. I would look away, although it was impossible to block out the horrible screams or the smell of roasting flesh, yet still people risk all in the pursuit of secret knowledge.

The duke's London mansion had become my home, although I found it impossible to make my mark on the place. I persuaded him to let me have my own servants and ladies-in-waiting, whom I chose with care, creating further enmity with his housekeeper by ignoring her recommendations. Although I had the rooms once belonging to the countess redecorated, there was no place I could truly feel my own. Then I found Humphrey studying a map of the city in his study and an idea came to me.

Ever since invading Danes anchored their long ships in the mouth of the Ravensbourne at Deptford Creek, visitors to London by the River Thames had their first view of the city at the open fields of Greenwich, a natural camping-ground. Open and easily defended, these green meadows lead to a high hill overlooking a sweeping curve of the river. Merchants and boatmen had built all manner of rickety piers and wooden shacks along the water's edge and it was not a place for a lady to be alone at night.

Humphrey planned to take control of this vital route to the capital, making himself master of the waterway. He inherited the Royal Manor of Greenwich on the death of Sir Thomas Beaufort, Duke of Exeter, former Chancellor and once Captain of Harfleur. It was not the title that interested him, but the land. Humphrey was now negotiating an exchange of valuable property elsewhere for two hundred acres of what had once been the donation of Princess Elstrudis, youngest daughter of King Alfred, to the Abbey of St Peter at Ghent.

Looking at the boundaries marked on his neatly drawn map, I saw they extended from Blackheath to the banks of the Thames and realised at once it was the perfect place to build our new home together. I dreamed of creating a fabulous palace, rather than the fortified castle the duke envisaged. We would turn the pasture and wasteland into beautiful gardens, with orchards of cherry trees and flower-lined promenades, as we had seen when we visited the gardens of the archery guild in Mons.

Humphrey was captivated by the idea and immediately began planning a design for a new building. He swore it would be the finest in England, with all the latest refinements and a much needed new library for his collection of rare and precious books. As well as my gardens, arranged in long, straight terraces down to walkways alongside the bank of the river, he planned a deer park, fit for a king. On the top of the hill he would also build a fortified tower, high enough so it would be seen from most of the city. I remember how we talked and made notes long into the night, discussing ideas for our new palace.

The next day we sailed down the Thames in his gilded barge, rowed by twelve liveried oarsmen, to view the planned site of our new home. It was a glorious day and our party turned into a flotilla of boats, as we were accompanied by minstrels and musicians, cooks with baskets of food and servants carrying flagons of wine. The duke was accompanied by his personal guard and invited his favourites and supporters, while I was surrounded by my full retinue of ladies, all wearing their finest new dresses.

Climbing to the top of Greenwich hill, we could see the whole of London, with the tall spire of St Paul's surrounded by a forest of smoking chimneys. Trestle tables were soon laden with our banquet and the music of our minstrels turned heads all the way down to the river. It was easy to forget the hardship we had suffered in Hainault. We had arrived. Our party was the talk of London, which pleased us

both well, for the duke was keen to restore his reputation—
and I suspected I would soon be with child.

I take my daily walk within the high walls of the castle and
feel a sense of loss. The beautiful daffodils are now gone. No
trace remains that they ever existed. I hope at least they
were picked by someone to brighten a room or even as a gift
for a sweetheart. I see one of the feral pigs has also met its
end, hanging by its hind legs from an iron ring fixed to the
wall outside the kitchens. I stop and stare into the pig's
unseeing eyes, wondering if it had a painless death. A long,
deep red slash across its throat tells its own tale.

Moving quickly on, with a nod to my ever-present escort
of bored looking guards, I climb the stone steps to have a
moment on the high parapet. The wind has picked up and
tugs at my threadbare cape, whipping my long hair against
my face as if in punishment. To one side the cold Irish Sea
stretches into the distance, misty and troubled by white-
crested breaking waves. A single fishing boat struggles to
reach the shelter of the harbour, making almost no progress
against the wind and tide and I feel some empathy with
the crew.

There is still a dusting of the last of the winter's snow on
the windswept Welsh hills and I remember how it was
snowing when my first child was born. Deeply suppressed
memories of my friend Margery Jourdemayne return to
haunt me. Despite our long liaison, it seemed the duke and I
could not conceive a child. I was unconcerned at first,
particularly before the annulment of his marriage to the
countess. In fact, I feared a baby could be a step too far for
Humphrey and his attentions would soon turn to another. I

was painfully aware there were plenty of scheming women waiting for the chance to steal him from me.

When we were established in London everything changed. The duke declared that he wanted a son and heir to inherit his fortune. Although we were yet to be married, each month he asked if there were any signs. It was always false hope I offered him, against my better judgement, as I had to keep in his favour. I confided this to one of my most trusted ladies, who told me of a woman with a reputation for her knowledge of herbs and potions to help women conceive. Thus it was that I first met my true friend and companion, Margery Jourdemayne, known of by the people of London as the Witch of Eye next Westminster.

I felt a bond with Margery from the moment we first met, as if we had known each other for years. There was an ageless quality about her. Although her hair was turning grey and her lined and careworn face told of a life not without hardship, her eyes shone with the vitality of a much younger person. Her voice carried the accent of the poorer parts of London, yet her words showed the depth and breadth of knowledge that usually comes with good education.

Margery Jourdemayne became a regular visitor to our London mansion, always arriving in secret and, at my request, taking care to leave unobserved by the duke or our servants. She brought me a special potion to drink and told me it was made from stinging nettles and red clover, with wild raspberries to sweeten the taste. I still wonder if the real gift she had was to help me know the best days to conceive, as I did soon after following her advice.

Back at the high window of my room, watching a gathering storm on the Welsh hills, I remember the attic rooms where I was to spend so much time before the birth of my first child. The duke decided we would spend the Christmas season in the old Greenwich manor house he inherited after the death of the Duke of Exeter. I was not feeling in a festive spirit, as there was still no word from the Vatican about the annulment of Humphrey's marriage to Countess Jacqueline. Humphrey wrote long letters to his brother, pleading with him to use his influence to support his case. I know John, Duke of Bedford, disapproved of me and hoped to persuade Humphrey to find a more suitable match.

The manor house was not as grand as our London mansion yet I felt at home there. The kitchen was the heart of the house, with steaming cauldrons of water always on the boil under the watchful eye of the good natured cook and housekeeper. Dark oak beams supported low ceilings and narrow, creaking stairways led to unfashionably small rooms, filled with the late Duke's old furniture and smelling of damp until we had a log fire roaring in the wide grate.

Humphrey retained the services of a midwife, who lived in a nearby cottage and checked the baby's progress for me each day. I forget her name but recall her as a shrewd, good natured woman, with sharp eyes that saw right through me without any sign of judgement. She told me she'd lost count of how many babies she had delivered in the parish. When the duke was called away to settle a dispute in the weeks before Christmas, I sent for the midwife and asked her to keep me company.

We passed the long hours with her tutoring me in the mysteries of childbirth. I was shocked at some of the things she told me, yet determined to learn as much as I could. In time our talk turned to knowing when the baby was due. The midwife asked me to remember when I was first aware of the child, then counted the days on her fingers. Between us we calculated that it would be a winter baby. I was also desperate to know if it was possible to tell if it would be a boy or a girl and asked the midwife if she could help me ask the help of Margery Jourdemayne, the one person I knew could have the answer.

More than a week passed before Margery was able to visit me. Laughing at the sight of my advanced condition, she placed a gentle hand over where my baby rested and confidently announced it would be the boy I longed for. She gave me a special potion of linden and chamomile flowers, mixed with honey, to ease the pain of childbirth and predicted it would not be a complicated delivery, knowledge for which I was extremely grateful.

The baby came late one night when the duke was away on business. I remember feeling a strange fear and excitement, then immense relief when I heard the newborn child cry out loud and strong. Duke Humphrey named our son Arthur and our lives changed again, now I had a baby to care for. He wished to keep news of his son secret until we were able to marry, so I had to stay at the old Greenwich manor house while he returned to his duties in Westminster.

The new servants became my constant companions, the wet nurse and nursery maid taking the place of my ladies, as I did everything in my power to ensure our son had the best care and attention. The waiting was made more bearable by regular visits from Margery Jourdemayne with the latest news and gossip from London. I was truly interested in her stories from people she knew in some of the poorer districts. Before I met Humphrey I lived and worked in the city and missed the excitement of the market-places and taverns. She was remarkably well informed and became my good friend and confidante, as well as my teacher.

As the weather improved Margery suggested we should restore the herb garden at the old manor. Much to the surprise of the gardeners, we set them to work with spades and hoes, rooting up the overgrown weeds, despite the cold. When spring finally arrived I also enjoyed long walks foraging for wild herbs and rare mushrooms in the woods with Margery. The fresh air and exercise was good for me and I learned a great deal about how to recognise and use special plants.

Arthur was barely a month old when he caught a fever. At first I thought he would soon recover, but then he began to cause me much distress with his sweating and shivering. I sent for Margery Jourdemayne and she came right away, despite torrential rain on a stormy night, to watch over him until he was well again. She told me he would have recovered well enough, yet I am sure she saved his young life with her special potions of willow and meadowsweet. It was a great comfort to me and sealed the bond of our friendship.

As I remembered her kindly face, a distant flash lights up the Welsh hills, followed soon after by a crack of violent thunder and I move away from the window to sit closer to the fire, my bones feeling the chill. I stare into the flames and the awful death of Margery Jourdemayne rests heavily on my conscience. I slept fitfully that night, my head full of memories I would rather forget.

Humphrey remained at his London mansion while there were meetings of parliament, returning to the Greenwich manor as much as he could through the summer. I noticed a change in him, as he was less ready to talk about his work or his progress in winning more support. Aware from Margery of speculation and gossip about my absence, I decided

Arthur was old enough to be left in the care of his nurse-maid and returned with Humphrey to be seen at his side.

I rode proudly through the streets of Westminster on a fine white mare, surrounded by my ladies in all their finery, with an escort of the duke's personal guard. The clatter of the iron-shod hooves of our horses on the cobblestones brought crowds of onlookers. If the people were going to talk, at least I would not give them the satisfaction of thinking I was in any way ashamed of my circumstances. We attended a banquet at Westminster Hall where I could feel all eyes were upon me and I knew this was how it would be from now on.

As the summer came and passed into autumn, Arthur grew quickly into a boisterous toddler, thriving in the fresh country air, and I realised I was again carrying a child. This time I prayed it would be a girl. Once again, the duke insisted I must return to my sanctuary at Greenwich, away from questioning eyes. I waited out a long winter, virtually a prisoner in the old manor house, although I was happy there and Humphrey visited me as often as he was able to.

This time it was not to be an easy birth. I remember the dreadful sense of foreboding at concern in the eyes of my midwife. She sent one of the young serving girls at once for Margery Jourdemayne while she stayed at my side day and night. Sleeping on a thin straw mattress on the floor next to my bed and her intentions were good, yet her snores kept me awake until the small hours of the morning. I knew she feared the worst for my unborn child.

The servant girl was unable to find Margery Jourde-mayne. I remember thinking this was a bad omen for the birth of my child. My pains came more frequently while we waited for her reply and I had to make my potions as best as I could to ease my suffering. The child was in the wrong position. It was as bad as it could be. At one time I over-heard the midwife muttering to one of the girls that she might be able to save me or the child but not both. She boiled white willow with mandrake to ease my pain yet I still suffered greatly. A whole day passed before the child was born, by God's grace a healthy girl. My prayers had been answered, although the midwife cautioned that I should not expect to bear more children in the future.

It took many weeks before I felt well enough to leave my bed. Even then I could only walk with the aid of a stick and still felt weak. Duke Humphrey was delighted with our beautiful baby and named her Antigone, from the Greek 'against birth', after her tumultuous entry into the world. Although she lacked the strength of her brother, she was bright-eyed and perfect in every respect, with my dark hair, her mother's daughter.

My writing was interrupted by the nervous young scullery maid bringing me my food, a bowl of luke-warm stew and stale rye bread. They don't allow me to have wine often now, so I must be content with the watery beer. I worried this would make me ill until I saw my guards drinking the same. As I ate alone I recalled the excess of the celebratory banquet when the message arrived from the duke's brother in Normandy.

The messenger had ridden hard from Dover to tell us Countess Jacqueline had agreed a peace treaty with the Duke of Burgundy and that Humphrey's marriage had been annulled by papal decree, on the grounds it was illegitimate. He carried the letter of annulment, bearing the seal of the pope. It was the news we had been longing to hear, for at last we were free to be married. I remember the excitement as the hasty arrangements were made for us to be wed in the chapel at Westminster.

I was to become a duchess, and knew how important it was for me to look like one. Seamstresses began work right away on my wedding dress while Humphrey busied himself with the details of the guest list. He saw this as his chance to set the past behind him and begin our new public life together. With our children discreetly hidden away at Greenwich Manor, we once more became the centre of attention. The ceremony itself was a simple affair, presided over by a stern-looking bishop, although the reception at the duke's London mansion afterwards was marked by excess.

I contrived to make a grand entrance, keeping all the high-ranking guests waiting for as long as I dared before giving the signal for a fanfare of trumpets for the new Duke and Duchess of Gloucester. The wine flowed and every type of meat and fruit was served in so many courses it would have been impossible to eat them all. Humphrey gave an impressive speech, talking of a future of peace and prosperity for England, which was rewarded by a rousing cheer from the assembled guests.

10

APRIL 1451

SINE CURA

The onset of spring in Beaumaris is heralded by a visit from Sir William Bulkeley, wearing a rich velvet cape with a polished silver breastplate over his tunic and carrying a fine new sword at his belt. My jailor seemed in good spirits and was unusually talkative, so I took the opportunity to ask if Lady Ellen would be able to visit, as she has not been to see me since before Christmas. I also asked him again if his wife could be so kind as to bring me a new dress to replace the now ragged gown I have to wear each day, as well as some fruit to vary my poor diet.

Sir William promised to see what he could do. I resent his condescending attitude towards me, yet I know from what Ellen has told me that he is a decent, honest man, trying to do his job as well as he can. He was as good as his word, for the next day I had a message from one of the guards that Lady Ellen was waiting to meet me in the court-yard. She was accompanied by a servant carrying a wicker basket laden with gifts for me.

Although she tried to hide her concern, I could see Ellen was troubled by how I looked after the hardships of the long winter. It was a bright sunny morning but a chill wind came straight from the sea, so we sought shelter in the porch of the chapel while she showed me what she had brought. My ever-present guards waited outside in the wind, watching with open curiosity on their faces in place of their normally bored expressions.

She took from the wicker basket a dark red dress with black lace, sparkling with small black beads at the neck and cuffs. It had a finely woven pattern of flowers and was the work of a skilled seamstress, like those I had worn so long ago at Bella Court. As well as the beautiful red dress, there were two cotton shifts and a pair of fine black boots with leather laces. I tried the boots on and fortunately they are a comfortable enough fit, much needed replacements for the badly worn pair I have been wearing for as long as I can remember. As I put them on I wonder if Sir William noticed my old shoes and mentioned it to her.

Ellen also gave me a sweet apple, a real treat at this time of year, which I suspect came from her personal supplies. I thanked her for her kindness to me and, as I held one of the apples, realised my body craves fresh fruit. I have lived on dry bread and the salty, barely palatable Welsh stew called 'cawl' for most of the long winter. Although the cooks sometimes added pork or mutton, more rarely even scraps of beef, my mouth watered at the sight of the apples. Lady Ellen nodded in approval and I ate the delicious apple while we talked, savouring every bite.

She told me how she worries that the lawlessness and unrest in London will soon spread to the rest of the country and eventually reach across the water to Beaumaris. I learned from her that Sir William has ordered the castle guard to be ready at short notice if required and has a man permanently posted at the door to their house, such is his concern for the safety of his family.

I understand why the people are angry at the king and government's failure to prevent further losses of English territory in France and dare to tell her Humphrey was right. The hard won victories of his father are being squandered by King Henry VI and his French queen. I feel the first glimmer of hope for a long time that others will draw the same conclusion and petition for my release.

Ellen sought my advice about herbal remedies for her youngest son William, who suffers with a persistent cough which keeps him awake at night. I recommended a drink infused with rosemary and thyme, if she can find any this early in the spring. This is the first time Lady Ellen has made any reference to my reputation. I can only see it as a positive thing that she trusts me to advise on the care of her young son.

Encouraged, I requested a favour, which as a mother I was sure she would understand. I asked her to make enquiries on my behalf to find my daughter Antigone. Even if Sir William could not allow her to visit me, it would put my mind at rest to know she is safe and well. I explained she is married to Sir Henry Grey, Lord of Powys, and may be living at his castle near the Welsh border. Lady Ellen said she could make no promises but would raise the question with her father when she saw him next. He is well connected and, being on the Welsh mainland, any enquiries he makes will not compromise her husband's position.

I think on her words back in my room as I put on my beautiful new red dress. It needs altering to fit me well, yet it lifts my spirits to wear something so well made after so many years of cast-offs. To my regret, I realise that in my delight at seeing so many gifts, I forgot to ask Lady Ellen for more parchment and writing ink. My last supply from the priest is running low and I have no idea when he will next come to see me or if he will be able to help me again. I try to conserve what little I have left by diluting it with a little rainwater and keeping my coded writing as small as I can, as there is so much to tell of the years after I became a duchess.

Standing at the high window of my prison, I remember the feeling of excitement when we were granted permission to build our new home in Greenwich. Humphrey didn't waste a moment, recruiting master builders from Italy, stonemasons from France and an army of labourers to clear acres of bracken. Giant old oak trees were felled to provide wood for the supporting beams and the scent of sap from freshly sawn timber carried on the wind.

So many workmen camped on the fields that the green hillside above the site turned into a temporary village of makeshift shacks and tents to house the labourers who toiled from first light until dusk. At night, their flickering fires looked to me like the light of hundreds of stars. The sound of their gruff voices, talking in several languages and sometimes singing drunkenly carried all the way to the darkflowing river.

Each day tan-sailed barges, laden with heavy blocks of stone, jostled for places at the newly rebuilt wharf, where men were busily unloading the daily deliveries from Portland. Carrara blue-grey marble was transported all the way from Tuscany and expert builders travelled from Florence and Milan to translate our vision of a palace into detailed plans. The air of the formerly peaceful fields of Greenwich filled with the musical ringing of stonemasons' chisels and the shouts of the labourers as they worked.

Duke Humphrey, restored to his former self, took

personal pride in the ambitious scale of the new palace. He rode around the site on a beautiful white horse, followed by his retinue of Italian advisors, checking on the progress of every detail. In no time at all the outline of the buildings emerged from the ground. His tower high on the hill, which he called Greenwich Castle, was finished first and provided the perfect vantage-point from which we could view the work on the house and grounds.

I was kept busy deciding and arranging the decoration of the house. In the centre was a great hall, where we could have banquets for over a hundred guests. The hall was lit by high chandeliers which could be raised and lowered by chains to light the huge candles, as well as oil lamps set on brackets along each wall. Before the building work had even started, the duke commissioned master tapestry makers from Flanders to weave colourful tapestries, each having some moral aspect for those with the learning to appreciate it.

The significance of one of the tapestries escaped me at first until Humphrey explained it depicted the struggle between two brothers, Cane and Abel, who became mortal enemies through jealousy, a clever reference to his brother John. Following the death of his wife Anne from the plague in Paris, Duke John had caused something of a scandal by marrying Jacquetta of Luxembourg, who at nineteen years old could easily have been his daughter. Worse still, he proceeded to bring her to London and proved surprisingly popular with the people and parliament, who perhaps saw him as a calming influence and begged him to remain.

Humphrey had been grateful and surprised at his brother's support in gaining the annulment that enabled us to be married, yet there was no questioning the rivalry between them. Duke John had been openly critical of Humphrey's conduct in almost every regard. He always seemed to have the upper hand, greater experience and more influence, despite the fact he spent so much time in Normandy and visited London so rarely.

My favourite tapestry of all those in our new home was on the wall of our sleeping quarters. Life sized and brightly coloured, it showed the temptation of a noble-looking Adam by a salacious and naked Eve in the Garden of Eden. It was well that only our servants would ever see the tapestry, for the figures depicted bore a striking resemblance to Duke Humphrey and myself.

The most important room in the whole house for Humphrey was his library, an oak panelled room with shelves filled with the greatest collection of precious books in England. Humphrey retained into our household Roger Bolingbroke, a respected and well educated scholar, who spent much of his time reading in the duke's library, although I was almost certain he was there to watch over the duke's priceless books.

Ruggedly handsome with a bushy beard, an infectious laugh and a deep, booming voice, Roger Bolingbroke was about the same age as the duke and had been at Oxford with him as a student. I remember he liked to wear a black cappa clausa over his tunic, which gave him an air of authority. The first of many poets, philosophers and writers to reside in our guest wing at Greenwich, he had an incredible memory and seemed to know every detail of all the books in the duke's collection. He soon became a favourite friend and companion of mine, with his ready wit and charming ways. I would seek his company when the duke was away on business and sometimes wondered if he was in love with me, although he was always a perfect gentleman and his behaviour most correct.

I also took it upon myself to oversee the creation of the formal gardens, the design of which was the subject of as much discussion and debate as the palace itself. Most of the two hundred acres at Greenwich were open, uncultivated grounds. They were mostly given over to become the duke's deer park, where he would ride and hunt the stags with his friends and guests he wished to impress. We regularly dined on venison, rubbed with bacon fat and marinated with spices, yet to live so close to so many deer was a mixed blessing. They would find their way into the gardens, damaging the tender young plants and jumping easily over the stone walls we built to keep them out.

Inspired by the gardens of the archery guild in Mons, my new gardens were rectangular, with straight paths and flower beds leading to an Italian marble fountain which formed the centrepiece. First drawn on a huge parchment, the planned layout was marked out with wooden stakes and lengths of twine before the workmen started digging into the hard ground. Fruit trees, shrubs and flowers of every variety were brought to Greenwich from all over the country for my garden.

My true purpose was to ensure that the grounds were well-stocked with all the herbs I would need, particularly those which were rare or exotic and had proven so hard to obtain. I sent for Margery Jourdemayne to advise me on the choice of herbs and plants, only to discover the king's sergeant-at-arms had taken her under arrest to Windsor Castle, to be examined before the Council on charges of witchcraft and sorcery. I at once pleaded with Humphrey to intervene on her behalf, which he did with some reluctance.

He returned some time later with the news that he had achieved her release following her promise to never again use witchcraft, and payment of a surety. Although he told me he used two gentlemen intermediaries, I am sure his involvement was at some personal risk to his reputation. In the circumstances, we agreed that Margery would not be seen again in Greenwich until the whole incident had been forgotten, something which we would later have good cause to reflect on.

It had taken nearly two years to complete our grand palace, which Humphrey allowed me to name Bella Court. I chose the name as the Italian foremen would refer to me as the 'Bella Donna' when they thought I was out of earshot, which I found was a great compliment. Humphrey pointed out that 'bella' was also the Latin word for 'wars,' so as the champion of the war party at parliament he liked the pun, however accidental. We celebrated the completion of the work with one of the grandest banquets London, or even England, had seen for many years.

The guest of honour was no less than the young king, accompanied by a retinue of his royal court followers, the great and the good of England. The only person of note not attending was our old enemy Cardinal Beaufort. Looking back, I realise that was the happiest time of my life. I was the Duchess of Gloucester, married to one of the most influential men in the land, with two beautiful children and a palace which was the talk of London.

One thing that still saddened me was how my husband's enemies repeated the lie that he had 'married a commoner'. It was well known that on his deathbed, King Henry V urged his commanders to fight to the end in defence of his claims to the kingdom of France that would now pass to his son. He had commanded them to keep the Duke of Orleans prisoner in England until the future king was of age. It pleased me greatly therefore, when the Duke of Orleans was transferred from the custody of the Earl of Suffolk, who had been ordered to France, to the care of my father. I knew Humphrey had contrived this to happen, yet word spread quickly, reminding everyone I was the daughter of a respected and worthy knight from a noble family.

My title of duchess was formally recognised when I was accepted at the royal court on the feast of St George at Windsor Castle. A fanfare of trumpets marked our arrival and Duke Humphrey took my hand and led me into the great hall, where we were welcomed by the king wearing his gold crown. I was presented with the robes of the Order of the Garter before all the important lords and ladies of England. At last, the troubles of my past seemed to have been forgotten and I had now established my position as the first lady of the kingdom.

Everything changed when a messenger arrived with the news that the duke's brother had died suddenly in France. Instead of mourning his death on receiving the news we raised a glass to his memory and began contemplating the consequences. First and foremost, his brother's demise put Humphrey in direct line for the throne. As the only surviving brother of Henry V he was heir apparent and only the weak young Henry VI now stood in the way of him becoming King of England and France, with me at his side as his queen.

John had been able to accumulate great personal wealth in addition to the lands and fortune he had inherited on the death of his father and older brother King Henry V. There had been no legitimate children from two marriages and it was to be expected that many of his titles and estates in England and France would naturally pass to Humphrey. As well as succeeding his brother as Lieutenant of the King in Calais, he was also granted extensive lands in Picardy, Flanders and Artois, all regions under the ambitions of the Duke of Burgundy.

The death of his brother made Humphrey one of the richest men in the country, so we did not doubt that this widow, Duchess Jacquetta and her family would contest his inheritance where she could. Instructions were given for the work at Greenwich to continue and our children were left in the care of their nursemaids, as they were too young to make the long and potentially dangerous journey to attend Duke John's funeral at the old cathedral of Rouen in Normandy.

The sea crossing to Calais was uncomfortable and our ship was crowded with Humphrey's guards, as well as our servants and my ladies-in-waiting. I was glad we had provided for our personal security when we arrived in Normandy, as it was evident there was much ill feeling towards the English. We travelled in fear of our safety, despite our armed escort.

The funeral service was long and dull, being conducted in both French and English, with too many speeches. At one point I looked across at his widow, young and attractive in her mourning clothes. Although I knew she had little say in the marriage, I believed her grief at the loss of her husband after two short years of marriage was genuine. In different circumstances we could have been friends, yet I suspected her husband had turned Jacquetta's mind against Humphrey and myself. It saddened me that she treated us with thinly-veiled disdain, despite Humphrey's reassurance she would be well provided for.

I was innocently pleased, therefore, to receive an invitation to meet with Jacquetta in her rooms that evening. Duke

John's presence still loomed heavily over their house and I could sense I was being watched as I was led through grand corridors to his young wife's personal chambers. I was surprised to find her there alone, without servants, and she welcomed me with a cool detachment I should have recognised as a warning of the shocking accusation to come.

Pouring two goblets of wine she handed one to me and, looking directly at me, asked how I thought a man with such energy and life as her husband could have died so unexpectedly. Taken aback, I hesitated to answer and she seemed to read my mind. I recalled the glint in Humphrey's eyes when he had reminded me of the story of Kane and Abel.

'Did your husband have his brother poisoned?' Her question was an allegation.

I saw a strength and determination in her I had not noticed before and froze in the act of sipping my wine, although my throat felt so dry I wondered if I would be able to speak. Jacquetta had not even raised her goblet to her lips and I realised she was perfectly capable of poisoning me as an act of revenge.

Noting my silence, she told me her husband had taken the precaution of retaining a loyal servant in our household, to keep him informed of our actions. It was through this servant they had learned of my regular visits from Margery Jourdemayne, who she called 'that witch of Westminster.'

'Did you wish my husband's death?' This time there was anger in her voice.

I had never discussed this with anyone, even Humphrey and certainly not with Margery, although the chilling truth was that although I knew I could not confess it, I had many times wished that John, Duke of Bedford, was dead. I also realised why Margery had been arrested for witchcraft. Humphrey's brother had acted on the information he received, regardless of the terrible consequences for my friend.

It was with relief that we returned home to Greenwich, sailing on the earliest tide despite the imminent threat of a storm. As I looked back at the dark shape of France disappearing into the distance it appeared strangely threatening. The allegations of John's widow Jacquetta deeply disturbed me. She was a vengeful woman and I was troubled by the knowledge she might yet seek revenge through threatening those closest to me. I had missed the children greatly and resolved never to leave them again, even though I knew Duke Humphrey would have to return to carry out his duties in Calais.

11

MAY 1451

ERUBESCANT CONTURBENTUR OMNES INIMICI MEI

W riting this journal in a shaft of warm early morning sunshine that comes through my window, my thoughts turn once more to freedom and how I could escape from Beaumaris. My only real advantage would be surprise, as I know my guards have become complacent as I am careful never to give any indication I would even consider trying to escape. Superstitious and simple men, they think I have powers of witchcraft, and fear I will curse them, something I encourage to keep them at their distance. I think that is how I still have my mother's gold ring and the last of my precious jewellery, sewn into a secret pocket of my old blue dress.

My difficulty is that this old fortress, which Lady Ellen told me was the last and largest of the castles built by the first King Edward in Wales to keep attackers out, is proving just as effective at keeping me in. When I have been allowed to climb the stone steps up to the high parapet, I have seen how cleverly it is built. With its sixteen towers and double rows of walls, Beaumaris castle is easy to defend and also easy to use as a prison.

My window is wide enough for my slim body and has no iron bars fixed into the stone that would stop me climbing out. There is no prospect of this, for my room is on the second floor. Even if I were able to plait some rope which could take my weight, I would then have to cross the wide open space of the outer ward, overlooked by the guards who patrol the top of the curtain wall which surrounds the castle on all sides. Outside the wall is the wide and deep moat, which I would not relish crossing even if I could.

I have learned to find privacy when I need it by standing to the right of the door of my room, out of the field of view of the guards who check on me through the small grill. I am also alert to the metal scrape of the bolt being drawn, as it is loud enough to wake me even when I am sleeping. The door is not always guarded, as I can hear when there is anyone in the narrow corridor outside, yet there is no way of escaping through it without it being unbolted.

This means I will have to choose my moment with care and wait until the door is opened by the cook with my food or the servants who come to clean my room and change my bedding. I would need to somehow distract their attention. I notice my small store of precious tallow candles, logs and sticks for my fire. It would be an easy enough matter to set a fire which gave off a lot of smoke. It would be best to do this at night, when I expect my guards would be at their least vigilant. A fire would easily be explained away as an accident and I could douse any flames with my jug of water if I am unable to escape.

I would also need to disguise my appearance in some way. I could blacken my face with the soot from my hearth and fashion a hooded cape from my old dress. It would be even better if I could somehow steal some men's clothing and cut my long dark hair. I have a sudden memory of when my hair was cut short for my penance. I am certain people would be less able to recognise me without it.

Once out of my room I still need to find a way through the gatehouse, the only way in and out of the castle. I have lived in this south-east tower since January, so there has been plenty of opportunity to observe the activity through the south gate. Sailing boats are often moored at the castle quay, noisily unloading as they bring supplies. Once a week the merchants of Beaumaris also set up their stalls and the space in front of the castle becomes a small market-place. At nights I hear the men shouting and the rumble of chains as the heavy wrought iron portcullis is lowered into place. Without fail it remains until morning, sealing us off from the outside world, presumably on the orders of Sir William Bulkeley.

Although never used while I have been here, the gate-house has two more portcullises and several sets of heavy wooden doors, all guarded by armed sentries. It seems impossible that I could ever pass unnoticed through the main entrance to the castle, and even then my island prison is separated from the tantalisingly close mountains of main-land Wales by the fast flowing Menai Strait. I doubt I would be able to stow away unnoticed on one of the boats in the quay. I expect I could find a small fishing boat left unat-tended on the shore at night, although I am certain I would not be able to make the crossing without assistance from an accomplice with knowledge of the currents.

There is another entrance to the castle which seems to be disused and therefore not well guarded. On my walks in the inner ward I have observed that the north gatehouse looks unfinished, without any barbican or portcullis, yet from my vantage-point on the parapet I saw behind it an old wooden bridge leading north-west across the moat, with a winding track running inland across open fields. The island of Anglesey is green and fertile, so I imagine it would be possible to hide somewhere inland and find food and water until any search for me is abandoned. Perhaps I could make my way to the far west of the island and then trade the last of my jewellery for a passage across the sea to Ireland, where no one would know or care who I was.

Later I will look more closely at the narrow passageways which connect my room to the chapel tower. There are tall window openings to the inner ward along one side and at the chapel there are stone galleries that once allowed people to observe those praying. The galleries have fine carving to the stonework and I wonder if these were built for King Edward's use or even for his young wife, my namesake, Eleanor of Castile, once the Queen of England. If I could somehow evade my captors, these corridors and galleries may offer some temporary hiding place, as they would not expect me to lie low so close to my room.

The risks would be much less if I had an accomplice, although I have no idea who, if anyone, could be taken into my confidence without bringing danger upon us both. The only people I have spoken to since I arrived are Sir William and his wife Ellen, the old priest, the cook who brings my food and the maids who sometimes clean my rooms and wash my clothes. I know Ellen would never do anything disloyal to her husband. The old priest seems a little disaffected with his work, although he has not visited me for three months now and I wonder if something has become of him. This leaves the servants, so I decide to discreetly speak to each when I have the opportunity to learn what I can of them.

I read my Book of Hours and find some comfort in Psalm 6 of the Penitential Psalms: *Let all my enemies be ashamed, and very sore troubled: let them be converted, and ashamed very speedily.* Memories of life at Bella Court return to my thoughts. Humphrey wasted no time on our return from Normandy and was soon able to identify the spy within our household. He refused to discuss how the man had been punished but I suspect it was most severe and he was never seen or heard of again. From that day on we were always more careful about what we said in front of our servants and there was always an element of distrust. We had learned the lesson that even the most loyal servants would have their price.

We had hardly settled into a routine when word arrived in London that an old enemy, Duke Philip of Burgundy, had invaded the English stronghold of Oye castle and hanged the men of the garrison when they surrendered. He was now advancing with an army and a fleet of warships against Calais and would hold the town to siege. As well as its strategic significance, the town of Calais had a special place in the hearts and minds of the people. It was thought vital to safeguard English trade that our last stronghold in France must be held for the crown, whatever the cost.

Humphrey, now the king's Captain and Lieutenant of Calais, was ordered to raise an army without delay and defend the town against the Burgundians. An experienced soldier from the king's household, Lord Welles, was appointed as his commander in the field and sent ahead in advance to reinforce the garrison of Calais. The king ordered every county in England to contribute men and money towards the protection of our interests and even our arch rival Cardinal Beaufort was persuaded by parliament to finance the expedition with a thousand marks.

I remember saying a tearful goodbye to my husband,

wondering if he would ever return. He was wearing his best sword with a new breastplate of shining silver and appeared confident about the prospects of delivering a swift lesson to the Duke of Burgundy, although I knew him too well to be fooled by his bravado. He told me his army was to sail to Calais in five hundred ships, the largest fleet assembled in many years, with over four hundred men-at-arms and more than four thousand archers. His retinue included the Duke of Norfolk and the Earls of Devon, Stafford, and Warwick, followed by many of the most experienced knights of the realm.

A worrying wait for news followed. We were well aware the Duke of Burgundy had plenty of time to prepare his forces and rumours circulated in London of a Burgundian army numbering over thirty thousand fighting men. It was reassuring to know the Calais garrison, the only English standing army, included experienced soldiers who had served in the French wars. The enemy army was thought to mainly consist of conscripted Flemish farmers, who could be expected to have little appetite for laying down their lives for the Duke of Burgundy.

I also knew that Humphrey was no military leader. He could hold the respect of his men, yet tended to react to the enemy rather than plan to have the advantage. We had only escaped our adventure in Hainault because of the experience of Sir John de Mobray, Earl Marshall of England and I feared for my husband's safety. Worse still, the thousands of archers with him were no battle hardened army. Most of the men had been hastily recruited from towns and villages all over England on the promise it would all be over within one month and many had probably never fired a single arrow in anger.

Fortunately, the harbour at Calais was easily defended

with cannons from the castle and the Rysbank Tower. Supply ships sailed every day from Sandwich and Dover, returning with reports that soon reached London. We learned that the Burgundian fleet had attempted to block the harbour entrance by sinking ships full of stone but the garrison managed to pull them clear—and salvaged the stone for good measure.

At last a letter arrived for me, bearing Duke Humphrey's personal seal. The news was good, as he wrote that when he finally arrived in Calais he found the siege already raised. The garrison had held the town and opened sluices to flood the open fields outside the city walls, making it impossible for their attackers to maintain their encampment. There was no sign of Duke Philip and many of the enemy forces had deserted on hearing the news of the arrival of his army, abandoning their guns, which were promptly captured, along with most of their supplies.

My husband should have returned right away to a hero's welcome, having never had to fight, yet the whole incident turned unexpectedly to our disadvantage, as rumours quickly spread through the city that he had failed to arrive in time. Calais was safe, yet the siege had been lifted and the battle with the Burgundian army won by none other than Sir Edmund Beaufort, Cardinal Beaufort's nephew and Humphrey's cousin. Once again, it seemed the cardinal had the upper hand.

Two long weeks passed with no further news, and then a second letter arrived for me from Humphrey. He had decided to take his forces inland through Flanders, capturing much booty. I knew there were risks in such an expedition, as the Duke of Burgundy would be expected to find the English an easy target once they were out in the open fields of his own country. The letter confirmed that

Humphrey had already returned to Calais and would be sailing home with rich prizes as soon as he was able to.

Now he was able to parade through London at the head of a victorious army, followed by his knights on their war horses and oxen dragging captured Burgundian cannons, wagons laden high with booty and grim-faced Flemish nobles, who would be held for ransom. The celebrations continued for days, with people cheering whenever he appeared in public and calling him 'Good Duke Humphrey'. We attended a magnificent banquet at Westminster, where it gave me great pleasure to see the look on Cardinal Beaufort's face.

When we were finally alone in Greenwich he told me the true story. A Burgundian prisoner revealed to them that Duke Philip had escaped to the city of Lille, where he was forced to wait while he rebuilt his army after so many desertions. This meant the towns and villages of Flanders would offer easy pickings. Humphrey ordered his fleet to follow by sea and chose a route close to the coast, yet although he was confident in the knowledge he could always escape in his ships, they had little sleep after they left the safety of Calais. They lived with the constant threat of being surprised or ambushed by Burgundian forces. Then he realised his captains had disobeyed orders and returned to Calais, leaving him stranded deep in enemy territory.

He confessed he had barely been able to control his men, who were hungry and ill-disciplined. They began sacking and burning villages and towns, looting anything of value, raping women and murdering prisoners as they went without mercy. Then, when they reached St Omer, they had nearly been overwhelmed by the forces defending the town. I was simply relieved to have him back safe in England and he confessed that he never wished to lead such an army again.

It was another bright morning on my walk so I asked to be allowed again to climb the high castle ramparts to have a view of the green fields of Anglesey and the deeper blue-green Irish Sea. I watched a pair of white swans. They seem to be building a nest against the edge of the moat which is far too wide and deep for me to cross, other than by the gatehouse. I looked again for the wooden bridge to the north-west. The narrow path through the fields leads to a stone wall with an unguarded gate. In the far distance the mournful tolling of a bell carries in the still morning air and I wonder if the path would be the way to the friary, so I must find a way to raise the matter with the priest when he next comes to see me.

One guard was ordered to follow me to the top and I recognised him as the man who reminded me a little of my son, Arthur. He has the same stocky build and unruly dark hair, with eyes that seem a little knowing for one so young. An idea formed in my mind that of all the men who guard me, this young soldier was the most likely to be able to help me. I recall how he stands apart from the other local men, as I have heard him speaking in English, rather than the rapid Welsh dialect I cannot understand.

I need more ink and parchment to work on my secret journal and know I cannot rely on the priest, who hasn't visited me since February. William Bulkeley has forbidden me to have anything that could be used to write letters, yet I decided to risk asking the young guard to help me, as I have little to lose. He looked at me, his face impassive as he seemed to be considering my request. My plan hung in the balance for that moment, and then he scowled at me and said to do so would risk his job. He ordered me to climb back down from the parapet.

As I was about to do so, he seemed to reconsider and said he would offer a trade. He would bring me some ink if I would show him how to read and write his name. I told him I would be happy to but he must keep our arrangement secret. He agreed, and feeling pleased with myself for the first time I can remember, we climbed down to the inner ward as the horses are being taken from their stables for exercise. I returned to my room in good spirits, daydreaming about riding one of the horses at the gallop out through the south gatehouse to freedom.

12

JUNE 1451

ALEA IACTA EST

I woke from a vivid dream that I was back at Bella Court when my children were small. I was happy then, with everything I could wish for. My husband was home safe and my little son Arthur was already beginning to look like his father, with the same determination and interest in learning. I like to think my daughter Antigone was more like me, adventurous and already charming everyone she met. I remember how she would shriek with delight when Humphrey would sometimes sweep her high off the ground and hold her above his head.

My husband returned from Flanders a changed man. Although he had to make occasional visits to Calais, he never spoke of war again and seemed finally content with our life in London. Our house was filled with clever and creative people, scholars and philosophers, who visited for discussions and debates. Humphrey also championed the merchant class of London, who had amassed great wealth through the wool trade and the prosperous new businesses of banking and commerce. This proved to be an astute move, positioning him as an influential intermediary between those who had inherited wealth and the newly wealthy, building his reputation both in parliament and in business.

Almost replacing the Royal Court, which had become sombre and formal under our pious young king, Bella Court had become the place for the nobility to be seen, the social centre of London. We would often hold banquets in the great hall, with music and entertainers of every kind. Humphrey had a particular liking for Italian music. Musicians and minstrels travelled from as far away as Florence and Milan to play for us. These concerts became the talk of London, so each time we tried to make them a grander spectacle, with more musicians and even choirs singing in our gallery.

The greatest banquet held at Bella Court was for our daughter Antigone's wedding. Many potential suitors had come and gone, now she was fifteen years old and grown into a beautiful young woman. None were good enough for me, of course, and Humphrey would remind anyone who cared to listen that his daughter could only marry an earl. Then he found a husband for her. Henry Grey, 2nd Earl of Tankerville and Lord of Powys was handsome, wealthy and charming. Nine years older than Antigone, his father Sir John Grey fought in Humphrey's retinue at Agincourt, being rewarded with vast estates in Normandy and the post of Captain of Harfleur. Henry inherited his fortune and estates in Normandy and Wales when Sir John was killed at the Battle of Baugé.

Antigone's wedding was in great contrast to my own. After the formal ceremony in Westminster we sailed down the Thames to Bella Court in the duke's gilded barge to one of the finest banquets seen in London for many years. The wedding guests were served with wild boar and venison, with the finest sweet wines from the Levant, and the centre-piece of the banquet was an enormous sugar sculpture of the figure of Venus, the Roman goddess of love, beauty, fertility and prosperity, emerging from the sea. As my daughter left for her new home at Powys Castle, Earl Henry's mansion on the Welsh Border, Humphrey took my hand and reminded me that we could wish no better future for her.

My husband returned to his love of learning once life returned to normal, inviting scholars and philosophers to Bella Court for long discussions and debates. It was at about this time that I was introduced to Thomas Southwell. An eminent doctor of medicine and the Canon of St Stephen's Chapel in Westminster, he was a close friend of Roger Bolingbroke, who shared his interest in astrology and was knowledgeable about the planets and constellations.

Thomas Southwell was an extremely bright, quietly spoken and likeable man, always impeccably dressed, with an interesting opinion on everything, so he soon became my personal physician, guide and tutor in the esoteric arts. His one failing was to rarely appreciate the witty remarks of his friend Roger Bolingbroke, who would amusingly often take advantage of this fact. Most interestingly for me, he was always ready to discuss such questions as how the universe came to exist, how it operates and man's place within it. He was also exploring how religion could coexist with the learning and knowledge that had been suppressed over the ages.

My curiosity about the magical arts had begun with seeing how Margery Jourdemayne could cure most ailments with her herbs and potions, and the spark that had been kindled by the passion of Friar Randolph now took another turn. My new companions had made a study of a rare and secret handbook Humphrey had procured from astrologers in Germany. I was intrigued at their plan to undertake certain 'experiments' to test the truth of the ancient writings.

The book looked disappointingly ordinary when they showed it to me, with a plain brown leather cover, several torn and missing pages and few illustrations. The secret book did not seem to have great age or to have been looked after particularly well. It contained what claimed to be faithful copies of secret astrological and occult arts from ancient times, much of it written in finely printed Latin, with some in Italian. The front part of the book was missing, leaving no details of its author, although some clue to the book's provenance came from notes in the margins by a Johannes Hartleib, who proved to be a counsellor and advisor to the Duke of Bavaria. These notes were cryptic and in old Germanic script, which Roger Bolingbroke was fortunately able to translate for us.

One of the experiments was supposed to help with gaining favour – and there was one person whose favour I needed more than any other, the young King Henry VI. Now fifteen years old, he was always polite to me, yet I knew it was because my husband had been Regent for as long as he could remember. In truth I suspected his mind had been turned against me by his mother. I had not forgotten that Queen Catherine, a woman of my own age, was Countess Jacqueline's sister-in-law through her first marriage to the Duke of Touraine, also of the House of Valois. They were close, and I was there when Jacqueline had been godmother to her son, holding the infant king at the font.

I remember it was by a messenger from Queen Catherine that my husband learned Countess Jacqueline had died of consumption, still childless. He took it badly and became drunk, cursing the day he ever met her, swearing that with Jacqueline's death Burgundian sovereignty in the Netherlands was assured, then admitting he had once loved her. I felt a powerful sense of guilt, as the countess had treated me well, given me her trust and shared her secrets with me, yet I had repaid her so badly. Her tearful face as we bid farewell still haunts me to this day.

I knew my place at court would never be secure without the favour of the king. Worse still, the king's mother and others who resented how I took the place of Countess Jacqueline, would now, with her death, do all within their power to discredit me in the king's eyes. I thought if the experiment from the secret book proved to work, it could do me great good. If it failed, no harm would be done to anyone. We would have to ensure the utmost secrecy, even from my husband, as we could not risk his enemies, or mine, ever learning of our experiment.

We met in the duke's library during one of the duke's regular visits to Calais. Roger Bolingbroke, having made certain we could not be overheard, read aloud from the German book, translating as he went, with Thomas Southwell and myself asking questions to make sure we understood the process correctly.

The invocation was not a complicated one, although it required me to write a magical Latin formula on virgin parchment in the blood of a white dove Thomas Southwell had procured for the purpose. I took a fresh quill and carefully wrote the secret words in a square, while wishing for the grace and love of the king:

$$S A T O R$$
$$A R E P O$$
$$T E N E T$$
$$O P E R A$$
$$R O T A S$$

Although I had seen him several times, I heard no more from the young guard regarding our clandestine arrangement for over a week, then one evening the bolt on my door slid back and he was standing there alone, a serious look on his face. He looked behind him to confirm we could not be overheard and produced a fold of parchment from his tunic. He reached inside again and handed me a small flask, which he said contained black ink of good quality, and he had been able to keep it a secret from the other guards, as I had asked.

He had to come in to my room to see what I was writing, so for the first time my door was left unbolted, a small but important step in my escape plan. Spreading out a sheet of the parchment on my small table, I asked the young guard's name. He told me it was Richard Hook, so I tested the ink with my quill and wrote the letter 'R', then handed it to him, asking him to copy it as well as he could. His hand was a little unsteady but he coped well enough, so I then wrote the rest of his name, showing him how to join each letter and he copied it out twice. He looked pleased with the result, so I presented it to him to keep, telling him I would be happy to teach him more, if he wished.

I asked him to tell me how he had come to be at Beaumaris Castle as a guard. He smiled and said he was the third son of a farmer, so could not expect to inherit and had always known he must make his own way in the world. He had travelled from his family home in England to Wales, taking casual labouring work, eventually reaching the island of Anglesey, seeking better regular work. He said he found the routine of a castle guard an easy if unrewarding life, as I was currently the only prisoner. He looked uncomfortable and I knew what it was he wanted to ask me. Was I really a witch, as he had been told?

I explained as simply as I could how I had been used by my husband's enemies to remove him from power. I didn't mention how he reminds me of my son or that he is the only one of my guards who treats me with any measure of respect. If they really believed I was a witch, guilty of treason against the king, I asked him, how was it that I am simply held prisoner in Beaumaris Castle, instead of being burned at the stake? He looked a little reassured at this and I realised how important it was that he should believe me.

I lay awake in the darkness after young Richard Hook had left, unable to sleep, his question troubling me. I tried to remember happier times and recalled the excitement on hearing that my daughter Antigone had given us a grand-son, Richard. When she was well enough to travel she brought him for us to see. I held this strong healthy boy, my grandson, just as I had held my Arthur when he was a baby, and wondered where all those years had gone.

I also remembered the sense of mystery of that first experiment at Bella Court. It seemed so innocent at the time, if only we were to know where it would lead. I carried the small secret parchment everywhere with me, concealed in the sleeve of my dress, even when I attended a mass in the chapel at Windsor Castle in the presence of the young king. He was as courteous to me as ever, yet seemed to pay me no special attention and I wondered if our 'experiment' had failed.

When I met again in secret with Roger Bolingbroke and Thomas Southwell, I told them it was my wish to experiment with a more powerful incantation, which we had previously ruled out. The secret book described a method to secure the supreme and undying love of any person with dignity and honour. Most importantly, this was described in the secret text as having been used by the Greek philosopher Parmenides to obtain special favour from the King of Persia. The 'spell' was also much more complicated, as it required the casting of two figures in pure silver. We discussed the involvement of others to do this difficult work but decided the only way to ensure secrecy was to share the tasks between us.

Roger Bolingbroke agreed to fashion moulds for casting the silver from the soft Portland stone left over from the building of Bella Court. The book described how the moulds should be made in two halves which fitted perfectly together. Roger professed he was no sculptor, although fortunately a good likeness was not required, as the images were symbolic. One was to be in the form of a man wearing a crown, to represent the king, and the other needed to be recognisably female in shape, one third larger than the first and holding a sceptre. I was to provide the silver from my jewellery, while Thomas Southwell had the task of procuring a small furnace from the London silversmiths.

After several weeks they finally announced they were ready to make the new experiment. The appointed hour for the casting for the first figure was the first hour of a Sunday, under a waxing moon. Roger Bolingbroke told me he had read that since ancient times the waxing moon has represented the goddess Artemis, one of the most widely venerated of the ancient deities. He said we must watch for when the moon grows larger in the night sky, moving from the new moon towards a full moon. That is the best time for spells that attract, bring positive change, spells for love, good luck and growth. It seemed a good omen for our experiment.

I was able to slip away in the darkness to where Roger Bolingbroke was waiting for me as we had secretly arranged. We rode silently in the night through the woods, across the old river bridge then through back streets and alleyways to the small London workshop where Thomas Southwell had been working on the pretext of learning the art of jewellery making. Twice we stopped to make sure we were not being followed, as it was vital to maintain absolute secrecy about our experiment.

I remember how the brilliant heat of the smelting furnace added a surreal sense of occasion to our experiment. Thomas Southwell had built it using charcoal and had to maintain the heat with a pair of leather bellows. It was hard work, and the sweat was running down the poor man's red face before the silver was molten. Roger Bolingbroke took the crucible of glowing liquid silver in long iron tongs and poured it with great care into the stone mould he had built, while I read the first incantation: '*I Eleanor, wishing to obtain favour and be revered by King Henry and honoured forever, form this image made and carved in his name, by virtue of which he should love me without measure forever*'.

When the mould was cooled we quenched the small figure in spring water, then he handed the figure to me and I could look at it properly for the first time. Roger Bolingbroke had been unduly modest about his skills as a sculptor. I held in my hands the figure of the king and there was a likeness, from the proportions of his body to the pious look on his face. The little crown on his head had been finely modelled and I remember that the gentle warmth still radiating from the silver made it feel like I was holding a living thing. Pleased with their work, I handed the small figure to Roger Bolingbroke who inscribed it with the magic words in the book, before wrapping it in a clean linen cloth until we were ready for the next.

Our plan was nearly ruined when, on the evening of the following Wednesday my husband returned late from a meeting of parliament. He was restless and was barely asleep before I slipped away into the night. The appointed time for casting the silver figure to represent me was the first hour of Thursday, so we reached Thomas Southwell's workshop with only moments to spare.

As before, the figure was cast with me saying the next incantation: '*I Eleanor, form my own image according to my likeness, by which I may rule forever over King Henry and be loved by him for all eternity*'. This time Roger Bolingbroke had chosen to flatter me with the proportions of his sculpting, for when I held the still warm figure it looked more like a girl in the flower of her youth than my more matronly shape.

On the following day we met together one last time to purify the images with a special potion of aromatic cinnamon, long pepper and the herb agrimony, saying the magic words three times. A prayer was read by Thomas Southwell as set out in the ancient text. Then followed a strange ritual. I had to use a small iron chain to bind the 'hands' of the king's image behind its back.

The arms of the little figure were quite thin, so Roger Bolingbroke was able to bend them in his strong hands without too much difficulty. I took the chain and carefully tied it around the little hands in a knot that would not easily slip off again. The next part of the ritual required the head of the figure to be bent to face down. Unfortunately the solid silver neck was too hard to bend, so Thomas Southwell took a small hammer and, while holding the little body firmly on his workbench, had to hit the back of the head until it bent.

Until then I had been happy to go along with the strange ritual, which reminded me a little of playing with dolls as a child. Now, watching Thomas Southwell's hammer do its brutal work, I felt the first stirring of conscience. I said a silent prayer that no harm would come to the king through our experiments, which were never intended to do anything other than win his favour. There was no going back by then, though, and I placed the figures together, saying: '*As this image, made in the name of King Henry, stands before me with bended neck, thus may he love me and revere me above all others and strive to praise me*'.

The last stage of the experiment required me to travel through the city with the images wrapped in linen to the king's residence at Windsor Castle, where I was to remain until evening, when I took the small bundle to a secret place and buried it deep in the earth so it could never be found again. Looking back, I cannot recall any sense of danger in what we were doing, although if anyone discovered our experiment it could so easily be mistaken for treason and witchcraft.

Throughout the Christmas festivities I watched and waited for any sign of favour. Then we received our New Year's gifts from the king. To Humphrey he presented a tablet of solid gold with an image of the Virgin Mary suspended by three gold chains, with six diamonds, sapphires and hundreds of pure white pearls. For me there was a beautiful brooch in the shape of the king holding a golden ball, set with five large pearls, a large fine diamond and three hangers adorned with rubies and pearls. As I held it in my hand I was a little shocked at the uncanny similarity to the figure which I hoped was safely buried in Windsor Great Park. These were without question the finest New Year's presents given to anyone by the king, a certain mark of his grace and favour.

It was of course not possible to say our restoration was linked in any way to the experiments, although my accomplices were content our efforts had not been wasted. I was the favourite of the king—and the duke was now predominant in the country. The sudden death of the king's mother, Queen Catherine of Valois, on the same day as our gifts arrived, also removed one more person who would most certainly have worked to reduce our influence with the young king.

Another queen was also lost to us that year, as Humphrey's stepmother Queen Joanna died at Havering-atte-Bower, a village near London, after a short illness. I remembered how I visited her with Countess Jacqueline before we set sail for France. Queen Joanna treated me kindly, even though I was merely a lady-in-waiting to the countess. She had also talked openly about her interest in astrology to foretell the future.

Humphrey's mother had died when he was young, so he had become close to his stepmother, who would regularly accompany him on his visits to the Abbey of St Albans. On the news of her death he decided he would meet the cost of her funeral and persuaded the king to make it a full state occasion. The same Italian craftsmen responsible for the fine stonework and statues at Bella Court were commissioned to create a life sized effigy of Queen Joanna, not as the old woman she was at her death but instead based on a youthful portrait, looking beautiful in her prime.

The body of Queen Joanna lay in state in Westminster Great Hall, wearing a golden crown under a red velvet canopy surrounded by torches, burning day and night in her memory. A hundred paupers held candles while bishops and priests read prayers for her soul. Many nobles and knights visited to pay their respects to the wife of one of our greatest kings. On the day of her funeral I travelled at Duke Humphrey's side in a grand procession behind her funeral carriage all the way from London to the cathedral at Canterbury, where she was laid to rest next to her second husband, Henry IV, in St Thomas the Becket's chapel behind the high altar.

I have always found some solace in her story as, like me, she was falsely imprisoned for necromancy and using witch-craft against the person of the king. Having endured her punishment, Queen Joanna was pardoned and released to live the rest of her life comfortably in Nottingham Castle, with a good pension. If I can endure the same, perhaps there is hope for me yet.

13

JULY 1451

HONI SOIT QUI MAL Y PENSE

R eflecting on my past life and adventures in this secret journal reminds me that, although I have seen much sadness, there are also many things I must be grateful for. I was once the first lady of the land, the favourite of the King of England and France, with everything I could wish for. My children were growing up in a palace, surrounded by beauty, music and learning and, after years of longing for what he could not have, my husband was finally content. He was also very proud when our daughter Antigone gave us a second grandson, and named him Humphrey.

My New Year's gift from the king was a beautifully crafted garter of real gold, with the motto made with letters of gold: *Hony soit qui mal y pense.* The buckle was decorated with a flower of precious diamonds, with two large pearls and a bright red ruby on the pendant and two perfectly matching large pearls with twenty-six smaller pearls on the garter. Surely this was the final proof, if it were needed, of the king's absolute regard for me? It is only now, all these years later, that the significance of the motto strikes me as particularly apt: *Evil unto him who evil thinks.*

Everything was going so well. I was finally given a beautiful little granddaughter, my third grandchild, named Elizabeth by Antigone and it seemed our lives could not be better. Then an ominous shadow passed over our lives, slowly at first, just as the sun passes behind a cloud and you gradually realise its heat has cooled. I used to look back and try to see what we could have done to prevent it, yet now I cannot help but wonder it was simply our destiny playing out. Perhaps we could no more have changed the course of those terrible events that blighted our lives than stop the clouds obscuring the sun.

My bored guards talk softly in their Welsh language as they wait outside the chapel entrance, more for the summer sunshine than through respect for my privacy. I sit alone on a wooden bench in the cool sanctuary of the castle chapel and read the devotional Book of Hours, brought to me by the kindly priest. I asked the young guard Richard Hook to enquire after him and learned that the priest has left on a pilgrimage to visit a holy place near St Davids in the west of Wales. I have added him to my prayers and hope he is well enough for such a long journey.

Translating the fine print as well as I am able to, I see new meaning in the words of Psalm 142, '*Enter not into judgement with thy servant: for every one living shall not be justified in thy sight. For the enemy hath persecuted my soul: he hath humbled my life in the earth. He hath set me in obscure places as the dead of the world*'. It is true that those who entered into judgement against me were themselves surely guilty of the same beliefs.

I grieve for those who died because of the events I set in place and will remember them always in my prayers, although I wonder why my God must be a vengeful one.

Was it our destiny, some grand plan that would have unfolded without regard to my actions or inaction? My life is surely humbled and I have lived these past ten years in such obscure places as I had never heard of.

The question which troubles me now is to understand my true destiny. The psalm says, *'Make the way known to me, wherein I may walk: Deliver me from mine enemies'*. Am I to submit to this unjust imprisonment, so I can dedicate my last few years to prayer? Should I risk my life attempting a reckless escape, knowing this could bring harm and pain to myself and others? I would have no concern for my jailor, Sir William Bulkeley, yet what would become of his good wife Lady Ellen and her family? For now, at least, the decision is not mine to take.

When I witnessed Queen Catherine being laid to rest in the Lady Chapel of Westminster Abbey I remembered her as a beautiful, confident woman of my own age and realised how fortunate I had been with the birth of my children. I thought that was the end of her influence on my life and now she would trouble us no more, yet it was not to be. Some ten years before, when still Lord Protector, Duke Humphrey had been concerned over rumours she intended to marry his own cousin, Edmund Beaufort, who had stolen the glory of the defence of Calais from him.

I remember how the prospect of a Beaufort being in a position of such power and influence caused my husband sleepless nights until he formed a plan to prevent it. As Lord Protector it was within his power to propose an Act of Parliament to prevent the Dowager Queen marrying without the king's consent. The true purpose of the act was to ensure that any future husband would face the loss of his lands and possessions. This would be certain to deter the ambitious Edmund Beaufort, who knew Humphrey would not hesitate to enforce the Act.

As we expected, there were those in the parliament who saw this as a move by my husband to protect his own position in the line of succession. His opponents were unable to win the day, although he was forced to concede that children from such a marriage would still be members of the royal family and not suffer punishment. Humphrey told me he was content with this, as the king's permission could only be granted once he reached his majority, and when the Act was passed that was still many years away.

Humphrey had taken the precaution of having the Dowager Queen watched, installing one of our trusted men in her household as a groom in her stables. Through him we learned, less than a year later, that his brother's widow had ignored the ruling of parliament and married in secret. Fortunately it was not to the cardinal's nephew, Edmund Beaufort. Our informant told us her illicit husband was a servant, a Welshman by birth named Owen Tudor.

He had the man investigated and found this was no ordinary servant. Owen Tudor was well educated, the same age as the Dowager Queen Catherine and from a noble Welsh family. He had also been a soldier and fought with honour in France, being made a squire by the king, who granted him the right to bear arms in England, the only Welshman permitted to do so. His position as keeper of the Queen's wardrobe had been well paid and placed him in close and regular contact with the Dowager Queen, so it was possible that by forestalling her marriage to Edmund Beaufort, Humphrey had made it possible for their relationship to become more intimate.

We were in no doubt there was a conspiracy by the Bishop of London and others to conceal this scandal, particularly from Humphrey and parliament, as the couple were living secretly at the bishop's palace in Much Hadham, Hertfordshire. The problem was how to deal with this knowledge. I begged Humphrey to let the matter pass and accept that the Dowager Queen had acted just as he had done with Countess Jacqueline. He had no wish to punish the queen in any way, as she was after all the mother of the king, yet Tudor had clearly shown a disregard for the Act of Parliament which Humphrey had taken the trouble to put in place.

While this marriage remained secret, it seemed prudent to simply let the matter rest. It remained so for some years, during which time they had three sons and a daughter, then rumours began to circulate in London about the illicit marriage. We had always known it was a matter of time before the truth was revealed, as the queen had influential supporters. The scandal would also be of great interest to those in Cardinal Beaufort's faction who were also opposed to Humphrey's rise to power and always seeking ways to weaken his authority.

At about the same time we heard from our informer in the queen's household that Queen Catherine was unwell. She had taken to her bed and was showing worrying signs of the instability and delusions that had afflicted her father, King Charles VI of France. It seemed she would occasionally forget who she was or sometimes think she was still Queen of England. Our man understood from overheard conversations that, as a consequence of Catherine's condition, Owen Tudor was now considering the future of his two eldest sons and planned to visit the king at Windsor Castle to ask for them to be recognised.

The time for Humphrey to act decisively had finally come. On his orders, the queen's husband Owen Tudor was arrested and brought to appear before the Council to explain his conduct. The hearing should have been a formality, as by marrying the Dowager Queen, Tudor had shown contempt for the ruling of parliament set out in the Act of Parliament. To Humphrey's surprise, a majority of the members of Council were persuaded by the Welshman that he had not acted dishonourably and that surely Queen Catherine should be free to choose whom she should marry. He was released, acquitted of all charges.

At first we suspected the devious hand of Cardinal Beaufort behind the Council's decision. Humphrey privately accused him of an attempt to discredit his actions and received the shocking reply that it was the king himself who had directed the Council. This was impossible to disprove without drawing more attention to the matter but we knew if it was true it meant we risked incurring the king's displeasure.

I hoped the matter was ended and proposed we should accept the inevitable and publicly support the Dowager Queen's marriage as legitimate. I should have known my husband better. He had taken Owen Tudor's acquittal as a personal affront. Without concern for the consequences, Humphrey again sent armed men to track down and arrest Owen Tudor as he made his way back to Wales. This time he imprisoned Tudor without further trial in Newgate jail, seizing his possessions.

We then faced the question of what to do about Queen Catherine, who was by then reported to be pregnant with yet another child. Humphrey arranged for her to be taken to Bermondsey Abbey for her own safety, where she could be under close observation by his own physician. It was soon after arriving at Bermondsey Abbey that she sadly lost the child and suffered complications which led to her death. Although he was innocent of any part in this, rumours began spreading in London that my husband precipitated the tragedy through his self-serving actions. Humphrey was dismissive of such talk, as he had personally ensured she was cared for as well as possible. There was nothing to be done about the rumour and gossip yet I knew it was the start of a shadow passing over us.

Then we learned Owen Tudor had escaped from his cell in Newgate Prison and was now presumed to be somewhere in Wales. My husband was furious, as he knew Tudor must have had help from someone in Newgate. He sent all the men at his disposal in search of him and held an inquiry, which failed to identify Tudor's accomplices. This time when Tudor was recaptured Humphrey would have imprisoned him in the Tower but was conscious that the whole business was potentially damaging to his own reputation. Humphrey instead had Tudor sent to Windsor Castle, where he remained in some comfort until the king was of age.

We expected King Henry VI to grant a royal pardon to Owen Tudor at the year end, when he reached the age of sixteen, yet were surprised when the king took him into his own household, ordering the restoration of his goods and lands. The king also recognised Tudor's two eldest sons as his half-brothers and his manner towards us changed. It was said he could not forgive my husband for such treatment of his late mother. Through no fault of his own, Humphrey had provided his enemies with the means to poison the mind of the king against him.

Worse still for Humphrey and against his advice, the young king assumed personal control over parliament, creating a new council with Humphrey at the side of

Cardinal Beaufort. Although he was awarded a salary of two thousand marks a year for life, it grieved him to see his power and influence eroded so greatly, as he was certain the cardinal had been behind the plan and now he must rely on his old enemy to secure any decisions.

With this check on his political ambitions, my husband returned to the study of old manuscripts, which he had begun in his days at Oxford, and seemed content to spend long hours in his library. I was also content to devote myself to raising my children and reminding London society of our importance by arranging banquets and riding in splendour through the city, followed by Humphrey's personal guard, all in their fine uniforms.

The king continued to show me favour and had grown into a handsome young man, tall and slim, intelligent and sharp. He loved hunting and gaming and spending money on fine hats and gowns, yet he was not popular with the people, who rarely saw him. He had never shown the spirit of his father and could have accompanied Humphrey to the relief of Calais, yet chose instead to spend long hours at prayer in his personal chapel.

Now dangerous rumours began to circulate in London as word spread about his late mother's mental condition. I had been close to the king and on several occasions observed how he would sometimes become as if his mind was elsewhere. One moment he would seem to be listening then the next he would have a far away look in his eyes. Thomas Southwell agreed it was possible the king could have inherited some form of madness from his mother's French family.

Such talk could, of course, be seen as treason, yet the truth of it was there for anyone who knew the king to see. It was only natural that people would start talking of the line of succession, and my husband was the heir apparent. Not for the first time I found I was dreaming of a day when Duke Humphrey could become king, with me proudly at his side as his queen.

Many untruths have been told about that fateful day when we cast the king's horoscope. It has been said that it was instigated by my friend Margery Jourdemayne. The good lady suffered greatly as a result of this allegation, yet I had not seen her for some months when I began wondering about the future of the king. Margery Jourdemayne might have been known as a witch but her talent was a good one, curing the sick with her herbal potions and helping the poor with innocent charms that gave them great comfort.

I confess that I approached my friend and astrologer Roger Bolingbroke about the matter and I alone was guilty, if it was a crime to be curious about my future prospects. I knew King Henry V had not wished Queen Catherine to be confined at Windsor Castle because of a prophecy, that Henry born at Windsor shall long reign and all lose. I had no idea if this was true or a fanciful legend, yet the idea that Humphrey could one day be king often returned to my thoughts.

It has been said that we chose to begin with my own horoscope, yet this was untrue. Like so many I regretfully had no record or knowledge of my date of birth, other than it was in the year 1400. My mother would of course have been able to tell me but she had taken the knowledge to her grave. My father was not able to help, as he could only recall that it had snowed the day I was born. He told me he had feared he would lose us both, as mine had been a difficult birth.

I was present at Windsor Castle as lady-in-waiting to Countess Jacqueline, so I was able to clearly recall the excitement and commotion when King Henry VI was born in the late afternoon of the sixth of December, 1421. We were able to discover from official records the exact time of the king's birth was at four minutes to four. This was the information we needed to produce the king's astrological chart, although we were aware of the risks of doing so. As before, I decided it must be done in absolute secrecy, without even the knowledge of my husband.

Roger Bolingbroke and I worked in the duke's library, late one evening, when we were certain not to be disturbed. First he drew a circle, much as Friar Randolph had done in our London house. He carefully marked on it the symbols of the zodiac and, consulting his books of astrological tables, drew the position of the sun and moon and planets in relation to the zodiac, which made it possible to calculate the horoscope with precision for the time of the king's birth.

He drew a series of lines, explaining that the interpretation is best done from the simple to the more complex. The king's horoscope revealed he was in Sagittarius, with one of his dominant planets being the sun. This, Roger told me, can indicate a sense of honour and dignity, with charismatic leadership qualities, yet also a weakness related to the sin of pride or to excessive authority. With Mercury among his dominant planets, the king's weakness could lie in his nervousness to follow his instinct.

The question of threats to the king's well-being proved to be complex to determine. Roger Bolingbroke said it was impossible to indicate a death point in an astrological chart and anyone who suggested otherwise was a charlatan. A horoscope could reveal areas that put someone at risk, although this would be a subjective interpretation. I was intrigued to learn more. With so much resting on this knowledge I suggested we should consult with our friend Thomas Southwell. After much discussion, it seemed from the horoscope that the king could suffer a life-threatening illness. Although it was not possible to be certain of the date, the calculations indicated the summer of 1441.

14

AUGUST 1451

CARPE DIEM

his is the warmest summer I can remember. The grass in the inner courtyard is parched from lack of rain and where there was once thick mud is now turned to a fine dust, which clings to my dress as I walk. My precious ink dries instantly on the page and the parchment feels almost brittle as my sharpened quill scrapes these coded words. I am grateful for the light breeze which comes through my window from the sea and, when I can, will return to my prayers in the chapel, the one place in this castle that remains cool despite the sun.

I have often had reason to mention the long standing conflict between my husband and what he called 'The Beaufort party', led by Cardinal Henry Beaufort. Both such strong-minded men, the conflict between them caused us endless problems as the two sides could never reconcile their differences. The Beaufort family were a rising power in England, yet while Humphrey retained favour at Court they could not claim to have the most influence with the king. Then in the spring of 1440 their arguments came to the fore when Cardinal Beaufort decided it was time to agree terms for peace with France.

Humphrey was one of the few who opposed this, not in anger against the cardinal's change of heart or even because his brothers had given their lives to secure England's position in the territories now being handed over so easily. I know he still yearned to be a Prince of Holland. Even yet, my husband signed his name with the titles Duke of Gloucester, Holland, Zealand and Brabant, Earl of Pembroke, Hainault and Flanders.

He cautioned the king that some were imposing on his youth. Then he called for the cardinal to be removed from his post on the King's Council, together with the Archbishop of York, who had also been made a cardinal by the pope. It was a test of who had most influence with the king and, unfortunately for us, the pious king supported the call for peace, not war.

Humphrey took it badly, as his political future and status were now shown to be in rapid decline. It seemed our enemies had won after all. With little to lose, Humphrey decided to publicly challenge the cardinal, asking the questions which no one had dared put into words. Where had the great wealth of the cardinal come from? It was not from his religious offices and he had not inherited his fortune. Was it through the sale of favours and grants of land that were rightfully the property of the king?

My husband also accused Cardinal Beaufort of arranging the marriage of his niece, Lady Joan Beaufort, to James of Scotland, then contriving his release without the authority of Parliament, illegally recovering his jewels when forfeited to the Crown. Humphrey produced damming evidence that the cardinal had also failed to pay the dues of his cathedral church at Winchester. The allegation was that

Cardinal Beaufort had grown arrogant by ill-gotten gains and now acted not like a humble servant of the church but like royalty, effectively governing the kingdom.

Looking back at the events of that dreadful year it seems we should have known the cardinal was a dangerous enemy who should never have been underestimated. He had already shown himself capable of the most unscrupulous acts, yet at the time Humphrey was furious with the cardinal and felt he still had enough power and influence in parliament and the royal court to put such questions and demand a response.

The cardinal's reply was unexpected. He called for the release of Duke Charles of Orleans, held by my father under an order from King Henry V that he was only to be released when his son had come of age and our domination of France was complete. Humphrey was outraged and protested most publicly that releasing the Duke of Orleans was against the wishes of his brother, the late king, and playing into the hands of the Duke of Burgundy. At last he aroused the popular support he wished for. The people could see the truth of his words and called for the king to act.

I first learned the news from my husband. I found him in his library, where I saw he had been drinking a good quantity of his best wine. The ambitious, successful man I married was gone, replaced by a tired grey shadow of his former self, and I knew that once again our lives were going to change. I remember how he took my hand and kissed it, trying his best to smile. When he spoke, his voice carried a great sadness. He said it was too late. The king was already too far under the control of Cardinal Beaufort.

He told me the king had issued a proclamation that he desired it to be understood the release of the Duke of

Orleans was at his own initiative and no one else was responsible. We knew these were Cardinal Henry Beaufort's words, yet there was nothing to be done. The king had asserted his wish to bring to an end to the war that had endured for over a hundred years. Duke Charles of Orleans was to swear an oath he would never take arms against England and would use his influence to remove the desire for war amongst those in power in France.

I must confess I felt a sense of relief, rather than anger. It was far from the outcome my husband had hoped for, yet I was as tired of English politics as he was. It would have been good to see him triumph over his old enemy, and it pained me to see him looking so broken. He had worked hard as Lord Protector, always looking after the best interests of the king, for his entire life. Never once had he sought to profit from his position by taking money for favours, yet his reward for all this diligent service to the crown was to be publicly humiliated.

For me, the king's decision to side with Henry Beaufort was the final proof my experiments with the secret arts were futile. My mind had been turned by the wonderful gifts from the king, coming so soon afterwards. They were a clear sign that at the time I was already highly in his favour. My presents were even grander than gifts he gave to his own mother, yet there was no reason to connect them with the little effigies buried deep in a secret place at Windsor. I resolved that never again would I risk such experiments.

Now I will write about the most wonderful yet saddest thing that has happened to me for the past ten years, while it is fresh in my memory. Lady Ellen was waiting for me at the entrance to the chapel when I took my walk. I could see right away she had something of much importance to tell me and was carrying a small bundle. She dismissed my guards, who retreated a short distance and watched us with curious interest.

Ellen turned to me. 'I would like to repay you for making my son well again.'

I shook my head. 'You have already shown me great kindness.'

'As a mother, I know how much you must miss your daughter.'

I looked at her, trying to understand her smile. 'Not a single day has passed that I don't pray for her to be safe and well.'

She took my hand in hers. 'I have found your daughter.'

I was shocked. 'Antigone? Is she well?'

'Yes, she is well. I wrote to her and asked if she can visit you.'

I hardly dared ask my question. 'Will Sir William permit it?'

'I asked him as a favour. He was reluctant, which is how it has taken so long to arrange. I reminded him you have been here more than a year now and never given him trouble.' Lady Ellen smiled again. 'He is a good man, Eleanor.'

I didn't know how to thank Lady Ellen and her husband. 'When can I see her?'

'They arrived in Beaumaris yesterday.' She saw my look and added, 'Antigone travelled with her son, your grandson.' She looked serious. 'There is something else I need to tell you, Eleanor.'

I sensed from her manner she had to tell me bad news. Had something happened to one of the children? Had my actions brought trouble on the last surviving members of our family?

'Your daughter's husband Henry, Earl of Powys. I regret to tell you he has died.'

Once again I was shocked, yet at the same time relieved it was not the children. 'I remember him as a young man, full of life. He can't have been more than forty. Do you know how?'

'No. I thought you should know before you see your daughter.' She looked towards the main gatehouse. 'I will bring her here, to the chapel. You must prepare, Eleanor. I will send a man to fetch you when your daughter is here.'

I thanked her again and returned to my room, hardly believing what had happened. I felt a strange mix of elation and apprehension about seeing Antigone after so long. My mind was full of questions. How had her husband died? Why had she never written to me? Had she tried to visit and been turned away without me knowing? How would she look after ten years, and how would she feel about what had happened to me?

It was important for me to look my best for my daughter. As I brushed dust from the hem of my red dress I realised Lady Ellen knew Antigone could soon be visiting when she gave it to me, yet decided to say nothing until she was certain. I combed my hair and plaited and coiled it in the new style I had seen Ellen wearing, and then an idea occurred to me. Taking the small blade the priest had given me, I made sure I wasn't being watched through the grill in my door. I carefully cut open the stitching at the secret pocket of my old blue dress where the last of my jewellery was concealed.

When I fled my home at Bella Court I filled a bag with gold and silver coins and my best jewellery. Over the years of my imprisonment these had been reduced to the rings I now wore, two gold brooches with large rubies and a pearl necklace given to me one New Year's Day by my husband. I had wasted the coins, rewarding my servants in the early days of my imprisonment, little realising I should have kept them to bribe my guards or pay for much needed food. The best and most priceless of all, the precious diamond brooch given to me by the king, was stolen from me. I curse the man who took my golden garter: *Evil unto him!*

For the first time in over ten years, I fixed the ruby brooch at the neck of my dress and fastened my pearl necklace around my neck. I wished I had a mirror to see the effect. Once I would have been worried my jewels would be taken by the guards, yet now it was a risk I was prepared to take. Lady Ellen would not allow it. It was strange but the simple act of wearing expensive jewellery again made me forget all the hardship and gave me the confidence I needed to face my daughter.

I heard footsteps and the bolt on my door slid noisily open. The guard gestured to me and I followed him down to the castle chapel, which had been lit with a dozen new candles, even though it was late morning. As I entered I saw Antigone, with a smartly dressed young boy as tall as her waiting awkwardly at her side. We stood for a moment, frozen in time, taking in the changes in each other over ten years. Still slim and attractive, she wore an emerald green dress and looked younger than her thirty years. I could still see the little girl who had squealed when Humphrey used to tease her.

She rushed forward and hugged me, sobbing. It was all I could do not to cry, even though I had not been happier since her wedding day at Bella Court.

'I thought I would never see you again, Antigone. It is so good to know you are well.'

She looked at me, tears in her eyes. 'My husband told me you were dead. He said you died of a fever, in Peel Castle.'

'That is why you never wrote?'

Antigone nodded, unable to speak. I wondered if that was what everyone had been told or if it was Sir Henry Grey's way to end my connection with his family. In a sudden insight I realised we married our daughter to the wrong man. Henry Grey might have been a wealthy Earl but he was no politician and, at least up to the time of my arrest, had never been called to parliament. If we had found Antigone a more influential husband he might have been able to plead with the king for clemency and negotiate my release.

'I am sorry to hear about your husband.'

'Yes. It has been a difficult time for us.' She seemed somehow angry about her husband and I wondered if he had treated her badly. Antigone dried her eyes as she gestured for her son to come forward. 'This is Humphrey. He is twelve now.'

I looked again at the tall and serious looking young boy who had been a baby when I last saw him. 'You remind me of your grandfather, Humphrey. Do you know your name is a tradition handed down from your de Bohun ancestors?'

'From my great grandmother's family.' He glanced at Antigone. 'Mother has taught us all the history of our family.' His voice was confident and echoed in the chapel.

I nodded in approval. 'Lady Mary was supposed to have become a nun. She was already living in a convent and was taken from there to be married to your great-grandfather, King Henry IV, when she was barely your own age.'

Young Humphrey smiled, the same wry, charming smile as I remember seeing so often on his grandfather's face all those years ago. I wish my husband had lived long enough to see his grandson. He would have been proud.

'Are your brother and sister well, Humphrey?'

'Yes, my lady. Richard is now fourteen and Elizabeth is eleven years old.'

Antigone added, 'Elizabeth is growing fast into the image of you. She already has suitors after her.'

I took Antigone's hand and led her to one of the long wooden benches which served as pews in the chapel, gesturing for my grandson to sit with us. His eyes were attracted to my ruby brooches as they sparkled in the flickering candlelight.

I unpinned one from the black lace and handed it to him. 'I would like you to give this to your sister, to remember me by.'

Young Humphrey took the jewel hesitantly. 'Elizabeth will be most grateful, my lady.'

I removed the second brooch. 'This one is for you, Humphrey. If you wish you may give it to the woman you will one day marry.'

He smiled as he looked at the ruby in its gold clasp, amused by the thought. 'Thank you, Grandmother.'

It was the first time I'd heard myself called that and I smiled back at my grandson. I removed my pearl necklace and handed it to my daughter, who looked at me in surprise. 'I would like you to have this, Antigone. I have never been able to count the number of pearls. I know it cost your father a great deal. He would have been happy for you to have it now.'

Antigone sat looking at the pearls for a moment and I

sensed she was thinking of her father and wondering whether to tell me something.

'Did they tell you he is buried at St Albans as he had always wished?'

I shook my head. 'They told me he was dead but not how, or where he was buried. I was going to ask Lady Ellen to find out for me.'

'The old Prior of St Albans paid for his chantry and burial vault and the monks said masses for him. When I last visited the priory, candles were still being lit every day on the altar in his memory.'

I hardly dared ask the question. 'Do you know how he died?'

She looked at me, a flash of anger in her eyes. 'They say it was a sudden illness. I don't believe it. He was arrested by men of the Duke of Suffolk. I think they murdered him.' Antigone scowled as she remembered. 'The queen took Bella Court the day he died. She has made it her own residence.'

I cursed Queen Margaret of Anjou and her henchman William de la Pole, glad now he had met an unhappy end. My husband Humphrey could still be alive but for the queen. She had seen a way to remove him and now had my home, which rightfully belonged to my daughter and her children. I hesitated to ask the next question. 'I was told by my jailor at Peel Castle that Arthur was executed by the Duke of Suffolk for treason. Is that true?' I held my breath, waiting for her answer.

'My brother was also arrested by the Duke of Suffolk, soon after father, with several good men of our household. Suffolk claimed he had evidence they were plotting to kill the king and place father on the throne, with you as his queen.' She frowned at the memory. 'There was no evidence or even a proper trial, yet they were all condemned to be hanged, drawn and quartered for treason.' She looked across at her son, who was following every word, even though he must have heard the story before. 'It was all a horrible plan by the Duke of Suffolk, for as they were hanged he arrived with the king's pardon. They were all cut down and set free.'

'Arthur is alive?' My heart was beating fast now.

'My brother has never been seen or heard of since. Henry, my late husband, said there was a rumour Arthur was murdered in secret.' She half smiled at me. 'I like to think he is hiding somewhere and will make himself known to me someday.'

'I will pray for it, Antigone.' We sat in silence for a moment as I remembered my son.

Antigone took my hand. 'The queen didn't have father's precious books. I made sure they were sent to Oxford, as he wished.'

I remembered how important that had been to him. 'When you were a girl our house was always full of scholars, translating the classics. Your father called you Antigone to show his admiration for Sophocles.'

Antigone smiled. 'He named me after a Greek tragedy.'

'He named you after a woman who was the rebel of her family, who valued spiritual laws above those of the state.'

'I have not been much of a rebel, although that is going to change.'

I turned to look at her, wondering what she planned to do.

Antigone appeared serious again. 'A Welsh noble named Gruffudd Vaughan was knighted on the battlefield for leading the men who protected King Henry V when he rescued my father at the Battle of Agincourt. He became a loyal follower of my father in France and when my husband's father was killed at Baugé, my father entrusted Sir Gruffydd to return the Earl's body to Powys and arrange his funeral.'

She stopped and ran the pearls she was holding through her fingers like a rosary, the same frown I had seen on her face when she was a little girl. 'My husband said Sir Gruffydd Vaughan, who had then been outlawed, had offended his honour by challenging his claim to the Lord-ship of Powys.' She hesitated to continue but I nodded for her to go on. 'My husband summoned Sir Gruffydd to Powys Castle and when he arrived, ordered his arrest. He had him executed, Mother. Sir Gruffydd Vaughan was beheaded in the courtyard of our home, without trial.'

I could see it was hard for Antigone to tell this story, but could see there was more, and pressed her to continue.

'Sir Gruffydd Vaughan's supporters in Wales swore to avenge his death. That was three years ago. We returned to our mansion at Pontesbury and life went on. Then we had a message there was trouble at Powys Castle, so my husband returned there in January last year. They said he died in a hunting accident. I doubt we will ever know the truth.'

I took my daughter in my arms and hugged her. 'You said things were going to change?'

Antigone looked at her son, my grandson, then back at me. 'My husband left a will, granting me his estates in Normandy. I am leaving for France, Mother. I don't wish for my son to be Lord of Powys. Richard will be the third Earl of Tankerville when he comes of age.'

I realised what she was telling me. 'It will be too great a journey for you to visit me again?'

Antigone nodded, tears returning to her eyes. 'I don't know if we will ever be able to return to Wales.'

15

SEPTEMBER 1451

VINDICTIS

I felt a strange mix of elation and sadness after my daughter's tearful goodbye on that summer afternoon. It was so good to know Antigone and the children, my grandchildren, were safe and well. At the same time, they would already be preparing for the long journey to Normandy. I knew I could never see her again. I also found myself thinking how different our lives would have been if Humphrey's campaign in Hainault had succeeded. He could now be a prince of Hainault, or even Burgundy. I felt a new sense of grief for the loss of my husband. Talking of Humphrey's death and seeing how much my grandson resembled him reminded me how much I missed him.

If my son lives he would have found a way to let me know or at least send a message to his sister Antigone. In my heart I know he was murdered, a mother's intuition, yet now at least there was a faint hope. He could also think me dead, if that was what everyone has been told. Lady Ellen said it had not been easy to find my daughter and send her a message. Somewhere at the back of my mind I cling to the thought that Antigone is right, Arthur is hiding until the day when he is sure it is safe to make himself known to us.

Now I have given away the last of my jewels I know that ends any foolish thoughts of escape. Even if I were somehow able to evade my constant guards and make my way across the island to the western coast, I could not hope to pay for a passage across the Irish Sea with just my mother's gold ring. Lady Ellen had been so kind to me. I would not repay her by bringing disgrace on her husband, so I am resigned to living out my days within these thick stone walls. I shall try to tell the rest of my story as fully as I can and hope one day anyone reading this will understand how my life was changed so cruelly and so completely.

Thinking back to those last happy days at Bella Court, I remember how the release of the Duke of Orleans against my husband's wishes proved he had less influence over the king than the cardinal, yet it seemed he had again survived. My father lost the good pension he received from the Crown for keeping the Duke of Orleans in custody, which he was relying on for his old age, but the Duke seemed to have respected his oath to the king. I suspected that after more than twenty-five years imprisonment, he was simply grateful for the chance to have a quiet life in France.

This memory gave me an idea. If it is true people think I died in Peel Castle, there will never be any call for my release and I will languish here forgotten by the world. I need to find a way to petition the king, without causing trouble for Lady Ellen and her family. Just as the Duke of Orleans swore an oath before the king in Westminster Abbey, I could do the same. I resolved I would offer to be exiled for life to Normandy, where I could live out my days in peace with my daughter and grandchildren.

I lay awake until I could hear the shrill calls of seagulls, marking the dawn outside my window, as I pondered how I could make my petition and who would be able to represent my interests. I decided I must first secure the permission of Sir William Bulkeley but I can hardly expect him to speak to the king on my behalf. Lady Ellen told me her father was well connected yet it seemed unfair to put her in a difficult position after all she has done for me. Only one person came to mind. The king will I hope remember my former secretary and chaplain John Home, the man who betrayed us all, if he still lives.

I realised the danger we were in one evening when I was having a late supper alone with Humphrey. We had dismissed the servants and I commented that he seemed unusually quiet. He didn't answer me, so to make conversation I said how happy I was that at least life could now continue as normal. My husband banged his hand on the table and raised his voice at me as he never had before, calling me a naive and stupid woman. He stormed out of the room, leaving me with the awful realisation there was something going on I didn't know about.

Later that night my husband confessed there was something he hadn't told me, which we must discuss. Far from forgetting the serious allegations against him, the cardinal was planning his revenge. He told me I must take care what I said in front of my ladies-in-waiting, the staff and the servants, and to let him know of any sign they could be spying on us. He made me promise not to travel anywhere in public without an escort of his personal guard. He had no idea when or how the cardinal would act against him, only that it was almost certain he would do so.

He said he was put in mind of Cicero's moral tale of Damocles, who, given the chance by Damocles to try life as a king, saw a sharp sword suspended over his head by a single hair from the tail of a horse. This, the king explained, was what life as ruler was really like. There can be nothing happy for the person over whom some fear always looms. People had already been warning Humphrey to take care and he confessed he was beginning to question the loyalty of everyone. I didn't ask if that included me, although I was glad we had maintained the highest secrecy when we made our illicit experiments.

As soon as I could I warned Thomas Southwell and Roger Bolingbroke to make sure no word of our secret activities ever got out. They both swore that nothing had ever been mentioned to anyone and I know they understood the seriousness of our situation. It seemed we had succeeded, as I was certain my husband would have imme-diately questioned me if he had heard so much as a rumour. I also asked them to destroy any potentially incriminating evidence and to let me know if anyone began asking questions.

Life did begin to return to normal again, although I was always looking over my shoulder, wary of the cardinal's spies. I was now suspicious of every servant, however long we had known them. My maids attended on me from the moment I woke until I closed my eyes to sleep at night, so it was not easy to always be careful what we said in their hear-ing. I had not forgotten how easy it had been to learn every-thing about Queen Catherine and Owen Tudor simply by retaining one man in her household.

Even my loyal ladies-in-waiting now also fell under suspicion. I was aware many of them came to Bella Court to enhance their social prospects. My own life changed completely when I became a lady-in-waiting to Countess Jacqueline, so I was under no illusions about what could hide behind their smiles. Everyone has their price and Cardinal Beaufort was a wealthy man. There was no question of dismissing them, for they were good company and entertained me with all the latest gossip, a constant reminder of how people loved to talk about the misfortune of others.

As the weeks passed Humphrey became something of a recluse, immersing himself in his studies, translating Greek classics. He only left Bella Court when he had to and refused my requests to organise entertainment for our friends. Our home, once so lively and vibrant, became sombre and tranquil, with few visitors, other than dull scholars who came to help Humphrey with his work. I became bored, missing the bustle of London and soon began returning to the city. Out of respect for my husband's wishes I always now had an armed escort when visiting, although this simply drew more attention to our grand procession through the narrow, crowded streets.

On a sultry day in late June I was dining with several of my ladies at The King's Head in Cheapside. The old inn had always been a popular place in the heart of the city, particularly on busy market days. On the upper floor was an overhanging gallery where I could often be found dining with my ladies. It became a favourite vantage place from where we could view the city's comings and goings, see and be seen by those who mattered. I felt in good spirits, finally beginning to put the troubles that had afflicted my husband behind me.

Humphrey's reputation had been undermined by his enemies at parliament and the royal court, yet was it truly a sin of pride for me to not let people forget I was the Duchess of Gloucester, married to the heir apparent to the crown?

The king remained unmarried, with no prospect yet of a wife, and his mother long dead, so I was the first lady of England. My husband continued to build our fortune through astute investments in land around Oxford and our palace at Bella Court could claim to be the grandest in London, rivalling even the king's own apartments.

I remember we were excitedly discussing how the ambitious Duke Richard of York was said to be crossing the Channel with an army of five thousand men. The much contested town of Harfleur had been besieged and re-taken for the king. I was hopeful that more victories in France would soon tip the balance back in my husband's favour. Even Cardinal Beaufort would have to admit he had been wrong to let our hard won territory be negotiated away so easily. The prospect of this restored my spirits and gave me hope that all would be well for us soon.

A breathless messenger interrupted our meal, handing me a folded note. I was drinking good wine and laughing at some silly joke as I broke the wax seal, without even looking to see who had sent the note. As I read the hurriedly scrawled words, I felt a chill run through my veins, a premonition of what was to come. I re-read the note, half hoping I had been mistaken but I had not. I recognised the distinctive signature of Roger Bolingbroke. We had been betrayed and he was about to be arrested, together with Thomas Southwell, on charges of treason against the king.

There is a sense of impending rain in the autumnal breeze drifting through my window. As I watch, relentless grey clouds cover the last small patch of bright blue sky. The hot dry summer has made this place more bearable, yet I fear another long winter, as I suffer in the cold which chills my bones. I see from this journal it was one year since that same Richard, Duke of York disturbed the peace of Beaumaris Castle with his unexpected visit. It was not for me he came, but to challenge the king and his scheming French queen.

Although now ten years ago, I still feel the shock of that dreadful moment in Cheapside when I read the note from Roger Bolingbroke. So this was how a respected man of God, a Cardinal of Rome, Bishop of Winchester and chief advisor to the king, attacked my husband, who had retired to his innocent studies. The cardinal had found the weak spot in the duke's defences, and it was me, his foolish wife.

Our enemies did their work slowly, with care and cunning, first arresting my friends. I ran from the inn and, followed by my escort, rode as fast as I could over London Bridge, all the way to Bella Court. Humphrey was waiting for me. The king's men had not only arrested Roger Bolingbroke and Thomas Southwell. Humphrey's personal secretary and chaplain, John Home, had also been taken to the Tower. My husband seemed to think it was a hollow threat dreamed up by the cardinal that could be easily resolved. We had, after all, he said, survived worse things in the past.

I was torn between believing him and telling the truth of the real danger we were now in. I was sure of the loyalty of my friends and knew they would do everything in their power to keep my secrets safe. I also knew the cardinal would not hesitate to use torture to make them talk if he thought it could bring down my husband. He would have already fabricated the case against them, so his aim would not be to extract a confession but to make them admit the names of their co-conspirators. I wondered how even the strong-willed Roger Bolingbroke would cope when shown the dreaded rack.

All we could do was wait, knowing Cardinal Henry Beaufort would make sure all of London soon knew about the arrests. Nothing travels faster than bad news. Tongues would wag, and the damage to our reputation done, even if the charges were eventually dropped. Neither of us could sleep that night. All I could do was pray for my friends in our private chapel. Humphrey could bear the waiting no longer and sent a dozen trusted men to Westminster to find out what they could. Some hours later one of his riders returned with details of the charges against our men.

My worst fears were realised. They were all accused of conspiracy to bring about the death of the king. We knew too well that anyone convicted of treason would suffer a most horribly painful death. It was but a short step to have them confess that their plan had been to put my husband on the throne in Henry's place. This was the work of Cardinal Beaufort. By arresting our known associates, he knew people would readily believe they were acting with my husband's full knowledge. The cardinal could easily pay for 'witnesses' to say whatever he wished them to.

There followed another long and difficult wait for news. Another of Humphrey's riders returned to tell us Thomas Southwell was now also facing a specific charge. It was being said he was accused of celebrating a mass unlawfully at the lodge in Hornsey Park. Our man could tell us little more, other than there was talk of Southwell being in possession of what were called 'strange heretical accoutrements'. I hoped this showed they had no knowledge of the truth.

Thomas Southwell was no heretic. We had known him for many years. He was Canon of St Stephen's Chapel in the Palace of Westminster, Rector of St Stephen's in Walbrook and the Vicar of Ruislip. At the same time it was a serious allegation. Humphrey had been present at the burning at Smithfield of a priest who denied the sacraments of the church. During his time as Regent my husband also oversaw inquisitions concerning heretics, traitors, and rebels, many of whom were executed for threatening the House of Lancaster.

Similarly I was at a loss to understand why our secretary and chaplain, John Home, also a man of the church and the Canon of Hereford and St Asaph, had been arrested with them. I could not tell my husband but to my knowledge he was innocent of any involvement in our experiments. Home was serious and scholarly, a tall, thin man with deep-set eyes and a strange habit of pausing over long before answering, as if weighing up all the possibilities before speaking. He did his work well enough yet I had never felt at ease in his company and would never have contemplated involving him in any of our secret experiments.

Then Humphrey's man told us the awful news that my poor gentle and innocent friend Margery Jourdemayne had also been arrested at her home in Westminster, accused of witchcraft and sorcery. I remembered how she was warned, last time we secured her release, that she would be shown no mercy if she was ever caught using witchcraft again. Although she played no part in our experiments and I had not seen her for some time, I was starting to realise the cardinal's plan.

Margery Jourdemayne was one of my 'known associates', not Humphreys. One way or another, Cardinal Henry Beaufort would find a way to accuse me, and through me bring down my husband. Too late, I recalled a quote from the Greek philosopher Antisthenes: *Pay attention to your enemies, for they are the first to discover your mistakes.*

The autumn rain I predicted has finally arrived in Beaumaris, quickly turning the paths around the inner ward to mud again. Instead of taking my walk outside, I passed through the passageways that link my room to the castle chapel. Once there I said a prayer for the souls of my friends and lit three new candles. One for the good-hearted Thomas Southwell, who was so swiftly removed from his proudly held position of Canonry of St Stephen's in Westminster. One for the deep-voiced Roger Bolingbroke, who had so patiently shared his knowledge of the heavens with me. One for my good friend Margery Jourdemayne, who never showed anything other than kindness to all she met.

I do not light a candle for John Home but no longer curse him as I have done so many times. Sitting alone in the contemplative peace of the chapel, I wonder if John Home knew the harm he would do by his glib allegations, made so easily. Did the cardinal put the words into his mouth, or was the falsehood all of his own making? He might not have been a spy for the cardinal, yet all the time he had been putting together his own distorted view of what was going on in secret at Bella Court.

John Home spent much time in the company of Thomas Southwell and Roger Bolingbroke. In his slow, shrewd way, apparently innocent questions in an unguarded moment could have led my friends to tell him more than they really should have. I can imagine John Home's fear when the cardinal's henchmen threatened to tear his limbs on the rack or worse, unspeakable tortures, unless he spoke of what he knew. With his own life at stake, I cannot blame him for sharing his ill-informed theories or agreeing to bear witness against my friends, as others also did. I wonder, though, if he is still alive, and if the lives of those who were once his trusting friends rest heavily on his conscience.

16

OCTOBER 1451

SANCTUARIUM

I t is hard for me to recall the details of how events unfolded during those dreadful weeks ten years ago, the reason I am here now, in Beaumaris Castle. It is also painful for me, as one who was once so proud of my reputation, to remember how the whole of London was soon buzzing with talk of our misfortune. My hope is that writing this story as well as I can may put my troubled mind at rest and leave those terrible times behind me.

The people love a scandal and the scheming Cardinal Henry Beaufort had given them one, a twisted, ill-informed version of events that would appeal to the superstitious and horrify the devout. We heard that Thomas Southwell was imprisoned in the Tower and, in addition to the charges of treason, Roger Bolingbroke, John Home and Margery Jourdemayne, had all now been formally charged with heretical practices and divination with magic and the black arts. Necromancy.

The good men and women of London were calling for my friends to suffer the harshest punishment before any trials had even taken place. Roger Bolingbroke warned me once; such is the fear and superstition of something which people don't understand, their only wish is to see it swiftly crushed, like a bed bug, without a moment of pity or remorse, no thought or care for its place in our world.

I knew there was nothing my husband could do to have them freed and no prospect of a pardon from the king. Shunned by even those who once supported us, our own position was under great threat. I argued with Humphrey that we should make urgent and secret preparations to go into hiding, somewhere far from London, until we could clear our name. He angrily refused, saying he had no reason to hide and to do so would confirm our guilt in the minds of our enemies. He swore he would remain at Bella Court unless there was no alternative.

Then we received disturbing news which took the decision from my hands. We heard of a declaration that Roger Bolingbroke was to publicly recant his crimes at St Paul's Cross, his revelations to be made before the King's Council. It was known that heretics could be shown leniency if they were to publicly recant their misguided ways, yet I found it impossible to believe Bolingbroke would do so before even a trial. I feared he had already made a confession, and had been somehow persuaded to reveal my own involvement and details of our experiments.

My husband was relieved he was not invited to attend the spectacle, so again he sent one of his trusted men on the appointed day to witness events and report back as soon as he could. It was during that awful wait that I secretly visited my husband's library and found the book we used in our secret experiments. Hiding it in the folds of my dress and making sure I could not be seen, I took it to my room. I did not even dare to open the book one last time and threw it on the fire, cursing the day I even knew of it as the parchment pages burned brightly in the orange flames. I covered the ashes with hot coals so no trace remained.

If events were to turn badly for me I needed to be ready. I wrapped my priceless golden brooch set with pearls and a large diamond, together with my gold garter, in some fine cotton cloth. They were gifts from the king but could also serve to pay for my safe haven somewhere no one would find me. I placed them in a bag with a change of clothing, my comb and a small but precious silver mirror. I took a needle and thread and sewed the best of my jewellery into a secret pocket in my favourite blue dress. As a final precaution I found my purse on a silk cord which could be worn under my clothes and filled it with as many gold and silver coins I could. My preparations made, I could only wait for the news I was certain would come.

Humphrey's man returned with a strange and worrying account of what had happened at St Paul's Cross. Crowds of curious onlookers gathered to first hear a sermon by Bishop John Low of Rochester, who spoke of the dangers of heresy and the foolishness of those who would claim to use magic. Our friend Roger Bolingbroke was placed high on a wooden platform, so everyone present could see him. Humphrey's man told us he looked dazed and seemed unable to stand without help. Instead of his black cappa clausa, the sign of his role in the church, he wore a colourful robe daubed with supposedly magic symbols.

Roger Bolingbroke was made to sit on a brightly painted throne-like chair, a wooden sword placed in one hand and a sceptre in the other. On his head they had made him wear a paper crown to mock his treason against the king. Cardinal Beaufort himself presided over the Council's questioning, surrounding himself with the Archbishop of Canterbury, the Bishops of London and Salisbury and the powerful earls of

Huntingdon, Stafford and Northumberland. The sign to the people was clear, the great and the good would prevail and justice would be seen to be done.

Our informant told us how Bolingbroke recanted his diabolical activities. His deep voice faltering as he confessed his actions were unlawful and against the teachings of the church. My husband urged the man to recall exactly the words he had heard. He remembered that there were jeers from the crowd and calls for him to speak the truth when he tried to argue he had never been a heretic and was a faithful servant of the church. The crowd had fallen silent as he prayed, his words echoing around St Paul's, for God to take pity on his mortal soul, and to have mercy on those who would condemn him.

I will never know what Roger Bolingbroke suffered before he agreed to take part in this carefully staged mockery of justice. I did know it was planned by Cardinal Beaufort to prepare the people of London for what would come next, a further confession that would set out the involvement of Duke Humphrey and myself. It was three long days and two sleepless nights before we had word that he claimed his actions were on my behalf. It was being said I had asked him to foretell my future, an act of treason if it could be shown I wished the death of the king, with charges of witchcraft and necromancy likely to be proven. I knew the terrifying punishment for such crimes. Men would be taken to Tyburn, where they would be hanged, drawn and quartered. The punishment for a woman was to be burned alive at the stake.

My one regret is I did not feel able to confess to my husband what I had done or discuss with him the true nature of our experiments. He deserved to know the extent of our actions and why I had to escape while I could, yet at the moment of truth I simply said I was going out to clear my head. Too many people were already suffering as a result of my curiosity and I had no wish to add my husband to the list of those accused as conspirators. I also knew there was no way I could say goodbye to him, even though there was a danger I could never see him again.

I put my purse, heavy with gold and silver coins, around my neck, with a light shawl over my shoulders to hide my face and, carrying the bag I had prepared, left without saying a word to anyone. It was a warm July evening as I took my last walk through my beautiful gardens at Bella Court in the setting sun. I remembered how the workmen had toiled to transform the rough pasture into my garden, one of the finest in the whole of England.

The borders were a riot of colour with flowers brought all the way from Holland and Zeeland; lands which my husband still claimed were his by right. It had been a good early summer and my fruit trees were already heavy with ripening apples and pears, purple plums and bright red cherries. Last of all I stopped to visit my herb garden and quietly said a prayer, not for myself, but for Margery Jourde-mayne, now so fatally caught up in my misfortune.

I made my way through our private avenues to the jetty on the Thames where boatmen were always waiting and paid one to take me upriver to Westminster. Looking back I know I should have asked him to row down the river. I could have escaped to one of the Channel ports and found a passage on a ship bound for France, where I could somehow have lived in exile until it was safe to return. There would have been dangers for a woman travelling alone and a good chance I could be robbed or worse, yet it would have been better to risk this than simply accept my fate. I decided instead to seek sanctuary in Westminster Abbey.

My husband called me a naive and stupid woman and perhaps he was right, for at the time I believed there was a right of sanctuary, where a person could seek protection, even from the cardinal and agents of the king, within consecrated ground. I knew the penalty for anyone forcibly removing people or committing violence against those in sanctuary was excommunication by the church. This would surely be enough to deter even the cardinal.

I was glad of a light breeze as I was rowed up the River Thames. The tide was in our favour and we soon passed the Tower of London, where my friends were imprisoned. I said a prayer that they would not suffer too much, yet even as I did so I knew how easily they could be made to betray me. I pulled my shawl over my hair and this simple disguise meant I drew no attention as we reached the busy jetty at Westminster. I made my way through the familiar, bustling streets of London. For once I was glad of the hard times I spent in the area, making a living as best I could before becoming lady-in-waiting to Countess Jacqueline all those years ago.

The sun had set and it was growing dark as I made my way as fast as I could to St Peter's Sanctuary, at the northwest corner of Westminster Abbey. The Sanctuary was a large square keep, two storeys high, with thick stone walls and a huge door made of heavy oak. It was built to withstand an attack and I thought was the safest place for me to escape from my immediate danger. My knocking on the door went unanswered, so I tried the handle and it opened to reveal a small chapel, with wooden pews and a simple altar lit by cheap tallow candles.

A surly looking man appeared from one of the rooms to

the side of the chapel and demanded to know my business at such a late hour. I explained I was the Duchess of Gloucester, seeking sanctuary. He looked at me with ill-disguised contempt. Word of the allegations made against me had already reached even into this sacred place. After a moment of consideration he said sanctuary was not permitted for the crimes of which I was accused. He told me I could use the chapel to pray for my soul while he consulted with the abbot.

There was nothing else I could do but take a seat in the chapel and contemplate the sorry situation I now found myself in. I was not expecting the warmest welcome but was shocked to learn I could be denied admission to the sanctuary. I did not have long to wait. The man had notified the authorities of my presence and the door banged open as two armed men entered to make my arrest. As they led me through dark, verminous streets with stinking, overflowing sewer channels, I heard a shout ring out that the Duchess of Gloucester had tried to evade the king's justice. The sanctuary I hoped for had turned into a trap from which there was no escape.

As we passed through a busier area of the city I noticed the men escorting me had been drinking and had an over confident swagger. It was late now and perhaps they had thought their work was over for the day, taking a quick drink in a tavern before turning in for the night when they were called to seize me from my supposed sanctuary. I let them walk ahead of me and watched for my chance. A heavily laden wagon which took up most of the narrow street approached us from behind. I waited until it was level with us and darted down a side street, clutching my bag with its precious contents as I ran.

The sound of shouts and heavy boots on the hard cobbles urged me to run faster until I started feeling out of breath. I stopped in a dark doorway and held my breath. My prayers were answered as they pounded straight past my hiding place and on into the night, still shouting to each other and calling my name. A heavily built woman in a grease-stained dress came out of the house opposite my hiding place and stated down the narrow street after the running men. I was certain she would see me and shout to raise the alarm. For once, luck was on my side. The woman muttered a curse and went back into her house, slamming the door behind her.

When I thought it was safe I found my way to the nearest river jetty, where there was a solitary boatman hoping to pick up his last fare for the evening. I paid him extra to take me to Greenwich as fast as he was able to. As his oars splashed rhythmically in the dark, fast flowing water I pulled my shawl around me and worried how I would explain to my husband that I was now a fugitive.

He would be aware by now that I had misled him, although I hoped he understood I would not have done so without good reason. I was expecting to face some difficult questions about my part in what had happened and knew he would be angry with me. My only saving grace was that I had shown the sense to keep him out of any part of our experiments.

It was little consolation but even Cardinal Beaufort knew better than to contrive false charges against the heir apparent to the throne. There still remained the question of what I was to do now. Bella Court would be the first place the king's men would look for me, so I resolved to go into hiding. There was no time to escape across the Channel, so I planned to ask Humphrey to help me make my way to some remote place where I could keep my identity secret until our difficulties were resolved.

As my boat neared the Tower of London my thoughts returned to my friends languishing inside those high walls. I wept at the thought that it was because of me they were now facing the most horrible deaths. There was a shout from the battlements. One of the sentries high on the wall called to my boatman to come to the Tower water-gate. I pulled my shawl higher around my head and urged my boatman to make all haste to Greenwich, offering him a gold piece to keep going. For a moment he hesitated, apologising to me and looking up at the waiting sentry, then he snatched the gold coin from my hand and pulled back hard on the oars, steering us on past the castle towards the safety of my home.

I looked nervously behind us to see if we were being followed as we picked our way through the jumble of boats moored on the ramshackle jetties at St Katharine's wharf. I feared that now, if I were captured, I would surely join my friends in the bleak, rat-infested Tower, a fate I must desperately avoid. It seemed luck was on my side, as I could see no boats pursuing us and we were soon around the bend in the river and the Tower disappeared from view.

At last the outline of Greenwich appeared through the gloom, with Humphrey's familiar tower high on the hill silhouetted in the moonlight. On the bank I could see burning torches, and at first thought it was revellers, then I realised they were soldiers. I should have realised that they would be watching for me at Bella Court as soon as my escape became known.

I could see there were only a few men posted at the jetty but I suspected more were waiting at the gates of my home. I reached the purse around my neck and took a second gold piece, which I handed to my boatman. He looked at it in his hand before thrusting the coin to join the first in his pocket and obeying my request to continue down the river to the jetty at Erith.

The Abbott of Lesnes Abbey near Erith was indebted to my husband, who was paying for the marshland around the abbey to be drained. I also remembered Humphrey remarking that the abbey's finances were in a dire state, so I hoped to be able to buy his silence and find true sanctuary for as long as I needed. It was as far from Westminster as I could travel in one night yet close enough to Bella Court that I could send a message in secret to Humphrey.

Gratefully thanking the boatman for his brave service, I skirted around the buildings at Erith and made my way to the abbey. I had only visited once, a long time ago and it was difficult to find my way in the darkness. At last I saw the black shape of Lesnes Abbey. I tried the door of the chapel. It was deserted and in pitch darkness. Exhausted from the night's exertions, I lay down on one of the wooden pews and, using my bag as a pillow, fell asleep.

It was light when I woke to find myself being regarded by several elderly monks. I explained who I was and that I had come to seek sanctuary. Then one of them said it was too late, as the king's men were already waiting for me outside. I was shocked they had found my hiding place so quickly, then realised there was one person who knew where I had landed. My boatman must have told them where I was, perhaps hoping for some further reward for his hard night's rowing.

This time those arresting me would not let me escape a second time, although their young commander seemed at a loss to know what to do with me. I had yet to be charged with any offence, so he decided to have me escorted by river back to the sanctuary at Westminster Abbey. Once again I was rowed past the jetty at Greenwich, so close to my husband yet still so far. Again I passed the Tower and on to the now crowded dock at Westminster, where a small army of soldiers were waiting to take me back to the Sanctuary.

A small, spartan room with a wooden cot and a rough blanket was found for me, so different from the luxury I had grown used to. For the first time since I read the note from Roger Bolingbroke I surrendered to self-pity and cried until my pillow was wet with tears. I cried out for my husband and children, whom I knew I might never see again. I cried for my friends, who would be tortured and were surely certain to be killed. I cried in fear for my life and the horrible fate I now faced.

I remembered how my husband's late stepmother, Queen Joanna, once faced the same charges. Her punishment for alleged witchcraft and necromancy was to be placed under house arrest for three years, during which time she told me she had lived in relative comfort. I resolved not to let Cardinal Henry Beaufort treat me with any less consideration than had been shown to Queen Joanna of Navarre. I was not a queen but I was a duchess and that must count for something.

I was further encouraged when I was visited by Edmund Kyrton, the Abbot of Westminster. A soft spoken, devout man, he seemed concerned at my distressed appearance. He first asked if there was any truth in the allegations made against me. I could see he was watching how I answered as I dismissed it all as a plot against my husband. The abbot gave no clue to his own views yet I sensed he saw the truth of my words.

The abbot told me he had not been long in his post although he knew the law of sanctuary. He asked if I was aware that by seeking sanctuary, I must now be tried by an ecclesiastical court. He must have seen I had not grasped the significance of this, so he explained that only a secular court could impose the death penalty. I thanked God, for the first time in ages, realising that my bid for sanctuary had not perhaps been quite so foolish after all.

17

NOVEMBER 1451

DAMNANT QUOD NON INTELLIGUNT

Relentless wind and rain lashes Beaumaris and keeps me from my walks, leaving me to dwell on the events of my trial. I was kept waiting for more than a week, confined to my room in the sanctuary, before I was told I had another visitor. I guessed it was my husband, come at last to offer me some words of comfort. I was sure he would by now have learned where I was, yet I was concerned to understand why he had not been able to send me a letter or even a note. I brushed my hair and tried to make myself presentable, waiting with an unexpected sense of apprehension for him to arrive.

I was to be disappointed. My visitor was not Duke Humphrey but a self-important clerk of the court, who told me I had to come with him for questioning before the bishops at the Chapel of St Stephen. My escort of the king's men led me out into the sunshine for the short journey across the road to the chapel. I carried my bag with my precious jewels hidden inside, wary of leaving it unattended, even in the Sanctuary. A small crowd of curious onlookers were already gathered to witness my disgrace and I scanned their faces, hoping to recognise any of my husband's trusted men, yet there were none to be seen.

On my many visits in the past I had never thought St Stephen's to be a remarkable chapel. Now I saw the ancient building through new eyes. As I entered the cool interior I raised my eyes to the vaulting of its wooden roof, which soared nearly a hundred feet above the tiled floor. I could now see why Thomas Southwell had been so proud and once said it was more like his cathedral than a chapel. Every inch of the interior that could be decorated was painted in bright colours of scarlet, green and blue, with gold leaf edging. Bright sunlight flooded the chapel with more colours, filtered through beautiful stained glass windows.

There, in front of me at a high table sat the most important bishops in England, all of whom were known to me through my husband. Archbishop Henry Chichele of Canterbury sat next to Robert Gilbert, Bishop of London. Humphrey's enemy, John Kemp, Archbishop of York, was next, then the ill-fated William Ayscough, Bishop of Salisbury and the Chancellor, John Stafford, Bishop of Bath and Wells. Finally, I came face to face with my old adversary, Cardinal Beaufort, wearing his robes as Bishop of Winchester. My eyes went to the large, ruby-studded crucifix on a heavy gold chain around his neck, so I didn't have to look for any longer than necessary at his self-satisfied expression.

I was led to a rickety wooden chair and sat facing the bishops, who regarded me with silent curiosity. If their intention was to intimidate me, it was not successful. It was important for me to show confidence in my own innocence and not be bullied into saying something I would later regret. It was the frail old Archbishop of Canterbury who spoke first, his tone revealing his many years as a lawyer, as well as man of the church. He looked at me sternly and asked me to state my name. Although they all knew who I was, I replied as confidently as I could, surprised at how my voice echoed in the high-ceilinged chapel. The archbishop said I was required to answer most serious allegations of conspiracy to bring about the death of our king, Henry VI. The archbishop waited for a moment, then with a nod from Henry Beaufort began to slowly read the list of the charges against me, so many I lost count.

It seemed my friends had done their best to keep secret the truth of our experiments. I wondered what tortures they had endured to try to save me. I tried to keep my mind on what I would say when the archbishop finally came to the end of his lengthy diatribe. I would not be like Roger Bolingbroke. He had played into their hands by staying in the painted chair and keeping the paper crown on his head, as no one in the crowd would take his words seriously. He should have stood and torn the paper crown to pieces in front of them, to show it was a mockery of justice.

I looked into the stern faces of those who presumed to judge me. Apart from Archbishop Henry Chichele, who barely looked up from the papers he was reading from, only Henry Beaufort was watching my reaction. The other bishops avoided my gaze as if troubled by their involvement in the hearing. William Ayscough, Bishop of Salisbury, looked as if he was in prayer, his eyes cast down.

Some of the charges were ill-founded yet close to the truth. I was accused of encouraging my accomplices in the making of wax effigies of the king and melting them in a fire during a black mass. I was also accused of making my own horoscope, with the assistance of Roger Bolingbroke, to see if or when I would be made queen. This was something

I could confidently deny under oath, if this was the extent of the evidence of my 'treason'.

Listening to the allegations made against me I realised another possibility. Someone with no involvement had been piecing together information, filling in the gaps as best they could. I suspected the hand of Cardinal Henry Beaufort, who would not be concerned about the accuracy of the allegations. He could have taken such information from my friends, revealed under threats of torture, and embroidered it to better suit his purpose.

Then another name occurred to me. I had wondered why our chaplain John Home had been arrested. Now I knew. He had been made an unwilling accomplice to the cardinal, spying on us and using his position to learn what he could. For some reason he had not wanted to give evidence against us and now he faced the same fate. I thought back to what I knew of the man. He would readily submit at the first threat from the cardinal's men.

At last it was my turn to speak. I placed the bag I had been holding on the chair and stood, taking one step forward. They seemed taken by surprise by my changed demeanour. Looking them straight in the eyes, I denied it all. I told them I was a loyal subject of King Henry VI and faithful to my husband and the church. I swore before God I had never required anyone to prepare a horoscope for myself, or ever been party to the making or burning of wax effigies of the king or anyone. I asked those present to hear the truth of my words and to see I was no witch, no necromancer or heretic. I reminded them I was present at the christening of the king. My husband had given him many years of loyal service as Lord Protector of the realm. I was the Duchess of Gloucester, first lady in the land.

There was a long silence afterwards. Archbishop

Chichele, an old friend of Humphrey's from his Oxford days, was regarding me with new interest. John Kemp, the Archbishop of York, now also a cardinal and Henry Beaufort's accomplice, was frowning, as if something in my reply offended him. Henry Beaufort spoke. 'Was it not true', he challenged, 'that as the wife of the heir apparent, I wished to one day be Queen of England?'

I hesitated, aware that whatever I said could compromise my position. I tried to clear my mind and realised I had already taken too long to give my answer. I replied that I had been aware of the possibility since the death of my husband's brother John, Duke of Bedford.

Now John Kemp, who, as chancellor, had once been such a thorn in the side of my husband, leaned forward. 'Was I not interested', he asked, 'to discover when that eventuality would occur?'

I was being drawn deeper into their trap. If I said no, it would not have the ring of truth, yet if I said yes it could be taken almost as a confession. I repeated that I was a loyal subject of King Henry and prayed every day for his good health.

Again Henry Beaufort challenged me, this time with the look in his eyes of a man who knew he was going to have his way. 'Was I aware that a man of my husband's household, Roger Bolingbroke, had sworn I had asked him to make use of a horoscope to foretell my future?'

Now I felt the panic rising in my chest. They had persuaded my accomplices to talk and were simply waiting for me to either confess or lie. I said I knew Roger Bolingbroke, who was a faithful man of the church and an accomplished scholar. He had once told me that anyone who said it was possible to predict the point of death using horoscopes was either deluded or a charlatan. Henry Beaufort raised his voice this time, demanding that I confess or I would face the consequences of my unholy actions.

I sat down on my chair again, not wishing to comment on his outburst. The chancellor, John Stafford, began asking questions I was at a loss to answer. 'Where was my husband, Duke Humphrey? He had not seen fit to visit me or send any message since I had arrived at the Sanctuary of West-minster Abbey? Why was he not here, now, defending the honour of his wife?'

I remained silent. The chancellor turned to Archbishop Chichele and addressed his next question to him. 'Could the absence of the Duke of Gloucester be a sign he believes his wife to be guilty of these charges?'

Archbishop Chichele considered the question for a moment. I remembered what Humphrey had once said about him. He told me Henry Chichele had been a highly influential advisor to his elder brother, King Henry V, and encouraged his war with France, saying that God was on our side. The man now before me was close to eighty years old, yet he seemed to have lost none of his sharpness. He announced that the hearing would adjourn for deliberation, and I was to be returned to the Sanctuary at Westminster until more secure accommodation had been arranged for me.

The captain of the king's men escorted me out of the chapel and I emerged back into the bright July sunlight to find a sizeable crowd gathered outside. Rows of soldiers armed with long, steel-pointed halberds lined each side of the path and all the way to Westminster Abbey. The captain noticed my surprise and explained it was on the personal orders of the king. He had declared no person was to hinder the bishops in the performance of their task, or to attempt anything against myself or my property in the meanwhile. This could explain why Humphrey and his supporters remained so silent, yet as I slowly walked through the avenue of soldiers I wished he would at least send me a letter.

I spent a sleepless night in the Sanctuary, which had now truly become my prison, with no appetite for the meal of rough bread and meat offered to me by the monks. I lay on the uncomfortable straw-filled mattress and went through the charges against me in my mind again and again, trying to see how I could defend myself against so many allegations. I realised my only option was to confess. Not to anything treasonable but to some of the lesser crimes, for which I could publicly recant.

The next morning I was again summoned to St Stephen's Chapel to face the bishops. I thought it had not taken them long to agree a judgement on me and I wondered what new questions they would now ask. I saw there was a witness waiting to testify against me, standing between two of the king's men, who looked ready to support him if he could no longer stand. It was barely a month since I had last seen Roger Bolingbroke, yet in that time he had aged ten years. His hair was matted and his eyes bloodshot, with a look of abject misery. He made no sign of recognition as I took my seat in front of the assembled bishops.

Archbishop Chichele instructed Roger Bolingbroke to repeat his allegation that I had encouraged him to make a horoscope to tell my future. Never once looking at me, he said I had instructed him to find by divination to what estate in life I should come, his deep voice wavering as he spoke. I was shocked at how my strong and intelligent friend had been so reduced by his captivity and wondered again what deprivations he had suffered. Chancellor John Stafford, Bishop of Bath and Wells, asked if I would now confess that this was true. I said it was. After seeing Roger Bolingbroke I had decided to admit the lesser crime.

If I hoped this would be an end to the matter, I was mistaken. After Roger Bolingbroke was led away, Bishop Stafford's next question took me completely by surprise. 'Was it true', he asked, 'that I had retained the services of a known witch, by the name of Margery Jourdemayne, as a sorceress, to concoct potions to induce Duke Humphrey to love me?'

I answered she was not a witch. Her knowledge of natural medicines simply helped the duke and to conceive my son, Arthur, then to relieve pain during the birth of my children many years ago. I added that I had not seen Margery Jourdemayne for several years since.

Archbishop Chichele asked me to explain how it was Margery Jourdemayne had confessed to the King's Council that she concocted magical potions to make Duke Humphrey marry me. I was about to dismiss this as nonsense, as I had not even heard of her when I met my husband, who had needed no encouragement from so-called magical potions. I realised what the archbishop was saying. He was offering a way for Humphrey to be excused his association with me, on grounds he was somehow bewitched. There was a chance I might be able to save Margery's life by admitting what again was a lesser, non-treasonable crime. With great effort, I said it was true.

Now Henry Beaufort, who had remained silent throughout, declared he had heard enough. He announced that the king had agreed for me to be committed to Leeds Castle in Kent under the custody of Sir John Steward, Constable of the Castle, and John Stanley, Usher of the King's Chamber, until the king and council had decided my punishment. This news seemed to surprise the other bishops as much as me, although some seemed relieved the matter was out of their hands, at least for a while.

At last the sun has returned to Beaumaris and I am able to have much needed fresh air. I have learnt storms are on the way when the squawking seagulls flock to the shelter of the castle, as they do now. Grey skies confirm that autumn is coming to an end and I can expect the chill onset of winter. One of my guards this day is Richard Hook, who reminds me so much of my son. I asked him if there is any news of the old priest, as I would like to see him. He offered to enquire on my behalf and let me know. I thanked him and said we could resume our writing lessons when he wished.

As I reached the chapel I entered the arched doorway and sat in silence for a moment, remembering my last bid to evade imprisonment in the Sanctuary in Westminster. I needed to somehow find a way to leave the Sanctuary of Westminster Abbey before my transfer to Leeds Castle, from where I knew I could never escape. My foray down the river had hardened the attitude of my guards, who were probably under threat of their own lives if they allowed me to evade them. For whatever reason, I could not count on a rescue by my husband or his supporters, so I knew it was up to me to find a way and I did not have much time.

The stress and anxiety of my situation had taken its toll, as I still had no appetite and felt quite unwell. This gave me the idea to feign illness, which could at least delay my transfer from Westminster Abbey and allow time for me to plan my escape. I was visited by a kindly monk who tended the infirmary and served as the apothecary to the abbey, who tried to encourage me to take some broth mixed with herbs. I drank the cup of warm mead he offered but would not eat until the commander of my guard agreed my demand to be seen by a physician.

It was late afternoon before the man arrived. He seemed wary and I doubted he could be trusted to help me but I had little choice. I hoped it was true every man has his price. As soon as we were alone I unwrapped the precious brooch in the shape of the king holding a golden ball, set with a large diamond and adorned with rubies and pearls. I could see from the look in his eyes he immediately appreciated its value and told him he could have it in return for helping me find a way out of the abbey to safety.

The physician shook his head, replying that even this fine jewel was not worth the risk of his life. He was aware of the declaration by the king and knew if he helped me, he too could face charges of treason and pay the awful penalty. It is not true, after all, that every man has his price. He was a good man, though, and told me I must eat to keep my strength for the difficult times I would face ahead.

18

DECEMBER 1451

PULCHRA CARCEREM

I listen to the crackle of unseasoned logs burning on my fire as the flames find the fresh sap. Glad of the warmth they bring to my room, I move my chair closer to the hearth and try to comfort my ageing bones. I have known colder Decembers yet in the middle of the night I wake shivering in the chill air. Once awake, I often find I cannot go back to sleep and lie listening to the howling wind blowing hard from the sea. If it is in the right direction I am sure I can hear distant waves, pounding on the shores of this remote Welsh island.

Sometimes I am glad to be away from the petty politics of court and parliament, away from the greed and corruption, the noise and smell of London. Even if I were now set free I would not stay in England. My home, my lands and fortune are all gone, confiscated or stolen by my enemies, so I would have nowhere now to stay, no money to last into my old age. My only hope would be to find my daughter Antigone in Normandy.

My mind returns to the reason I am here and the terrible events of ten years ago that haunt me still. I remember how I abandoned my faith in God and cursed the bishops who sat in judgement over me one by one, wishing them all dead. I think those who know the truth would find it in their hearts to forgive my curses, for these highest men of the church, two of them cardinals of Rome, knew full well the deceit and cruelty of what they did.

I will never know if it was my curse that finished Archbishop Henry Chichele. He was old and frail. I thought at first, as my husband's former friend, he simply wished to distance himself from the disgrace being brought on Duke Humphrey. Then I heard the Archbishop had suffered a seizure while at his prayers and breathed his last. I do not know what became of John Stafford, Bishop of Bath and Wells, Robert Gilbert, Bishop of London, or Humphrey's enemy, John Kemp, Archbishop of York. I hope their cruel and vindictive actions rested heavily on their conscience, keeping them awake at nights.

I shed no tears for the nervous William Ayscough, Bishop of Salisbury, when I learned from Lady Ellen that he was hacked to death by rebels who stormed the Tower. She told me his head was severed from his body and carried through the streets of London on a pike as a grisly trophy. Adam Moleyns, who rose to the position of Lord Privy Seal and Bishop of Chichester, was also lynched by an angry mob. I must confess to taking some small comfort from hearing that my greedy and dishonest old enemy, Cardinal Beaufort, died begging God to forgive him for his sins, his wealth and power no longer any use to him.

Trapped in my small room in the Sanctuary of Westminster Abbey I had nightmares of being chained in dark, rat-infested dungeons. My feigned illness became real as I still refused to eat or drink everything the worried abbey monks brought to me. If it were not for the abbot, Edmund

Kyrton, I fear I would have died on that rough straw mattress in that small, whitewashed room. He came to see me, placed his hand on my brow to see if I had a fever, then made the sign of the cross and asked God to have mercy on my soul. I realised the kindly abbot thought I would soon be dead. That was what saved me.

Leeds Castle in Kent was where my husband's stepmother, the Dowager Queen Joanna of Navarre, was held for two years on charges of witchcraft. She told me once it had been no real hardship and she was eventually released. This was my first thought as my long and uncomfortable journey from Westminster came to an end. The carriage provided for me was old and found every bump in the road. We travelled faster than I would have wished, each moment taking me further from my husband and my home at Bella Court.

My first sight of the castle took my breath away. Surrounded by a beautiful, tranquil lake, we crossed a paved stone bridge to reach the impressive gatehouse, emblazoned with the royal coat of arms. I could see why this was where King Edward the first chose to live with my namesake, his beloved wife Eleanor of Castile. I remembered this castle was also where the Dowager Queen Catherine of Valois began her scandalous affair with her lover Owen Tudor, who had given so much trouble to my husband. Now it was to be my prison.

My jailor, Sir John Steward, Constable of the Castle, was waiting when I arrived and showed me to a well-appointed room, with views over the water and a fine Flemish tapestry of women at work in a vineyard on one wall. An ambitious, self-important yet charming man, he seemed refreshingly unconcerned about the allegations against me. Sir John told me he hoped to make my stay at Leeds Castle a comfortable one. He had served in the king's household as master of the horse and knew my husband, as well as my father.

In return for my promise not to try to escape, he offered to send to Greenwich for my servants and one of my ladies in waiting to keep me good company. I was grateful, as I knew they would bring me news of my husband and hopefully a letter from him. It was all quite a change from my bare little room in the Sanctuary at Westminster. I could almost forget I was his prisoner, although he had taken the unnecessary precaution of posting an armed guard at my door.

In truth, all thought of escape had now left me. I was much closer to the Channel ports and the prospect of a sea crossing to France, yet I knew the next time I was captured I would find myself locked away with my friends in the Tower of London. Despite my reluctance to be moved to Leeds Castle it was by far the most tolerable of prisons.

I was relieved to be allowed a little freedom, although I was always followed by my guards, something which I knew I would have to become used to. I therefore took the opportunity to explore my new home. Once a Saxon fortress, the castle was built on two islands, each surrounded by a high wall, rising some thirty feet from the water and reinforced with bastion guard towers.

Far from making me feel trapped, the wide expanse of the lake served to create a sense of peace, with only the echoing cries of distant waterfowl to break the silence. The large walled area in front of the castle contained green lawns, kept short by a flock of little brown sheep, and an oval walkway, where I could take my exercise when the weather permitted.

Not to be compared with my beautiful gardens at Bella Court, the simple yet well-tended gardens at Leeds Castle had been planted with English roses and supplied the castle kitchens with onions and leeks, as well as fruit and berries from an orchard of stunted trees and shrubs. I was pleased to see a well-stocked herb garden, sheltered from the winds and frost inside the walls.

I would pick bunches of late flowering French lavender, a favourite of mine for its intense fragrance and violet flowers, to dry for its perfume. A second drawbridge connected the main island to a smaller one with its Norman keep and royal apartments, called the 'Gloriette' in memory of Queen Eleanor. I was never allowed to visit this island, although I could imagine it would have been a home fit for a queen.

My apartments were at the north end of the main island, close to the high-ceilinged great hall, where I took my meals. I was also allowed to visit the adjacent chapel, my new sanctuary, where I could always find peace to think. Each day I would visit the chapel and pray for the souls of my friends, for my husband to contact me, for the safety of my children and for the health of my grandchildren. Although Arthur had yet to find a suitable wife, Antigone now had three children and I prayed for the day when I would see them all again.

Summer turned slowly to autumn and my life at the castle in Kent settled into a routine. The forty mile journey from London meant news travelled slowly, so in return for his approval of its contents, Sir John Steward allowed me to write a letter to my husband. I found it difficult to find the right words. I told Humphrey how sorry I was to have left as I did, although now I was well treated and eagerly awaited his reply. I was disappointed as the days became weeks with no word from him. I began to fear he was also under arrest or that Cardinal Beaufort had somehow intercepted my letter.

My servants finally arrived from Bella Court, two maids, a cook, a cleaner and a scullery girl, though none of my ladies in waiting had been prepared to make the journey to Kent to keep me company. One of my maids was Mary, a thin-faced shrew of a girl, only a little older than my daughter. I suspected she had been chosen to spy on me and noted how she eyed me warily as she cleaned my room. The other was a cheerful, buxom woman named Martha, with a loud laugh and a tendency to curse when she thought I couldn't hear. Martha was much closer to my own age and had been in my service for almost as long as I could remember.

An inveterate gossip, Martha had entertained me in the past with her colourful stories. Her extensive family seemed to have spread throughout London and she could usually be relied on for an account of what was being talked of in the taverns. She would tell me of scandals and gamblers, swindlers and murderers, the dangerous world of the London poor where life was hard yet somehow strangely exciting.

At first even she was uncomfortable in my presence but as she settled in to the new routine her naturally talkative nature got the better of her. She told me Bella Court had become a different place after I left. I was not surprised to hear Duke Humphrey had reacted angrily to my flight to seek sanctuary, swearing loudly and drinking heavily, long into the night. Then, after he heard of my arrest and appearance before the bishops, seemed to have fallen into a deep melancholy and began taking his meals alone in his study.

Martha said he rarely left the house and was refusing to see anyone other than my son Arthur, who was dealing with all his business matters. She had no idea if my letter had been delivered to the duke or if he had tried to write to me. Even when my husband must have known she was leaving to join me he sent no message, and neither had my son.

I was also disturbed to learn that soldiers of the king had made a permanent camp at the gates to Bella Court and were regularly to be seen patrolling the grounds and guarding our jetty on the river. It seemed my husband was under the closest watch. I knew the declaration from the king meant he could also face charges if he made any attempt to rescue me.

Worse still, I learned from Martha the reason none of my ladies in waiting had made the journey with her to Kent. My husband had dismissed them all, sending them packing and telling them never to return. This made no sense to me and Martha was reluctant to explain, but I pressed her to tell me. She admitted it was as if I was already dead. My name was never mentioned and my rooms had been shuttered and declared out of bounds to all the household staff and servants.

Martha also told me the talk in London was that I had confessed to the bishops of using witchcraft and necromancy. I should have known Cardinal Beaufort would turn my words. In my heart I knew whatever I had said or not said, the bishops would still find me guilty of the charges. Somehow I still hoped that admitting to the lesser crimes would enable them to show leniency, yet now I doubted it.

I resisted the temptation to give in to the sense of despair that tugged at my heart whenever I thought of my family or prayed for my poor friends in the Tower. Whatever people said in the taverns of London, I was still the Duchess of Gloucester, first lady in the land. Just as Queen Joanne had survived the same cruel allegations, so would I.

Sir John Steward had not visited me for some weeks, as he had been away in London, so I was pleased when he came to see me on his return. I could tell right away the news he brought was not good. A royal commission had been instructed to enquire further into the alleged plot against the king. The commission included the earls of Huntingdon, Northumberland and Stafford, Lord Fanhope and Lord Hungerford, all members of the King's Council, as well as the mayor, aldermen and several commoners of London.

The king had, he said, stipulated that I was not to be tortured and, whatever else happened, my life was to be spared. Then he told me the commission was to be led by Lord Ralph Cromwell, Treasurer of England. Lord Cromwell fought at my husband's side at Agincourt and once tried to mediate between my husband and the Beaufort faction. Humphrey then decided Cromwell was undermining his position at parliament through his position as Chamberlain of the Household. When Cardinal Beaufort was away on diplomatic business in France my husband removed Cromwell from his lucrative post.

Since then Lord Cromwell had opposed my husband with a vengeance, supporting Henry Beaufort at every opportunity. His reward had been to be made Treasurer, much to Humphrey's annoyance. From this new position of power Ralph Cromwell had become one of our most outspoken critics. This was the man who now controlled the finances of England – and the commission that would decide the fate of my friends.

I knew this was all Cardinal Henry Beaufort's work. He had cleverly distanced himself from this commission yet controlled it through Lord Cromwell. A lay commission would be able to impose the death sentence on my friends and would have done the same to me. Not for the first time I realised how fortunate I was that only an ecumenical court could try me.

It is now almost Christmas in Beaumaris and I am pleased to have had a visit from Lady Ellen, who brought me a gift of a bottle of red wine mulled with precious aromatic spices. The news from London is that the queen is still not with child. Ellen hinted at rumours that the queen is barren and the king is incapable of begetting a new and future king. She well knows such talk could be seen as treason.

I warm a little of the mulled wine in a cup by my hearth and one sip takes me right back to happy times at Bella Court. Then I remember how the Queen of England, Margaret of Anjou, always planned to steal my palace at Greenwich from me and my husband. First she removed me, so I could no longer keep my husband safe from her henchman, the Duke of Suffolk. She had tricked Duke Humphrey and somehow ended his life, as well as that of my precious son, for I know he is dead. Alone in my room I raise my cup of wine and curse the health of the queen and any sons she may one day bear.

Such bitterness had its roots in the long wait as September turned to October at Leeds Castle. The leaves were falling from the trees yet still there was no news from London. It was as if we were cut off from the world, surrounded by our placid lake. I passed the time with my embroidery and learning to play simple tunes on a lute I found in the corner of one of my rooms. It was an old, well-crafted instrument with a gentle and sweet tone. I wondered who once owned and played it in the same room I did now. As a child I learned to play with somewhat basic technique, realising it would take a lifetime to truly master the instrument. Now I had all the time in the world. More than I needed.

My lute became my favourite pastime and my skill improved a little. I was tuning the lute one cold October day when the door opened to reveal the constable of the castle, Sir John Steward. I could see straight away that he was not his usual charming self. Guards followed on each side of him as he entered my room, as if he expected me to attack him. I set the lute to one side and stood, the air between us tense. I braced myself for the bad news I had been dreading those long weeks ever since he had informed me of the royal commission.

Sir John looked serious as he told me my associates Roger Bolingbroke and Thomas Southwell had been indicted of sorcery and treason. They had been found guilty of using magical figures and invoking demons and evil spirits to anticipate when the king should die. His face was grim. He said they confessed that I encouraged them in this and promised gifts in return. I was to prepare myself for my return to London to appear before the Council at Westminster. Without further discussion he turned and closed the door behind him, leaving me to realise one more chapter in my life was coming to an end.

19

JANUARY 1452

VERITAS VOS LIBERABIT

A new year dawns and at last a letter has arrived from my daughter Antigone in France. It was delivered by Sir William Bulkeley in person when he came to see that I am well. He apologised that the letter had been unsealed, explaining he had to read it under orders from his superior, the Constable of Beaumaris, Sir William Beauchamp. For the first time I saw the trace of a smile from my jailer as he clearly knew how much this simple fold of parchment would mean to me.

I thanked him and as soon as he had gone I read the letter quickly, then slowly and more carefully, hardly able to believe its contents. My daughter and her children had made the long sea crossing from Portsmouth to the harbour of Honfleur in Normandy. When they reached the village of Tancarville, on the banks of the River Seine, they found her late husband's chateau and estate had been allowed to become too run down to be habitable. Undaunted, they travelled to Paris, where she had met a handsome cavalier, the master of the king's horse, named Jean d'Amancy, whom she intended to marry.

Antigone wrote that her future husband was a good, honest gentleman, well respected with excellent prospects, who hoped one day to become the French Ambassador to Venice. He had a fine house in Paris and more than enough money for their needs. Most importantly, he wished to marry her not because of who her father was, for her title or fortune. It was that rarest and best of reasons—a love match.

My husband would have been aghast at the thought of his daughter marrying a Frenchman, an alliance utterly against his policy and all he had fought for. Worse still, her intended husband, a servant in the household of King Charles VII of France, was not even of noble birth. I know if Humphrey lived he would already be thinking of ways to prevent this marriage, demanding Antigone's return to England on the next available ship.

I am simply happy for her. Like me, she has survived through the most difficult times, seen the opportunity and taken it. My only regret was I knew the chances of her ever returning to visit me in Beaumaris were now greatly reduced. I read Antigone's letter yet again and could tell, reading between the lines, she asks my blessing. I wrote my letter in reply, wishing her every happiness and success in her new life in France and telling her she must follow her heart and marry.

I waited until I saw the young guard Richard Hook, then handed him the unsealed letter, asking him to be sure it reached Sir William, who would have to read it before sending it to my daughter. As I did so I felt a new sense of closure. I no longer needed to worry about what could happen to my daughter Antigone or my grandchildren, Richard, Humphrey and little Elizabeth. They would be safe in France, where no one would know or care who their grandmother was or what she had done in the past.

Once again my carriage made the long, uncomfortable journey to Westminster, this time with my little retinue of servants, escorted by a troop of the king's mounted cavalry. I wondered if this could be a sign they expected an attempt to rescue me on the road to London. I wished in vain for my husband to send a band of his ruthless mercenaries to carry me away to safety, although my royal escort did help clear a path through the onlookers blocking the busy streets as we entered the gates of the city.

As we neared Westminster I hopefully scanned the faces in the crowd for any of my husband's trusted men, yet if they were there I could not see them. My carriage drew up in front of the Palace of Westminster, where I was handed over to colourfully liveried soldiers, men of my new jailer, the Constable of the Tower of London. Fortunately I was not destined for imprisonment in the Tower, as I had feared, instead being shown to a sizeable room within the palace apartments.

I had a restless night's sleep, waking early, my head full of dread for what lay ahead. I knelt in prayer for the strength and resource to stand up to yet another interrogation by the bishops. These men, supposedly the greatest and most devout in the land, now took on the faces of demons in my troubled mind, holding my life in their corrupt hands.

I was led down a passageway, across a cloistered, cobble-stoned courtyard and through parts of Westminster I had never seen before. I could only guess it was to avoid the crowds I heard already gathering in the streets. In front of me was a heavy wooden door, studded with iron, which opened for me to enter. I found myself back in the high-ceilinged splendour of St Stephen's Chapel. Before, the chapel had been almost empty, our words echoing in the silence. Now I had an audience. People filled the chapel pews, talking amongst themselves as if waiting to be entertained.

An expectant hush fell over them as I entered, a few whispered comments as they realised who I was. I again took my seat in front of the court of bishops, keeping my head high and my back straight, looking neither left nor right. I did not wish to see who had come to witness my shaming and disgrace, my former friends or my husband's enemies.

Instead of Archbishop Chichele, the officious Dean of Salisbury, Adam Moleyns, clerk of the King's Council, read the lengthy charges against me. I listened in silence to his litany of sorcery, necromancy and treason against the king. Before me were the bishops of London, Salisbury and Lincoln, as well as the Bishop of Norwich and several masters of divinity I recognised only by their robes and golden chains of office. I was not sorry to see no sign of the Bishop of Winchester, Cardinal Henry Beaufort, or his disingenuous henchman John Kemp, Archbishop of York.

When he had finished, Adam Moleyns asked if I would plead guilty. He sounded almost hopeful, as if to save them further inconvenience. For a moment I considered refusing to grace this corrupt court with any response. I knew this would not help my case in front of so many witnesses, so again I decided to admit the lesser charges. As before, I strongly denied any thoughts of treason against the king, reminding them again I was the Duchess of Gloucester, loyal wife of the king's uncle. The bishops appeared to be expecting this and had no further questions.

It seemed no progress had been made during my long wait in Leeds Castle. Despite having every opportunity to reach their judgement, the bishops had brought no new evidence or even any fresh questions for me to answer. The clerk Adam Moleyns announced that the hearing was adjourned and I was led under escort back through the rear of the chapel to my room in the Palace of Westminster, to be detained to wait once more to hear my fate.

Now I had become a prisoner. I was not allowed to leave my apartment or permitted any visitors, with only my servants and ever-present guards for company. I was allowed to write a letter to my husband, yet I sat with the quill in my hand, unable to ask my many questions or to explain how I had found myself in this dreadful predicament. I knew whatever I wrote would be read by the cardinal and used as evidence against me. I also doubted it would ever reach my husband.

Several long and lonely days passed before I returned to St Stephen's Chapel to face the same bishops, with their spokesman the Dean of Salisbury. I wondered if we were going to repeat the process again until I confessed to all the charges, then I heard a commotion behind me as a soldier shouted at someone to walk forward. I turned to see Roger Bolingbroke and Thomas Southwell being dragged before the court in chains. Behind them staggered an old woman, bent double and hardly able to stand. It shocked me to realise this was my once proud friend Margery Jourdemayne.

They were each in turn brought forward and made to confess their crimes in front of me, although it seemed to me they hardly knew where they were or what they were saying. Adam Moleyns had the task of asking the questions and, each time, the accused would condemn themselves by admitting to be guilty of all charges, which the clerk of the King's Council duly noted in his ledger.

Roger Bolingbroke swayed unsteadily on his feet and looked a shadow of the strong and clever man I had known. He was told to repeat his assertion that I had encouraged him to use the black arts to find if I would be queen. He said that was true. Then he was asked to say he had tried to foretell the death of the king. When he hesitated to answer as he must have been instructed the guard struck him on the side of the head and he collapsed to the floor. I could see his fingernails had been torn out.

Thomas Southwell was carried forward by two burly guards and sat in a chair, as he was unable to stand. His sad, bloodshot eyes looked at me from a bruised and swollen face and he shook his head as if to tell me he had no choice but to condemn me also. He stumbled through the rehearsed words, his speech slurred as if something had happened to his tongue. I could hardly hear him, yet none of the bishops paid much attention and I realised why the cardinal was absent. This was simply a formality, a show for the record, in front of witnesses, to prove that the condemned were guilty and deserved their fate.

Margery Jourdemayne was the last to be brought forward. She tried to stand straight and there was a trace of pride in her voice when she answered that she was the woman known as the witch of Eye. She was no fool and answered the questions well until it came to the question of my own role in her witchcraft. She confessed in a wavering voice that I had employed her to concoct magical potions to induce Duke Humphrey of Gloucester to marry me.

When at last the staged confessions were over I was told

I would appear again before Archbishop Chichele to finally receive the sentence of the court. Escorted back to my room I found out from the king's men guarding they were commanded by Sir John Holland, Duke of Exeter, the Constable of the Tower of London. Sir John is a first cousin of my husband, so I asked my guard if a message might be sent requesting that I could meet with him.

I had not forgotten the questions of the chancellor, John Stafford, who had asked where my husband was, why had he yet to visit me or send any message and why he was not defending my honour. The surly guard looked doubtful but agreed to pass on my request and I allowed myself a little hope for the first time since I had returned to London. Sir John Holland was another of those who had fought at the side of my husband at Agincourt. Now he was my jailor and the one person who could arrange for Duke Humphrey to visit me. Once my husband heard what a travesty Cardinal Henry Beaufort had made of the ecclesiastical court he would soon be able to intervene on my behalf.

I found little appetite for the food provided and spent a sleepless night on the wooden cot in my room, trying not to remember the desperate faces of my friends. The next day passed without any word or even being allowed out for any exercise, although I was able to eat a little of the beef stew and dry bread I was brought.

On the second day I heard from one of my guards that Thomas Southwell had died in the Tower, supposedly of despair at his crimes. I knew poor Thomas to be a physician, with a skilled knowledge of medicines, so I hoped he had found a painless way to end his life. That night I said a prayer for him, and for the others who would not be so able to escape their terrible punishment.

Then my servant Martha returned from a visit to her

family with terrible news. Despite publicly recanting her sins, Margery Jourdemayne had been taken from the Tower to West Smithfield and burned at the stake, her awful screams silencing the curious crowd which filled the market square and many of the side-streets. She had been shown the mercy of having tar poured over the faggots piled around the stake, so they burned more quickly.

I know she would have suffered horribly and to this day wish I had asked the bishops that she could be allowed to be strangled first. At the time I stayed silent, yet I had known that Margery Jourdemayne was innocent of any of the charges against her. It rests heavily on my conscience that I did not argue more strongly in her defence. She had no part in our experiments and it had been some time since she even visited me at Bella Court.

I resolved to do what I could for my faithful friend Roger Bolingbroke, who as far as I knew was still held in the Tower of London. My difficulty was that I had witnessed his full confession to the ecclesiastical court with my own eyes, even though I was certain it had been obtained through cruel tortures. The punishment for men was far worse than that for women and now I had little to lose by at least trying to help him.

A plan formed in my mind by the time my guard told me Sir John Holland, Constable of the Tower, was on his way to see me. I made myself look as presentable as I could and put from my mind the knowledge that Sir John was the man behind the torture of my friends. When he arrived, I even found the strength to smile in welcome, for the sake of Roger Bolingbroke, the man who had unwittingly risked his life to make me happy.

Sir John Holland was red-faced and portly. He looked a little older than my husband, yet displayed the same air of confidence that comes with royal birth. I recalled once seeing him much the worse for drink when he had attended our grand banquets at Bella Court. I also remembered Humphrey confiding to me that Sir John inherited his father's title but no income to go with it. He had solved the problem by marriage to a rich widow, yet was notorious for his many young mistresses.

Sir John was curious to know why I needed to see him, so I asked if we could be alone to discuss a personal matter of some sensitivity. He readily agreed, dismissing the guards. Unlike the honest physician in the Sanctuary at Westminster, I knew I was looking at a man who definitely had his price. I showed him the golden garter, my gift from King Henry VI, and saw his eyes light up with instant recognition of its worth. I asked first if he would be so kind as to contact my husband and arrange for him to visit me. Sir John looked surprised at my request. It was not, he admitted, an unreasonable thing for me to ask.

He was still looking at the precious garter, its buckle of diamonds, the large pearls and red ruby on the pendant. I told him I would give it to him in return for one more favour, his promise of a painless death for Roger Bolingbroke. I remember how I held my breath waiting for his answer. I knew he was torn between his duty and his greed, although not for long. He took the golden garter from my hand and said I had his word that my accomplice would not suffer more than necessary.

After Sir John had gone I stood at my window and looked out in the direction of the Tower of London, wondering if I had done the right thing for my friend. I had, after all, now signed his death warrant, as I knew I would soon hear he had also died in custody. I had saved him from the worst death, although I fell sobbing to the floor at how my selfish action had brought such misery to such good men and such a good, honest, clever woman as Margery Jourdemayne.

Now I must write of my own punishment. I had been spared the agony suffered by my friends. I was the first lady of the land, the Duchess of Gloucester, and by seeking sanctuary, had escaped the death penalty. I had been given hope by the Dowager Queen Joanna, yet I had underestimated the cruelty of the bishops. My husband warned me that Henry Beaufort would have his revenge on us, and of course he was right. The blow when it came destroyed me as utterly and completely as if I had been tied to a stake and burned alive.

It was the sixth of November, 1441. A date etched into my memory. Brought before the panel of bishops yet again, I thought I would at last hear the details of the penance for the crimes I had confessed to. I remember Archbishop Chichele had returned to speak for the bishops. The old archbishop looked unwell and unhappy with the task before him. Not so the evil Cardinal Beaufort, who could barely contain his satisfaction at seeing me brought so low.

The archbishop read a declaration, which had been unanimously agreed by the ecclesiastical court. His slow words echoed and I felt my whole world, everything that was important to me, all I cared about, slip away. Archbishop Chichele solemnly declared that, as it had been proven I had made use of sorcery and necromancy to procure his favours and effect my marriage to Humphrey of Lancaster, Duke of Gloucester, Earl of Pembroke. The court decreed my marriage annulled. I had been divorced.

20

FEBRUARY 1452

PAENITENTIAM

The long, cold winter nights have set in at Beaumaris Castle with a vengeance. This morning I found a bedraggled seabird sheltering on the ledge outside my window, its feathers fluttering in the relentless, freezing wind. The bird's bright yellow eye watches me warily as it repeats its feeble cry for a mate that will never hear it. The mournful sound reminds me of my misery and shock on that fateful day in St Stephen's Chapel.

The old Archbishop of Canterbury, Henry Chichele, continued to read loudly from his papers, hardly bothering to look up at me. I heard nothing, my mind repeating the same questions over and over again. How could the bishops divorce me from my husband? Surely Duke Humphrey would never allow such a thing? Numb and uncomprehending, I have no recollection of the rest of that day, other than being led back to my room in a daze, as if I had been struck a physical blow. I collapsed onto my bed and remained there, unable to talk or even think.

I woke in the middle of the night, my questions answered in a rush of awareness. Alone in the darkness that night in the Palace of Westminster, I knew why my husband never visited me, never replied to my letters, never even sent me a note. The answer was as stark and clear as if it had been written in red blood across a whitewashed wall. It had been obvious all the time, yet I had chosen to ignore the painful truth. After all we had been through together, how easily had he been persuaded it would be better for him to be rid of me?

A memory returned of the time at Leeds Castle when I questioned my servant Martha. She told me it had seemed to her as if I was dead, my rooms in Bella Court shuttered and placed out of bounds. How typical of Humphrey. I had not forgotten how he abandoned poor Countess Jacqueline to her uncertain fate outside the city of Mons, tears in her eyes as she begged him on her knees not to leave her in France. I did not love him less. To do so would only give more satisfaction to Cardinal Henry Beaufort.

My life did change from that moment, though. I finally accepted there would never be a royal pardon, no hope of a compromise or a legal defence that forced them to release me. There was now no prospect of a daring rescue by a band of Duke Humphrey's armed mercenaries. I no longer had the protection of my noble title but I still had good health and I had always been resourceful. I realised I would have to do whatever it took to remain alive, even though it would almost certainly mean surviving long years of lonely imprisonment.

The punishment ordered by the cardinal's ecclesiastical court aimed to bring as much public shame on me as was within their powers. The bishops had no authority to order my death, so they tried to make my life as miserable as they could. First they commanded that my long hair must be cut short, saying I must learn humility and know that the sin of pride is considered the original and most serious of the deadly sins, the source of the others.

It was ordered that I would be shamed by making public penances, carrying a candle through the streets of London, to a different place of worship on three separate days. The bishops wished for all to see how I recanted my crimes and how low I had fallen. On each occasion the Mayor of London and the Sheriffs of the City were to meet and escort me with two knights through the streets. After my penance it was decreed I must be imprisoned for life, under the care and stewardship of senior knights of the royal household.

The men who came to cut my hair were rough soldiers, who cursed loudly and smelled of drink. They seemed disappointed when I mutely submitted to their task. I think they would have preferred for me to scream and resist, yet I would not give them the satisfaction. They had it instead by groping my body and unnecessarily holding me down, calling me names and insulting me as they hacked at my head with their blunt scissors until I looked like a newly shorn sheep.

After they had gone I cried for the loss of my beautiful long hair. The bishops had known, of course, it was no evidence of pride. Long, well-kept hair was the sign of a woman of good and noble upbringing. Without it I would look like some poor scullery maid. Worse still, I heard one of the soldiers say he planned to sell my silken locks in the market-place as keepsakes. I looked around me. They had been truly diligent. Not one hair of my head had been left behind.

I was made to wear the coarse black woollen robe of a penitent nun, although they fortunately permitted me to cover my head to hide the poor work where my hair had been so roughly cut off. Then I was taken by my guards down the River Thames on a barge to the Temple Stairs and led to the Temple Bar gate, the most important entrance in the city from Westminster. I had witnessed the custom of the king being welcomed into London at Temple Bar by the mayor and was determined to use this to keep some dignity.

News of my downfall must have travelled throughout the city. The crowds of Londoners jostling noisily to see me recant reminded me of those I had seen at a bear-baiting. There were so many that the king's soldiers had to hold them back with their long, sharp-pointed halberds to create an open space where I would walk. Street vendors called out hopefully, offering cakes and ale, while urchins with grubby faces and bare feet followed behind my entourage, mimicking the marching soldiers of my escort.

There seemed to be a face at every window of the closely-packed, narrow houses with people leaning out from their overhanging balconies to have the best view of me. The bishops had unwittingly turned my public penance into a rather grand pageant. I recognised the Lord Mayor of London, Robert Clopton, a member of the draper's guild, who had been our guest at Bella Court when first appointed to his post. An ambitious and unpopular, thin-faced man, he chose to wear his full mayoral regalia, with a red velvet cloak trimmed with cloth of gold.

The sheriffs of London also took the opportunity to show their importance, as if competing with each other to have the finest clothes and the most servants in attendance. Rows of the king's men in their brightly coloured livery added to the effect of a royal procession. The two knights of the garter proudly escorting me looked more like my guardians than my guards. Wearing swords and shining silver breastplates, they seemed to have forgotten this was supposed to be a humbling punishment for me.

As I approached the formal reception there was a peal of bells from Westminster Abbey and someone in the crowd gave a cheer. 'Long live the king!' The cry was soon picked up by others and I have no doubt some thought the king himself had come to the city. The waiting mayor seemed unsure of how he should receive me. No doubt conscious of all the eyes upon him, he bowed and welcomed me to the city in much the same way as he had greeted the king. I thanked him for his kindness, which confused the matter further.

A large white church candle was placed in my hand. I was to carry the heavy candle through the streets for my penance. My arms ached with the weight before I had walked more than a hundred steps. Fortunately the late November breeze soon extinguished the flame, so my candle had to be exchanged for a lighted taper, which burned more easily in the windy streets. Someone behind me carried the symbolic candle, another small victory over the bishops.

The ecclesiastical court had chosen busy market days for my penance, to ensure the population would be increased by visiting merchants and men from the outlying towns, yet they would be disappointed. The people lining the narrow streets as my entourage passed by were not the jeering, accusing crowds the cardinal would have wished for. Instead I felt nothing but compassion from those who came out to witness my penance. They fell silent as I walked past them and I hoped it was because they knew how cruelly I had been treated.

Led by the mayor and aldermen of London, my two knights, and followed by my guards, my procession made slow progress as I walked first to the magnificent cathedral of St Paul's, with its towering spire. I stopped for a moment as I realised I was in the open courtyard of St Paul's Cross, where Roger Bolingbroke had been made to recant, seated on his brightly coloured chair. Then I was ushered on through the towering doors of the cathedral.

The heavy church candle was lit from my taper and I carried it slowly through the silently watching congregation, down the long aisle to place on the high altar. As I did so I planned to curse every one of the cruel bishops who divorced me; instead I said a silent prayer for those who died through my foolishness. How could I have ever thought the king's favour worth such a price?

The people of London who saw me make my penance would have known me still as a duchess, standing straight and proud as I walked in my procession through the narrow, dirty streets. Even though dressed in the rough black woollen robe, my head wrapped in a cloth, I had their respect. In my heart, though, my heart was broken and I was on the verge of the deepest misery, with little now to live for. All that kept me going was the thought of my children and grandchildren, and a new determination not to give Cardinal Henry Beaufort the satisfaction of seeing the truth of my despair.

On the following Wednesday my barge took me to what are known as the 'swan stairs' in Upper Thames Street. It has, I think, been a long time since swans were seen in such a place. I saw it is now a favourite spot for Londoners to illegally empty foul-smelling slop buckets into the river. I looked back at the old London Bridge and shivered as I saw the sightless, rotting heads of traitors fixed to poles. The current was running swiftly as it headed out to sea, on its way past Greenwich, Bella Court and Duke Humphrey.

I stared into the dark depths and considered jumping

from the barge to take my chances in the murky water. I never learned to swim and knew I would drown before my guards could pull me out. It would be a way to find if it was my destiny to live or drown, yet I lacked the courage. The opportunity quickly passed by as I was ushered up the stone steps to where a new crowd of onlookers waited to witness my disgrace.

Once again, I was made to walk through narrow streets of strangely silent crowds who had come to witness my penance, all the way to the Christ Church in Aldgate, known as the priory of the black canons. There I knelt in prayer in front of the altar while the lit taper I carried was used to light twenty-eight candles, one for each of the charges made against me. I prayed my children would be kept safe and well. I prayed for Duke Humphrey to have the strength to go on without me.

On the Friday I was landed at the old dock at Queen Hythe and walked through the busy streets of Cheapside, where I had so recently been dining in such style when I received the fateful note from Roger Bolingbroke. The third and final destination of my penance was the parish church of London, St Michael's in Cornhill. Someone in the crowd dared to shout in support for good Duke Humphrey as my procession made its way to the church. Their shout was soon echoed by others and I wondered if it might turn into a riot.

The king's soldiers ushered me into a carriage and quickly back to the Palace of Westminster. I had made my penance with some dignity, although I knew the ballad writers would already be trimming their quills to note my fall from first lady of the land. The record of history was, as 'good' Duke Humphrey once reminded me, always written by the victors. Cardinal Henry Beaufort would personally ensure that, if I was remembered at all, it would be for how I was most publicly disgraced.

My punishment was as nothing compared with the fate of my friends. It was some comfort that I had been able to persuade the disreputable Sir John Holland, Constable of the Tower of London, to promise me that Roger Boling-broke would not suffer unduly. So far I had not heard of his death in custody, so I asked my maidservant Martha to visit Tyburn on the appointed day he was to be executed, to see that Sir John was as good as his word.

When Martha returned she told me a tale of such horror and sadness I can hardly describe it, and only do so that the truth of how he suffered is not forgotten. Roger Bolingbroke had been a wise and caring man, so full of life and wit he brought out the best in all who met him. He was proud to be a man of the church, steadfast in his faith in God and always ready to help those less fortunate than himself. How could I not love him?

It saddens me to think how he must have suffered at the hands of torturers to make him confess. Once he had, the trial was simply a formality, his execution a certainty. Sentenced to death, he was dragged from the Tower through the streets of London, still made to wear the strange and colourful 'magical' garments, tied to a hurdle pulled by a black horse. Martha said Roger Bolingbroke had loudly protested his innocence of treason against the king. He was still shouting as he arrived at Tyburn, right up to the moment he was hanged.

He called to God for forgiveness as the thick noose of rope was pulled over his head. Martha had also known him as a good man, who always treated her more as a lady than a maidservant. She sobbed as she recalled how he had not been calling for his own salvation but for the souls of those who had judged him, for the men who now had the task of ending his life. With his last strength, he cried out for the Lord to show mercy. He called on God to forgive them.

Martha was reluctant to tell me more. I told her I must be told the truth of what happened that fateful day at Tyburn. For whatever reason, Sir John Holland had not been able to keep his promise to me. Roger Bolingbroke had been cut down from the gibbet while he still lived. A bucket of water was thrown into his face to revive him, then he was stripped and held down on a wooden table. They cut him open, removed his bowels and burned them on a brazier while he was made to watch.

This poor man, who would have dearly wished to be laid to rest in his peaceful Oxford churchyard, suffered the worst abuse. His still beating heart was cut out and thrown on the flames, to a cheer from the crowd. His head was severed, carried off to be placed on a spike on London Bridge, where black crows would peck out his eyes. His poor body was butchered into quarters, sent to be displayed on ropes at the gates of Oxford, Cambridge, York and Hereford, as grisly, maggot-riddled warnings to heretics and Lollards.

21

MARCH 1452

MUNUS REGIS

N o word had been said by any of the bishops about
where I was to be imprisoned, although I had
begun to be convinced it would be in the dark
dungeons of the Tower of London. Instead I found myself
returned to my rooms at Leeds Castle, a place I thought I
may never see again. I wondered if this was where I was
destined to end my days, in honourable confinement like
that accorded to the Dowager Queen Joanna. I even began
to hope that, like her, I would one day be released.

I had forgotten my imprisonment was a way to keep my
husband out of power. The cardinal must have worried that
even Leeds Castle would not hold me, as I was put into the
custody of Sir Thomas Stanley, Controller of the Royal
Household. Sir Thomas had been chosen to be responsible
for me because he was also the Constable of Chester Castle,
so it was no surprise that it was there he decided I should
be held.

I said my farewell to Sir John Steward and gave him my
gold ring with a large, valuable diamond to thank him for

making my time at Leeds Castle as comfortable as he could. A good man, he had always been most charming to me. As I was about to leave he kissed my hand, then beckoned one of his servants. Sir John presented me with the beautiful lute, saying he had witnessed how my playing had improved and wished me well for the future.

He told me I was to make the long journey from Kent to Cheshire escorted by a dozen of the king's soldiers. Arrangements had been made for the sheriffs of each county to be held personally accountable for me. They were under orders from the Chancellor, John Stafford, Bishop of Bath and Wells, that my journey was not to be delayed for any reason, particularly by feigned illness. My last memory of Sir John Steward is when I looked back and saw him watching my entourage leave. He raised a hand and I did the same in return, certain I would never see him or Leeds Castle again.

My first escort was John Warner, a talkative and wealthy landowner and Sheriff of Kent. Accompanied by my servants, including my loyal maidservant Martha, and the young maid Mary, I carried with me only the few possessions I had taken when I sought sanctuary and the lute, a present I was most grateful for. A horse-drawn bier had been provided for our long journey and we had not travelled far when snowflakes began drifting from the sky. It was late January, in the middle of what was to prove one of the worst winters for several years.

The road ahead was soon obscured with the falling snow, which made the going dangerous and difficult for our horses. The sheriff was leading our small procession when he gave a shout as his horse strayed from the track we were following and fell into a roadside drainage ditch. He was determined to rescue his favourite horse, a fine grey mare, and soon all the soldiers were trying to pull the poor creature. It was no good. The ditch was deep and full of icy water and the horse's struggling made it sink deeper into the slippery mud. The men tried lashing together reins and bridles and almost succeeded, yet despite their best efforts we could see the horse was stuck fast. There was no hope.

We watched as the sheriff took a knife from his belt. I could hardly bear to look as he leaned over his horse and affectionately patted it on the head one last time. Then he sawed through the thick leather straps and salvaged his valuable saddle from the horse's back. I can still picture the forlorn look in that horse's eye when we were forced to abandon it to take its chances. It reminded me how I had also been abandoned to my fate by my husband.

The loss of his horse put the sheriff in a sombre mood as we made our cautious progress to London. He told me his orders were not to delay our arrival in London for any reason, yet we had lost a lot of time. The winter sun set early and it was dark by the time we reached Westminster, sodden through from the melted snow. John Warner looked greatly relieved as he formally handed me over to the Sheriff of London.

My latest custodian was an arrogant young merchant with the memorable name of Richard Ryche, new in his post and clearly unused to being in command of so many soldiers. We were exhausted from the cold and had to rest for the night, so the sheriff decided to house us at the Abbot of Westminster's manor house at Neyat, within sight of Westminster Abbey. The manor was old and poorly maintained, with moss-covered shingles sliding from the roof and unglazed windows. The poorly fitting shutters did little to keep out the cold, but I was allowed to have my servants light a fire in the hearth.

As we huddled for warmth by the fire, with only a bowl of oat potage and a crust of rye for sustenance, Martha reminded me of the lavish Christmas banquets we would have at Bella Court, with a roasted boar's head carried round the tables by carol singers and minstrels. I recalled the menus for our grand New Year's Day celebrations. I missed the hot mulled wine and longed to taste again the sweet gingerbread, full of rare and precious spices few of our guests could afford, cinnamon and cloves, brought by merchants from the mysterious east.

Most of all, I deeply missed seeing my family. I missed my husband, who would always be a little drunk on fine brandy by the end of New Year's Day. I missed my beautiful daughter Antigone, with my grandchildren, all growing up so fast, and of course I greatly missed my son Arthur, the image of his father. I lived in hope of word that they were safe and well and would one day be able to visit me, wherever I was to spend the rest of my days.

The weather had not improved by the morning, with another fall of snow turning the roads to slippery slush. We had some two hundred miles still to travel before we would reach Chester, so the young sheriff decided we must wait until the weather was good enough to continue. There was nothing to do to pass the time, other than cook and eat, and try to have some sleep. It was little wonder that my thoughts would turn to escape.

Once inside the castle at Chester there would be a slim chance of evading my ever-present guards, yet in the abbot's manor there was only one man posted outside our door through the night. I examined the shuttered windows of my room. One was more than wide enough for me to climb through. Unfortunately my room was on the first floor, so the drop to the snowy courtyard below would be too much for me. Looking out into the darkness I saw it was a moonless night, with no sign of my guards in the courtyard outside. This could be my only chance of escape.

Gathering some of my possessions together into a bundle I tried to plan what I would do and where I could go once I was free. I was not sure exactly where I was although I knew Westminster well and would soon recognise familiar streets and buildings. A greater problem was to decide where I should be going, Sadly there was no point in trying to reach Bella Court, so I resolved to find London Bridge, cross the River Thames and hurry as far from London as I could.

There would be few people around at such a late hour and I pulled a shawl around my face to keep warm and reduce the chance of being recognised. I opened the old shutters wide and was about to climb through the window when I realised the drop was greater than I had thought. I could break a leg or at the least twist my ankle in the fall to the hard cobbles below. I would need a different plan.

If I was going to escape, I would somehow have to distract the guard at the door. For a moment I considered trying to bribe him with some of my jewellery or the money I still carried in my purse. There was no sound from outside my door, so I cautiously opened it a crack and saw the hallway and stairs were in darkness. My guards had become complacent and did not expect me to attempt an escape.

Taking my bundle, I crept out into the hall, stopping as one of the floorboards creaked under my foot, to listen for the guards. Feeling for each step in the dark, I made my way down the stairs to the floor below. I guessed the front door would be locked and barred, so headed through to find a way out through the back. A glimmer of light came from the kitchen hearth, left burning through the night, and I could see an old door. I had come too far to turn back now and tried the handle. It opened and I slipped through into the cold darkness outside.

I almost tripped over the man guarding the back door. He shouted in surprise at seeing me and I was soon surrounded by soldiers. Sheriff Richard Ryche was angry at having been called from his bed. He reminded me I was the guest and responsibility of the Abbot of Westminster and asked if I had given any thought to the consequences for him if I had succeeded in my plan. I could see from the look on his face that, in truth, the young and ambitious sheriff feared the consequences for himself. He was right, though. I had not spared a moment's thought for the men who were guarding me that night or how harshly they would have been punished. I promised I would not try to escape again.

The weather improved a little in the morning and we continued on our way north-west to the old Roman town of Chester. Even though the snow had cleared from the roads, the slush turned them to slippery mud and we made slow progress, being forced to stop often. I was handed from one sheriff to the next and stayed in a succession of inns and manor houses as we made our way through each county, taking nearly a week to complete the journey.

Sir Thomas Stanley greeted our party as we arrived at his castle. A gruff, portly man with an abrupt manner, Sir Thomas was in a surly mood and made no secret of the fact he was aggrieved to have me in his charge. He complained he had only been granted a hundred marks a year for his duty, one tenth of what he had been expecting, so I was not to expect the same comfort and privileges as the Dowager Queen Joanna.

Chester Castle stands on a low hill within a bend of the River Dee, a stones-throw from the border with Wales and within sight of the prosperous old walled city. At first I had high hopes, as we crossed a drawbridge over a deep moat through an impressive gatehouse and across an outer bailey. The castle, with walls of reddish-pink sandstone, looked well maintained and I thought my rooms would compare favourably with Leeds Castle. I could not have been more wrong. They thought there was a risk of my attempting to escape, and Sir Thomas Stanley was not a man to take risks.

The ancient stone gateway to the inner bailey of Chester Castle is called the Agricola Tower, after the general who led the Roman conquest. Underneath this high, square building was a vaulted-ceilinged crypt, where I learned Humphrey's father had imprisoned King Richard II, his first cousin, when he first took the throne of England. With his cruel sense of irony, Sir Thomas decided there could be no more fitting place for him to keep me safe.

Damp and miserable, the old crypt had bare stone walls and nothing but dirty rushes on the floors. The rooms were small and dark, with only the most basic furniture and a hall which was cold and drafty, despite the fire we lit in the hearth. I did my best with my servants to clean and tidy my new home and hoped it was only temporary, while proper arrangements were made to find somewhere more suitable for my imprisonment.

Unlike Leeds Castle, I was not permitted by Sir Thomas to explore the grounds, other than to occasionally have some fresh air within the small inner bailey and visit the high ceilinged chapel of St Mary de Castro, on the first floor of the Agricola Tower. The walls of the chapel were decorated with colourful images of saints, painted in red and blue, with gold leaf ornament. Although by this time I had lost my faith, I would spend as much time as I could in the chapel, watched over by these long dead saints, where it was at least clean and dry, if not particularly warm in winter.

If I had known I was to be held there for nearly two long years, I think I would have gone half mad with boredom, as there was nothing to do apart from survive from one day to the next as best I could. The distance from London meant there was almost no news. Even when I sent Martha out into the provincial city of Chester with some of the coins from my purse to learn what she could, it seemed I had been forgotten by the world.

One morning Martha came to tell me that the young maidservant Mary had returned to London, as her father was ill. I was surprised Mary had left without saying good-bye, as she had been in my service since I was first at Leeds Castle in Kent. I had never trusted her though and always wondered if she had been placed in my service to spy on me.

Something nagged at the back of my mind about Mary's sudden departure and I pressed Martha to tell me the truth. She reluctantly confessed that it had been Mary who raised the alarm when I escaped from the abbot's manor house at Neyat. Later when I was tidying my room I found my price-less New Year's gift from the king was gone.

I knew right away my servant Mary must have found my hiding place for the beautiful brooch in the shape of the king holding a golden ball, with its priceless diamonds, pearls and rubies. I cursed her disloyalty. My first reaction was to call for Sir Thomas to have her hunted down and punished. Fortunately Martha persuaded me to think on it. I still had the jewellery I had sewn into my blue dress, as well as the gold and silver coins in my purse.

That night I lay awake and realised the king's gift would have been of no further use to me. I had abandoned any future plan to escape or bribe those guarding me. Too many good people had already suffered because of my foolish actions. Instead, the golden figure could now change the life of my former servant and her family. If it was true her father was ill she would now be able to provide for them all.

It was not until the end of the October of 1443 that Sir Thomas Stanley came to see me with news he had received orders from the king to take me to Kenilworth Castle, in Warwickshire. I visited Kenilworth with Humphrey when we were making plans for Bella Court and knew his grandfather, John of Gaunt, had spent a small fortune turning the old castle into a fabulous fortified palace. Kenilworth became the main residence of Duke Humphrey's father, King Henry IV, and was truly a castle fit for a king.

At last I was to be leaving the boredom of my dark, damp prison in the crypt, and I wondered if it was a sign the king was finally beginning to have sympathy for my awful situation. I had, after all, been his favourite for many years, so for the first time in ages I felt a glimmer of hope. Perhaps Duke Humphrey had been secretly negotiating for my release and this was the first step towards the granting of my freedom.

Sir Thomas made elaborate arrangements for my protection on the journey, leaving nothing to chance. As well as the king's men, my escort was to be led by his own personal guards, sworn to ensure I had no opportunity to escape. He agreed I could take twelve servants with me, including several from his own household, my maidservant Martha and the cooks who had been with me for as long as I could remember.

The late autumn weather was good and once we cleared the Chester road, busy with over-laden carts and packhorses, we found ourselves in the open countryside. The roads were quiet, with only birdsong to accompany the tramping of the soldiers boots and the rumble and creak of our wheels. My spirits lifted. I have learned that everything is relative. Compared to the crypt in Chester, Kenilworth could only be a happy relief.

We travelled the hundred or so miles south-west without incident, stopping for the night at Hulton Abbey, where we were made welcome, and arriving at Kenilworth on the fifth of December. Although I was still the responsibility of Sir Thomas, he remained in Chester and I was now to be guarded by the Constable of Kenilworth castle, Sir Ralph Boteler, a Chamberlain of the Royal Household and newly appointed as the Treasurer of England.

I had known Sir Ralph almost as long as I had known Humphrey, as he had been made a councillor to the infant king. His mother, Dame Alice, had also been chosen by Queen Catherine to be the king's governess. Sir Ralph now held one of the most influential positions in the land, a sure sign he was in league with Cardinal Henry Beaufort. He had also fought at the side of Humphrey's brother John, who would have had every opportunity to poison his mind against me.

Like Leeds Castle, Kenilworth had extensive gardens. Built on naturally high ground, the streams that fed a nearby lake were dammed to create the largest artificial lake in the kingdom, over a mile long, surrounding the castle. I was led in to the former royal apartments and shown a surprising gift from the king. He had provided an ornate curtained canopy of red velvet fringed with gold over my bed, as a welcome present to my new home.

22

APRIL 1452

FEBRIS

Spring has at last returned, bringing new life to Beaumaris. I wake to a bright sunny morning and my spirits are lifted by the cheering sounds of birds singing outside my window. For a moment I keep my eyes closed and imagine I am waking at Bella Court and all this has been a dream. At any moment, my maid will come to ask which of my many dresses I will choose to wear today. I open my eyes and see the same familiar stone walls of my tower, yet I feel no sense of disappointment, for a new challenge occupies my mind now. I am helping my guard Richard Hook with his reading and writing.

I look forward to the days when he is on duty and I hear his familiar knock at my door. Young Richard is good company for me and it warms my heart to at last be doing something worthwhile. He makes slow progress with his reading and his writing needs much work, yet I admire his determination to improve himself. He is bright and has many questions, not all of which are answered so easily. In return for my lessons he sometimes brings me fresh supplies of ink and parchment I need to write this journal.

Richard Hook seems to be a man I can trust, so I have also asked him a favour. I took my mother's gold ring from my finger and asked him if he could sell it for me in Beaumaris, and use the money to buy a good strong box, large enough to hold my secret journal, with a lid that can be sealed with wax. He held my mother's ring in his hand for a moment and returned it, smiling. He promised to bring me the box, as well as the latest gossip from Beaumaris.

Occasionally, he also brings news of the world beyond this isolated and remote Welsh island. It seems the Duke of York remains at Westminster and has at last been persuaded to take his rightful place on the King's Council. I hope and pray this means an end to the corruption and self-interest within the troubled government of this country. The king seems to have accepted this arrangement and, for once, go against the wishes of his wife. Richard Hook tells me the Duke's cause is popular with the people. Even in the taverns of Beaumaris there is hope for better times ahead.

Now the king is no longer under the influence of Cardinal Henry Beaufort I can't help feeling a moment of regret. If only Duke Humphrey lived, he would have found a useful ally in the Duke of York. If it is true, as Lady Ellen heard, that the king is not capable of begetting a son and heir with his scheming French queen, Duke Richard is now the heir apparent. One day, God willing, we could see him rule all England.

Again I wonder if he will be too busy to remember the injustice done to me. I know I am not foremost in his mind or he would have demanded to see me when he arrived in Beaumaris last year. I have decided not to leave it to chance. I will prepare a letter to the Duke of York, pledging my support and beseeching him to look favourably on me now I have more than served penance for my mistakes.

Looking back I can say in ten years of imprisonment I found the closest to contentment at Kenilworth Castle, my beautiful, elegant, ornate prison palace. My jailer, Sir Ralph Boteler, was often absent with his duties as chancellor and treasurer in London, so I was left much to my own devices. Although watched over by the ever-present castle guards, they went about their daily duties at a discreet distance, so I began to feel more like Sir Ralph's house guest than his prisoner.

I returned to playing my precious lute, my practical memento of Leeds Castle, so nearly abandoned in my reckless escape from the abbot's manor in Westminster. Encouraged by Sir John Steward's kind words, I practiced for many hours each day until the notes come without effort. The sweet music kept back the dark thoughts from my mind as, with each passing week in my new home, I began to put the sadness of my recent past behind me.

My favourite room to play in at Kenilworth was the great hall, every bit as grand as the hall in the king's own residence at Windsor Castle. The wonderfully carved roof of the great hall is one of the widest and highest in England, soaring cathedral-like with its gold painted stars above me. My lute sounded clear and pure in its stillness of this great open space.

Towering leaded glass windows provide wonderful views out over the tranquil green waters of the Great Mere. I would sit by the window in my cushioned armchair watching nesting swans as they reared their brood of grey-feathered cygnets in the reeds at the water's edge. Once I might have envied the swan's uncomplicated lives yet now my own life was much the same, as I could do as I pleased, apart from leave this beautiful palace.

After the bleak unpleasantness of Sir Thomas Stanley's damp and miserable crypt at Chester Castle, I also now had a little hope to sustain my spirits. I could at last be certain the king had not completely forgotten me. His present of my bed canopy a much needed sign I was still in his favour, his way to let me know he rejects the cardinal's false charges of treason against him.

When the weather improved I decided to keep busy creating a garden in the inner court. It would never match the wonderful gardens at my home in Greenwich but the soil was good and high stone walls provided shelter from the wind, even in winter. Sir Ralph allowed me to have his men dig over the rough lawn and I sent servants out with some of the silver coins from my purse to buy fruit trees and the herbs I needed. It took a whole summer but I was slowly turning what was once a patch of grass and stones into a place of beauty.

In the spring my maidservant Martha suggested purchasing some laying hens, so we could have fresh eggs and the occasional chicken to eat whenever we wished. I liked her idea, so I gave her some money and she rode off to town in the horse-drawn cart. She returned with half a dozen healthy looking young pullets and a scrawny cockerel, which promptly began to wake us at dawn each day with his raucous crowing.

Martha was of course a city woman and had never tended after laying hens before. She gave them all names, calling the strutting cockerel 'Sir Ralph' after my often absent jailor. The chickens soon grew fat and ran wild, spending their day foraging for food in my gardens, scratching the ground looking for insects and seeds. They were in danger of ruining all my hard work until we found a way to pen them in.

Life settled into a simple routine, walking in my garden, caring for our little flock of chickens and playing my lute music. Martha had always observed her place most diligently, yet now I asked her to take her meals with me and we became good friends. In an unspoken pact we never discussed or mentioned what had happened at Bella Court and I almost started to forget why we were even at Kenilworth.

I also decided to improve my French by reading the old books I found in the state apartments. I doubted I would ever need to appreciate the finer points of manners and etiquette in the French court, although I was intrigued to wonder who left the leather bound books for me to discover. One was embossed with the red, blue and gold of the Royal Arms of England.

As I turned the pages of this precious old book I wondered if it belonged to Duke Humphrey's brother King Henry V, who once lived at Kenilworth Castle and wished so dearly to be King of France as well as England. Henry also had his own stepmother imprisoned after he accused her of using witchcraft to try to poison him. There was no need to curse Humphrey's elder brother. By all accounts he died a miserable, inglorious death.

Relentless rain kept me in my apartments on the day I began to feel unwell, so I retired to my bed early, a dull ache spreading through my bones. I lay awake for hours before I was able to sleep, then woke in a sweating fever. At first I felt so cold I huddled under the blankets of thick wool, my whole body shivering as if my bed was made of ice. I called for Martha to bring me more blankets and build up the fire in my room, yet as soon as she did so I had a raging thirst and began to sweat as if I was burning up.

I could eat little of the food brought for me and Martha became my constant companion, making cold compresses of elderberry and rosemary as I had told her. Despite her best efforts my fever became worse, so that I could hardly tell if it was night or day. I began to have delirious dreams. I called out to my friend Margery Jourdemayne for help and she appeared before me, not as I had known her but blackened and burned.

It may have been my fevered mind but I welcomed the somehow familiar hooded figure of death that now beckoned me to follow. I dreamt I was back at St Paul's Cathedral, carrying a lit candle up the long aisle. All the people I had ever known were seated in the pews to each side of me, even those who were now departed. I recognised the frowning John, Duke of Bedford, with his first wife Anne of Burgundy, her face disfigured with the plague, to one side and the self-satisfied young Jacquetta of Luxembourg to the other.

Countess Jacqueline cradled her dead baby in her arms and smiled at me as I passed, seeming to forgive my disloyalty to her. I tried to explain to her it was love, not disloyalty, that brought me into the arms of her husband. The countess laughed when I told her Duke Humphrey had now abandoned me, a wild, unearthly cackle that sounded sacrilegious in such a hallowed place.

I felt compelled to continue towards the altar, where the grim-faced bishops who sentenced me to imprisonment for life waited in their finery. I looked up at them and saw Cardinal Henry Beaufort grinning in evil welcome. The black-garbed figure of death called to me again. As I came closer his black hood fell back and I could see it was my friend and mentor, Roger Bolingbroke. His eyes black holes where ravens had pecked them out.

Jolted to consciousness by the shock of my visions I found I was in my bedchamber with its gold-edged velvet curtains. A white-bearded stranger was seated at the side of my bed. Dressed in a simple black tunic with a leather belt at the waist, he was reading a Latin text by candle light. He didn't look up and seemed unaware I was watching him as he turned the page, tracing the words with his finger, his lips moving silently as I had once done as a child.

Not sure if he was real or I was dreaming, I worried he had come to administer the last rites to me. Still a little confused, I asked if he was a monk or a priest, my voice sounding hoarse and weak. The stranger looked back at me and smiled with kindly eyes. He said he was neither, as he was a canon from the priory of St Mary. His voice was calming, with the warmth of someone experienced in caring for the sick. He marked the page in his book with a length of red ribbon and placed it on his chair.

He leaned over, placing his hand gently to my brow and nodding in approval. I told him I thought I was going to die and saw a moment of concern in his eyes. I called out for my maidservant Martha and listened for her answer from the next room, where she had been sleeping to keep close watch over me. There was no answer. The canon said my servant had sent for him when she could do no more, and he had watched and prayed over me until my fever lifted.

I asked him why he dressed like a monk and he explained the canons of the priory of St Mary live under the rule of St Augustine, taking vows of chastity, poverty and obedience. Unlike a monk who lives a cloistered, contemplative life, or a priest who tends to the needs of his congregation, he had sworn to follow the example of the

Apostles, preaching and giving hospitality to pilgrims and travellers, as well as tending the sick.

He said at first he thought he had been called too late, as my fever was the worst he had seen. For two days I had been close to death but it seemed I was destined to live. I asked him if he could summon my maidservant Martha and he looked serious, as if making a judgement. He said she had also contracted my fever, the day before, and was sleeping in the next room, much the worse for it.

The tone of the canon's voice told me he did not expect her to live, so I resolved to do whatever I could for my good companion. I took turns with the canon at her bedside, yet we could see her fever was growing worse. I sent servants in search of white willow bark, which I boiled with a little honey to make a potion, just as Margery Jourdemayne had taught me so long ago. The canon placed his faith in prayer, and read aloud in his gentle voice, which seemed to calm her a little.

We will never know if it was my potion or the canon's prayers that was the cure, but we were both greatly relieved when Martha began to slowly return to her jovial former self. I know if she had died I would have found it hard to continue alone, yet she was strong in body and spirit. I was grateful to the kind and gentle canon for helping to save us, and gave him the last of the gold coins from my purse as a donation to the priory.

~

Martha was in my thoughts as I made my daily walk around the inner ward in the spring sunshine at Beaumaris. Even now, after all these years, I clearly recall her humour and sense of joy in the smallest things as we found ways to pass the time at Kenilworth Castle. I barely gave it a thought at the time, but she made great sacrifices for me, never marrying and never asking to visit her only relatives in London. Her pay was meagre and Martha endured the same poor conditions in Chester crypt as myself, although she did so with much fortitude, which helped me in no small way.

I valued her loyalty above all else, when even my husband abandoned me to my fate. It warmed my heart to know there was at least one person who dismissed the bishop's cruel allegations. She served me, not truly as a maid but as better company than any of my ladies in waiting had at Bella Court. I loved her stories of the London taverns, a life I could have lived were it not for my father arranging my introduction to Countess Jacqueline all those years ago.

I remember how once she served a fine chicken dinner, a special treat after many weeks of mutton stew. She waited until there was not one scrap of the tasty meat left on the bones before telling me the strutting cockerel 'Sir Ralph' would no longer trouble our early mornings with his endless crowing. I truly miss my good friend and servant Martha and wonder what became of her.

Our three years at Kenilworth passed all too quickly. In July of 1446 I had a letter from Sir Thomas Stanley, who was still charged by the king to oversee my imprisonment. The messenger had ridden through the night and I broke the seal with a sense of deep foreboding. Sir Thomas wrote he was concerned at rumours of plans to free me, so I was to be transferred forthwith to his castle on the Isle of Man, where he could be more certain of what he called 'my safety'. Almost as a postscript, he added at the end of the letter that he regretted to inform me my father, Sir Reynold Cobham, was dead.

I remember my tears as I sat at my favourite window in the great hall at Kenilworth, the folded letter in my hand. How had my father died? Who was behind these rumours of plans to set me free? I dreaded the prospect of returning back into the charge of the man who kept me in his dark and damp crypt, with barely the chance to walk in the fresh air. The only person I could trust was my servant Martha, so I decided she must travel to London right away, with the last of my silver coins, to find the answers for me.

23

MAY 1452

AD UNDAS

I resisted leaving Kenilworth Castle for as long as I could by claiming I was too unwell to make the long journey to the Isle of Man. In truth, I prayed each day for my servant Martha to return from London, where I had sent her to bring me news of rumours regarding my release, as well as to learn what she could about my father's death. She had been gone for nearly a month and there was still no word from her. To my regret I never thought to teach Martha to read or write, so she would have had to find a scribe to send a letter to me, something I knew she would not want to risk.

Sir Thomas Stanley was a notoriously impatient man, so as June turned to July, it was with great regret I had to pack my things and prepare to leave. Although I had fled Bella Court with only what I could carry, over the years I had accumulated various possessions. My lute was wrapped in muslin cloth, as I was most concerned it could be damaged on the long journey or on the sea crossing to the Isle of Man.

We departed for Peel Castle at the first light of dawn.

My vain hope was that my maidservant Martha would somehow be able to join me on the road north. I was desperate now for news and sure she would do her best. In my heart I doubted it would be easy for her to find us, although we drew attention wherever we went. I rode in a high-sided wagon, with an escort of twenty armed soldiers of the royal household in front and my remaining servants following behind. I must have looked like a queen on a royal progress.

It was with sadness that I watched the last of the towers of Kenilworth Castle disappear into the distance. It was there I had learned to put the nightmares of the past behind me a little and to live simply, for the day. Ahead of me now lay nothing but uncertainty. The only thing I could be sure of was that Sir Thomas would not treat me with the same courtesy as shown to me by Sir Ralph Boteler. The thought, nagging at my mind as we travelled north, was that my unwilling jailor would find it more convenient if I were dead.

It had been a dry summer and clouds of dust rose to the skies in our wake. We made good time on the arduous journey to the coast, travelling all hours of daylight. I kept a constant watch for Martha, although in my heart I knew there would be no sign of her. I suspected Sir Thomas had ordered the details of my transfer to be kept a closely guarded secret if there were rumours about having me freed. He might not want me as a prisoner, but he would not risk being an unwitting party to my liberation either.

My destination could scarcely be more remote and still be counted as being in England. Peel Castle is in the middle of the Irish Sea, on a small, inhospitable and rocky island connected to the Isle of Man by a narrow stone causeway. Apart from that it belonged to Sir Thomas Stanley I knew little else about the place to which I was now headed. I had never wished to visit the island and expected I would likely now die there, forgotten by everyone I knew.

Dusk was falling by the time we reached the village seaport of Whitehaven, on the Cumbrian coast. I was tired from the long journey and grateful when we rested for the night. I was given a room at the small but well-ordered Benedictine Priory of St Bees, where black-garbed, tonsured monks went about their work without speaking. Fortunately it was not a closed order and the abbot had agreed to accommodate us, although with some reluctance.

I lay awake in the darkness, unable to sleep, listening to the mournful tolling of the priory bell that ruled every moment of the monks' lives. I wished for my comfortable bed at Kenilworth with its velvet curtains from the king. I missed the company of my maidservant Martha and knew she would never find me now, so far from London. I wondered who could be behind the rumours I was to be set free. I mourned the death of my father and cried myself to sleep.

In the morning I was expecting to sail in a high-masted galleon like Duke Humphrey used to cross the Channel from Dover. Instead, I was worried to see an ancient fishing vessel moored at the quayside, its rigging painted with black tar, the sails mended so many times they were a patchwork of canvas. The crew of rugged, bearded fishermen dressed in grimy rags and their captain leered and made some remark in their Gaelic language, his men laughing coarsely as I was ushered aboard. There was little room below decks and I found myself crammed with guards and servants, nets and wicker baskets, in the open hold which reeked to high heaven of herrings and fish guts.

A freshening breeze filled the tattered sails as we headed

out into the choppy Irish Sea and cold seawater soon sluiced over the deck. Larger waves spilled into the hold, where I cowered with my servants in fear of our lives as the boat pitched in the worsening swell. Over the noise of the wind and waves I heard some of the crew complaining loudly that it was bad luck to have me on board their boat. Their captain had no time for such talk and cursed them all and swore it was merely a squall.

Then a crashing wave struck the boat violently on the side and it heeled hard over, throwing us together in the hold. One of my maidservants screamed, the shrill sound echoing eerily as our boat ploughed heavily into a second, giant wave. I tasted salt as freezing water again poured over us, soaking our clothes and stinging my eyes. There was a shudder and the sound of ropes straining dangerously against creaking wood as the helm was pushed hard to turn us into the breaking waves.

I remember preparing myself for the moment when the pounding water would fill the open hold and take us to the bottom of the sea. My mind became strangely calm in the middle of the squall, despite the desperate sounds all around me, ready to accept my fate. I recall thinking that death by drowning would be preferable to imprisonment for the rest of my life. I had never learned to swim and, even if I could, there was nowhere to swim to, no chance of rescue in the middle of this deserted sea.

Then I heard a deep-voiced cry. 'Land ahoy!' The Isle of Man was sighted on the horizon and almost immediately the weather began to improve as we entered its sheltered waters. I should have felt immense relief, yet I had a deep foreboding about my new island prison. I sometimes wonder if I can foretell the future, as I sensed this would be the worst place for me to be held. It was not just Sir

Thomas Stanley who wished me dead. I had become an inconvenient reminder to all those who so falsely condemned me.

My new room was little more than a whitewashed cell, much as where a monk would live. I looked out through my little window, having my first real view of Peel Castle. This island fortress covers some five rugged acres, with high, embattled walls. Towers of different shapes and heights, made of the coarse grey local stone, are quoined and faced in places with red sandstone. In the middle of Peel Castle is the parish church of St German they call the 'cathedral' and close by a building known as 'the lord's palace', neither of which deserve the name.

Much of the enclosed area was turned to a rough pasture of grass too coarse for even sheep to graze and beyond the walls I could see nothing but rocks and the cold blue-green expanse of the Irish Sea. A stone jetty reached out into the sea, providing mooring for boats when the weather permitted, although the prevailing winds meant most sought shelter on the main island. There were almost no visitors, as the people tended to avoid Peel Castle other than when bringing supplies.

My servants soon tired of the harsh remoteness of this windswept place and departed one by one, until I had only my surly guards and a well-meaning cook for company. She did her best to make something of the cod and herring, which were plentiful in the seas around the island and smoked or dried to make them keep. Sometimes she managed to obtain a ham or even a fresh rabbit, although I longed for fruit or anything sweet to eat. There was no prospect of a garden as the soil was poor and I had no money now for plants.

The main problem was I had nothing to occupy my mind, as my lute and other possessions, brought with so much care all the way from Kenilworth Castle, were gone, stolen or lost. My new servants, hard, grim-faced Manx women, were no companions, barely speaking and eyeing me warily as they worked. All I could do was follow the path around the long perimeter wall and watch the fishing boats out at sea as they fought to make a living in the island's strong currents.

I had learnt to be grateful for small mercies, however. After the crypt at Chester Castle my little cell seemed more than adequate. I lost my few possessions yet I still had my blue dress. It was torn and stained with dirt but still had the secret pocket where I could feel the hidden weight of the last of my precious jewellery. It crossed my mind this could be a way to my salvation, enough to bribe one of my guards and pay for a passage to the Irish coast and freedom.

Now I had a new plan, to watch my guards and choose which to approach. The soldiers of Peel Castle were a garrulous lot, unhappy in their work. At first I thought none seemed worth the risk, until I noticed how one looked at me. His eyes showed curiosity, rather than the contempt or the wariness of one who believes I am a sorceress. While I waited for my chance I carefully unpicked part of the stitching of the pocket in my dress and chose a diamond pendant to use as my bribe.

At last the moment came when the guard I had chosen was alone at my door. Although anxious, I had nothing to lose, so I quickly explained my proposition. He studied the precious pendant and I saw from the glint in his eye he knew it was worth more than he could earn in a lifetime. He said he would need to think on it. All those guarding me had been told it would be considered treason, with the full punishment accorded to traitors, if any helped me to escape.

A week passed before I heard from the guard again. It was a moonless night and he demanded more jewellery if he was to risk his life for me. I handed him the pendant and agreed to make him richer than any man on the island. He seemed to know I told the truth and told me to wrap my dark cloak around me, then led me to a doorway near the lord's palace. We entered a long narrow passage which he said was for escape if the fortress was under siege. The walls dripped with water and were carved from the solid rock.

I heard waves crashing below as we felt our way down a flight of roughly hewn steps and emerged in a cave facing a rocky inlet. We waited in the still night air for the boat to make landfall until almost dawn before abandoning hope it would ever arrive. It was with a heavy heart that I climbed back up the steps, although we had agreed to try another time. Sadly our plot was discovered before we had the opportunity. The first I knew of it was when I was arrested and locked in the cathedral crypt.

Underneath the transept, the descent into the crypt is by a flight of steep steps some twenty feet below the ground level. The roof is vaulted by thirteen stone ribs, which form pointed arches, supported by pillars. The ground is rough stone and in one corner is an old well, fed from a natural spring, which adds to the gloomy dampness. The only light is from a small window set deep into one wall.

I cannot now bring myself to recall the awful conditions I had to endure as I languished in this dungeon, waiting for Sir Thomas to visit and deal with me. My health suffered in the damp and I developed a wheezing cough that troubled my sleep. Fat brown rats scurried in the small, bleak courtyard where I took my exercise and there was nothing to do, so I waited, with no idea how much longer I would remain there. I began to lose count of my days in this dreadful prison, until I found a rusty nail, embedded into one of the old oak beams and worked it back and forth until it finally came loose. Each morning I scratched another line in the grimy, thinly-plastered wall of my crypt prison, crossing each set of four with the fifth.

My faith in God and my fellow man now gone, I sank into a deep pit of despair, withdrawing into myself until I wondered about my own sanity. At one point I held the rusty nail to the vein in my wrist and tried to take my life. Either it was too blunt or I lacked the strength, although I felt barely alive by autumn when they let me return to my little cell. The row of deeply scored sets of lines in the wall told me I had suffered there for more than two long months. My hair was matted and my clothes dirty. I could not remember when I last had eaten anything other than greasy stew and stale crusts of dark rye bread.

A hard winter passed and it was the following spring before Sir Thomas Stanley finally arrived and brought the worst news. He told me Duke Humphrey had been arrested by the king's men in February and fell into a state of coma, for three days not moving or ever speaking. At his end, Sir Thomas gravely explained, Duke Humphrey recovered sufficiently to confess his sins and receive the last rites of the Church. I did not believe a word of it. My husband, for such he was to me, was cruelly murdered by his enemies. It was some small consolation that my husband's death had been followed within six weeks by that of his lifelong enemy, Cardinal Henry Beaufort.

It was clear Sir Thomas saw me as nothing but a liability and I suspected he knew Peel Castle was too poorly defended. He had sworn loudly when told of my escape attempt and said he had enough of me. As soon as he could he planned to arrange for me to be moved to the island of Anglesey in Wales, where I would no longer be his concern. I was not at all sorry to leave that sad rock in the Irish Sea, although I remained there for almost a whole year more before the ship arrived to take me to Beaumaris.

I believe in omens, good and bad, so the flat calm sea and favourable wind that carried me southwards to Wales boded well for my future. My ship was a fat-bellied carrack, with great triangular lateen sails. The Welsh crew seemed in good spirits and sang tunefully in their native language as they heaved the sails high up the mast. Their captain was courteous to me and explained we would dock at Beaumaris Castle before nightfall, God willing.

I was allowed to stand at the rail, enjoying the fresh sea air. It was late March and the worst of the winter had passed. I felt a sense of anticipation that the worst days of my life were now also being left behind me. All I knew of Wales was that my daughter Antigone and my grandchildren lived there, and her husband was the Lord of Powys. I dared to hope one day she would now be able to visit me.

Looking up into the clear blue sky, I wondered about the truth of the story Sir Thomas Stanley had told me. He said that as well as the duke, some twenty-eight men of his household had been arrested and tried for plotting against the king. It raised so many questions in my mind and I doubted I would ever know the answers. I was also deeply worried for my son, Arthur, as I knew how unjustly such charges could be contrived and the dreadful punishments that would follow.

At last, the dark mountains of Wales appeared on the horizon and we approached the green and welcoming island of Anglesey. Seagulls wheeled at our bows and small boats bobbed in a shallow sea, reflecting red and gold in the setting sun. There ahead, lay the golden brown towers of my new home, the great castle of Beaumaris. As our ship manoeuvred into the castle dock my eyes were drawn to the brightly coloured royal standard flying proudly from the top of the gatehouse and I knew this was where I would end my days.

I kneel alone in the chapel at Beaumaris and say a prayer for the soul of my husband, my beloved Humphrey, who could have spoken out in my defence yet remained silent as I was brought low. I had kept any knowledge of my actions from him, abandoned him without even saying goodbye. Telling him about my foolish experiments might not have saved me from my downfall, yet he would have been more able to understand why I did these things which caused such grief and pain.

My Book of Hours teaches me to forgive. *Judge not, and ye shall not be judged. Condemn not, and ye shall not be condemned. Forgive, and ye shall be forgiven.* I cannot forgive the cardinal, Henry Beaufort. At best, I can learn to pity him. In truth, the cardinal took not only my liberty from me; he also took my faith in humanity, my faith in God. I no longer believed there could be any justice in a world where good men are so cruelly murdered.

It was no surprise to me to learn that on the same day Roger Bolingbroke was so savagely executed, our secretary and chaplain John Home was given a special pardon by the court. I know he was innocent of any crime, simply caught up in the cardinal's net, yet when I heard he had been set free I cursed his mortal soul. I wished he would burn in Hell for an eternity for the betrayal of my friends.

Slowly, over the years, I have learned to replace my anger with understanding. Now I know I must remember how the cardinal's men would have threatened our chaplain. He must have been told he would suffer with the worst tortures unless he told them what they wanted to hear. It was the only choice he could make. I never liked him yet he was an honest man, trusted with the safe keeping of my husband's seal. The consequences of his testimony must have haunted him ever since. I look up at the wooden cross on the simple altar of the chapel and forgive John Home.

I prayed for the soul of Roger Bolingbroke, who is never forgotten. I also remember my good friend Thomas Southwell, who I hope was not killed by his torturers but found his own painless escape. I say a prayer for Margery Jourdemayne, and ask that she will not be remembered by history a witch, but as a good woman who helped the sick with her knowledge of herbs and potions.

I forgive King Henry VI, who could have granted a royal pardon to us all. The king was surely acting as he thought best, urged on by his corrupt and self-serving advisors. I have learnt how to forgive the pious bishops who sat in judgement in their gold-trimmed robes and condemned me for my vanity, while knowing in their hearts I was no traitor. I even find it in my heart to forgive the well-meaning men of the civil courts that sentenced my friends, all caught up in a sticky spider's web of intrigue and half-truths, spun so cleverly by Henry Beaufort.

As I come out from the chapel into the inner ward of the castle I see the grey clouds are gone. It is that rarest of days when the sun shines low in the sky, so bright I can scarcely see without shielding my eyes. Although now quite weak I am allowed to climb the stone steps to the high parapet one more time, where I stand looking out over the glittering expanse of the blue-green Irish Sea. I wish for the old priest to return soon, so that I can tell him my faith in God is restored.

24

JUNE 1452

EGO TE ABSOLVO

When the priest came back at last to Beaumaris Castle he found me in my bed, reading from the Book of Hours he had given to me, my candle burned almost to the end. He greeted me warmly and pulled a chair to the side of my bed, lighting a new candle for me. He looked well for his advancing years, his skin tanned brown as leather by the sun, although he still leaned heavily on his stick. I had so much to tell him and so little time. I realise I need his approval, for him to know that the years of bitterness have finally been overcome. The old priest has played an important part in opening my eyes, now only he can give me absolution. First, though, I knew I must hear of his adventures.

'They told me you've been on a pilgrimage to the far west.' I was truly pleased to see my old friend after so many months. 'I am glad to see you are safe, although I wondered if you would ever return.'

His brown forehead creased at the thought. 'There were times when I wondered if I would ever see this old place again.' He spoke slowly, his voice rich with the Welsh accent.

I smiled at him. 'It is a long journey for anyone but for a man of your age, a real achievement.'

The priest's eyes twinkled at my compliment. 'Almost two hundred miles.' He looked at me, a question in his eyes. 'You wonder why I would make such a journey?'

I sensed an air of peace and contentment about him I had not seen before. 'Your journey has been... a spiritual one?' I could hear the weakness in my voice but the priest did not seem to notice.

He nodded. 'It was my lifelong ambition.' The priest looked away from me, out of the window into the far distance, his eyes misty. 'I always wanted to visit the shrine of Dewi Sant, my patron saint.' He lowered his voice, as if afraid someone would overhear. 'I confess it has also served as penance for all the sins I have committed in my long life.' There was unexpected emotion in his voice.

I was touched by his admission. 'I doubt your sins required... such a penance.'

He frowned at an old memory I had no wish to make him recall. 'I understand why you wished to make your pilgrimage. It is more than atonement.'

The old priest nodded again. 'You are right. It was an affirmation of my faith.'

'I have also been on... a spiritual journey.' My voice sounded weaker now.

The old priest looked at me and silently took my frail, blue-veined hand in his.

Now at last I could say what I had been longing to tell him. 'I have learned to forgive those who wronged me... and rediscovered my faith in God.' My words were almost a whisper.

He sat looking at me in silence as he reflected on this

and I saw tears form in his old eyes. 'God bless you, my lady.'

EPILOGUE

AMEN

Eleanor Cobham died peacefully in her sleep on the 7th day of July, 1452. As a convicted sorceress and necromancer she was to be buried in unconsecrated ground. When Lady Ellen Bulkeley, wife of the sergeant-at-arms of Beaumaris Castle, heard of this, she persuaded the constable, Sir William Beauchamp, to permit Eleanor's body to be interred in the churchyard of St Mary and St Nicholas, the parish church of Beaumaris, Anglesey.

It was a tranquil summer day as the parish priest conducted the simple ceremony, witnessed only by Lady Ellen with her young son, William, aged seven, and a castle guard named Richard Hook. After everyone had left, Richard Hook marked Eleanor's grave with a wooden cross, on which he had carved her name in neat capitals, and placed against it a single red rose, the flower of Lancaster.

In St Albans, Abbot John Whethamstede arranged for a memorial, high on the wall that closes the south aisle, above the shrine, with the coat of arms of his late friend and bene-factor Duke Humphrey of Gloucester, surmounted by a coronet. Underneath the Abbot added a Latin inscription, accusing Eleanor of destroying the duke and 'thinking him barely worthy of this humble tomb'.

In Westminster, Eleanor's legacy would be as the catalyst for an important change in the law. Parliament declared that peeresses charged with treason were to be judged in the same way as everyone else, by judges and peers of the realm, just like English peers. This was little consolation to Queens Anne Boleyn and Catherine Howard a hundred years or so later.

In France, 1452, a cavalier named Jean d'Amancy became a nobleman and was granted the castle of Rumilly-sous-Cornillon in Haute-Savoie by Duke Louis of Savoy. He was sent to Venice in 1459 as the Royal Ambassador of King Charles VII of France.

"Eleanor was beautiful and marvellously pleasant."
Aeneas Sylvius Piccolomini,
Secretary to Pope Pius II, 1452

AUTHOR'S NOTE

My wife researched her family tree and discovered Antigone Plantagenet of Gloucester was her 19th great grandmother. Further research revealed Antigone was the daughter of Humphrey of Lancaster, Duke of Gloucester and the younger brother of Henry V, who became Lord Protector of England.

There proved to be much debate about the identity of Antigone's mother, although historian and author Alison Weir suggests both Antigone and her brother, Arthur, could have been the children of Humphrey and his mistress Eleanor Cobham, whom he later married. In her book *Britain's Royal Families: The Complete Genealogy* Alison Weir notes that 'Eleanor Cobham became Humphrey's mistress sometime before their marriage and might have borne him two bastard children'.

Curious, I looked into this, discovering the tragic details of Eleanor Cobham's life in the course of my research. It is a fact that Humphrey of Lancaster acted as a father towards Antigone and was definitely with Eleanor Cobham since at least 1425, if not earlier (records were seldom kept of mistresses), marrying her in 1428. Alison Weir's suggestion is therefore extremely plausible but I found no positive evidence to support it.

The only sure way to settle the question of whether Eleanor was Antigone's mother would be if some new documentation comes to light. That is how the idea for this novel came about. With the exception of the maidservant Martha and the guard Richard Hook, who represent the twelve staff and guards with Eleanor in her imprisonment, the people, places and events named are real and carefully researched.

There are many accounts which state important details incorrectly, most notably that Eleanor died at Peel Castle. It is well documented that her final two years were at Beaumaris. My wife and I spent a summer afternoon searching the churchyard of St Mary and St Nicholas, within sight of Beaumaris Castle. Inside the church lie the medieval ornate tombs of Lady Ellen and Sir William Bulkeley. We found no sign of Eleanor's grave, although she will never be forgotten.

Thank you for reading this book, which I hope you enjoyed as much as I did writing it. To find out about my other books please visit my website at **www.tonyriches.com**

Tony Riches, Pembrokeshire, Wales

Sources and Further Reading

The Trial of Eleanor Cobham: An Episode in the fall of Duke Humphrey of Gloucester, By Ralph A. Griffiths, 1969

Humphrey Duke of Gloucester, A Biography by K.H. Vickers, 1907

Humphrey Duke of Gloucester, by Maud C. Knight, 1903

A Mediaeval Princess, Being a True Record of the Changing Fortunes Which Brought Diverse Titles to Jacqueline, Countess Of Holland, Together With an Account of Her Conflict With Philip Duke Of Burgundy (1401 • 1436) by Ruth Putnam, 1904

Sorcery at court and manor: Margery Jourdemayne, the witch of Eye next Westminster, by Jessica Freeman, 2004
Forbidden Rites: A Necromancer's Manual of the Fifteenth Century by Richard Kieckhefer, 1998

Cultural politics in fifteenth-century England - the case of Humphrey, Duke of Gloucester, by Alessandra Petrina, 2004

King and Country: England and Wales in the Fifteenth Century, by Ralph A. Griffiths, 1964

Henry Beaufort, Bishop, Chancellor, Cardinal by Lewis Bostock, 1908

OWEN - Book One of the Tudor Trilogy

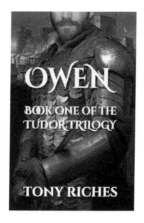

England 1422: Owen Tudor, a Welsh servant, waits in Windsor Castle to meet his new mistress, the beautiful and lonely Queen Catherine of Valois, widow of the warrior king, Henry V. Her infant son is crowned King of England and France, and while the country simmers on the brink of civil war, Owen becomes her protector.

They fall in love, risking Owen's life and Queen Catherine's reputation, but how do they found the dynasty which changes British history – the Tudors?

This is the first historical novel to fully explore the amazing life of Owen Tudor, grandfather of King Henry VII and the great-grandfather of King Henry VIII. Set against a background of the conflict between the Houses of Lancaster and York, which develops into what have become known as the Wars of the Roses, Owen's story deserves to be told.

Available as paperback, audiobook and eBook

JASPER - Book Two of the Tudor Trilogy

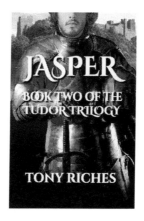

England 1461: The young King Edward of York has taken the country by force from King Henry VI of Lancaster. Sir Jasper Tudor, Earl of Pembroke, flees the massacre of his Welsh army at the Battle of Mortimer's Cross.

When King Henry is imprisoned by Edward in the Tower of London and murdered, Jasper escapes to Brittany with his young nephew, Henry Tudor. With nothing but his wits and charm, Jasper sees his chance to make young Henry Tudor king with a daring and reckless invasion of England.

Set in the often brutal world of fifteenth century England, Wales, Scotland, France, Burgundy and Brittany, during the Wars of the Roses, this fast-paced story is one of courage and adventure, love and belief in the destiny of the Tudors.

Available as paperback, audiobook and eBook

HENRY - Book Three of the Tudor Trilogy

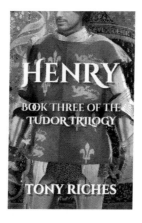

Bosworth 1485: After victory against King Richard III, Henry Tudor becomes King of England. Rebels and pretenders plot to seize his throne. The barons resent his plans to curb their power and he wonders who he can trust. He hopes to unite Lancaster and York through marriage to the beautiful Elizabeth of York.

With help from his mother, Lady Margaret Beaufort, he learns to keep a fragile peace. He chooses a Spanish Princess, Catherine of Aragon, as a wife for his son Prince Arthur.

His daughters will marry the King of Scotland and the son of the Emperor of Rome. It seems his prayers are answered, then disaster strikes and Henry must ensure the future of the Tudors.

Available in paperback, eBook and audiobook

MARY ~ Tudor Princess

Midsummer's Day 1509: The true story of the Tudor dynasty continues with the daughter of King Henry VII. Mary Tudor watches her elder brother become King of England and wonders what the future holds for her.

Born into great privilege, Mary has beauty and intelligence beyond her years. Her brother Henry plans to use her marriage to build a powerful alliance against his enemies – but will she dare to risk his anger by marrying for love?

Meticulously researched and based on actual events, this 'sequel' follows Mary's story from book three of the Tudor Trilogy and is set during the reign of King Henry VIII.

Available in paperback and eBook

34385130R00172

Printed in Great Britain
by Amazon